DISTORTED PERCEPTION

by Jonathan R. Snowling

2022 Great Story Network Hardcover Edition
Copyright © 2022 by Jonathan R. Snowling

Published in the United States by The Great Story Network.
Hardcover ISBN 9798985581362; Paperback ISBN-9798985581317

Special thanks to the editing team:
Lisa Mathews; Tanya Egan Gibson; Jacob King;
Brian Saliba; Robert Runte; Adria Laycraft;
Casey Phillips

Title page and interior design by Rafael Andres
Cover design by Richard Ljoenes Design LLC

"Media can at times reduce human beings to units of consumption or competing interest groups, or manipulate viewers and readers and listeners as mere ciphers from whom some advantage is sought, whether product sales or political support; and these things destroy community. It is the task of communication to bring people together and enrich their lives, not isolate and exploit them."

— Pope John Paul II, Message for the 32nd World Communications Day, 1998.

PROLOGUE

The rusted security door squeaked as it jammed partway open. Edgardo Blades leaned into it with his shoulder and pushed until it swung the rest of the way, banging hard against the cinder block wall. A light flickered from a single long tube bulb on the ceiling. The floor's layers of dark red and blue epoxy had worn away in front of the door, exposing a patch of bare cement. Edgardo stepped inside, the click of his heels echoing across the room.

At first glance, it appeared empty save for a pile of cigarette butts near the door, as the ceiling light was only strong enough to illuminate a few yards in each direction. Edgardo peered further into the darkness until he could see the faint outline of a man seated on the floor at the far end of the room. He strode toward him, then paused under the light. There was a large splotch on the center of the left wall. The bulb hummed above him. He squinted at the splotch. Fresh blood. A lens flare streaked across Edgardo's goggles. Hot, sweating, and blinded by the distorted light, he felt disoriented. A sudden sense of claustrophobia came over him.

"Hey," a voice called.

Edgardo scrabbled urgently at the edges of his gas mask, released the straps, and quickly pulled it off his face.

"Why I am here?" the man at the far end of the room shouted.

Edgardo dropped the gas mask onto the floor and offered the man a bitter stare. What the hell was *he* doing in this place? Edgardo hated Honduras, yet here he was, deep inside a moldy abandoned industrial building on the outskirts of Tegucigalpa. Even more, he hated the level of exposure that came with working in this country. Too many eyes watching and keeping tabs. Too much attention brought on by the prominence of the drug trade and every other form of organized and disorganized crime.

He wished Temmy had chosen someone else to handle this, but it had been the first time he'd ever seen Temmy that shaken. He'd been adamant that Edgardo personally extract the information.

"What's going to happen to me?" The man waved his hand in the air, begging for Edgardo's attention.

Edgardo remained silent and kept his expression stone-faced to avoid engagement. He'd deal with the man soon enough. He calmly laid a thick manila folder down on the cement floor under the light. Inhaling a large breath of the stagnant air, he knelt in front of the folder. A bitter metallic taste permeated his mouth as he reviewed its contents. He rose to his feet and spat on the floor. The foul taste returned with his next breath.

"Who are you?" the man asked.

His birth name wasn't Edgardo Blades, of course. He'd changed names and identities often in his early days. Back when he'd been Roberto Samaniego, he'd overheard a young pregnant woman at a café discussing with her husband the root origins of the name *Edgardo*. She'd said it meant "one who is fortunate and powerful, or a wealthy man with a spear." He'd loved that. All of it.

A year later, he became Edgardo. He'd added Blades later out of appreciation for the Panamanian salsa and jazz musician Ruben Blades. Only recently had Edgardo taken to carrying a lucky stiletto, a vintage Italian Maniago.

He pulled the knife from his pocket, flicked it open with a snap of his wrist, and walked in front of the man, who cowered in an undershirt and boxer shorts. He was slender except for the bulge of his gut. His hands and feet were wrapped with duct tape.

"Whatever you want, friend, I'll do it," the man pleaded. "Please, just let me out of this place." Edgardo squinted as he tried to discern the features of the man's face, but he was too far from the light. Then he saw the gleam of the man's beady eyes and the bald spot on his head. Yeah, this is the one.

Edgardo pointed the knife down at him. "Escúchame!" An-tic-ipating a blow, the man turned his head. Edgardo obliged the man's fear, sinking the blade deep inside his leg, poking under his knee-cap. "Let you go? There is no escape from this."

The man cried out in pain and struggled to wrench his sweaty hands free of the tape. "Hijo de la gran puta." He turned his gaze away from Edgardo and rolled over on his side. "You have no reason to hurt me like this," he whimpered. "I told you, I would do whatever you wanted."

Edgardo waved the knife over the man's head. "Is this not what you deserve?"

"I didn't do anything to you. Why can't you just set me free."

"I may decide to grant you a quick death, if I choose."

The man hid his face against the cool concrete floor and cried.

"Or drag it out ever so slowly and painfully if I don't."

"You're not the one in control, then?"

"Control? More rests under my domain than your mind could possibly grasp. As for what happens to *you*, I most certainly have all of the control."

The man turned his head upward. A sticky mixture of snot and tears dripped from his face and clung to floor. "Let me go, then."

"I can let you walk out this door any minute I choose."

"Please, please!"

"Why?"

"Because I don't know anything. I'm just a teacher."

Edgardo kicked him in the ribs. "And a scientist, too, yes?"

He raised the knife again and drove it down through the tape between the man's wrists. The ripping sound of the tape echoed through the space as Edgardo freed his hands.

"Oh, thank you," the man said, tears pouring from his eyes. He rolled over and clamped his hands over the wound above his knee.

"Crawl over to the center of the room."

He looked up at Edgardo. "But my leg."

Edgardo stepped behind him. What was with this piece of shit? *His leg?* In a moment, that would be the least of his worries. *"Rápido!"*

He delivered a fierce kick to the man's spine.

The man placed his palms onto the floor and dragged himself forward. After a moment, Edgardo walked ahead and stood under the light.

"Over here, where I can see you better." He waved the man closer, picked up the folder from the floor, and flipped through it.

"It says here that you were a scientist of agriculture." Edgardo lifted a page out of the folder. "This was before they made you a professor, right?"

The man halted his crawl, put a hand over his wound, and took a deep breath. "Yes, that is where I started."

"It says you pioneered some advancement in the process of genome editing, using synthetic viruses placed within insects."

"Yes. It allows us to change the properties of crops that are already planted in a field. The virus is engineered to alter the DNA of the plants. They instantly become less susceptible to pests or drought."

"What a noble endeavor," Edgardo replied. He waved the professor closer. "Come here."

The man inched his way under the light. His legs, still bound, were drenched by the blood seeping from his knee. It left a streak across the concrete.

"Who are you?" the professor asked again.

"From what I've read in this file, I'm not sure I can trust you to keep secrets."

"What secrets?"

"Professor. Professor," Edgardo said. "That is the title they gave you, right?"

The professor proudly titled his chin up. "The university, yes."

Edgardo feigned a nod. "You teach classes and receive a paycheck from the university, but we both know you don't work for the university."

"What are you going on about?"

"Quite a complex endeavor, this work you're involved with. You created insect-resistant plants through the gene editing of grown plants. Seems like a high bar to set. Are you sure you didn't try to develop any other, more easily achievable uses for such a technology first? Something simple, like how to sterilize grown plants? I may not be a scientist, but if I had to guess..."

"The research has other applications, it is true."

Edgardo raised his eyebrows. *Other applications? Unbelievable, this guy*. Edgardo rubbed his chin and mocked the professor's response with a sarcastic nod.

"People are much more interesting test subjects than plants, aren't they?"

The professor shook his head. "Those weren't my decisions."

"These 'decision makers,' as we will call them, they were people you met after being invited to a conference, yes?"

"I didn't do anything wrong."

"Interesting weekend," Edgardo replied. "Looks like you may have fallen in with a bad crowd. Your new friends bought you a prostitute or two, did they?"

The professor used his knuckle to dry the areas under his eyes and slid the back of his hand across his nose to clean away the remaining snot. He wiped his harvest onto the floor. "Some things happened. So what?"

"First time, the prostitute was about, what, seventeen? Not the second one, though."

"It wasn't my fault."

"How old was she?"

"I don't know."

"Oh, wait, it says here in the file that you preferred the boys."

For a moment the professor held still, his unblinking eyes wide open. He quietly lowered his head and adjusted his hands around his leg wound. Tears dripped again from his face, leaving wet dots on the dry cement floor.

"And on the next one of these trips of yours, the boys were even younger, weren't they?"

"That wasn't me," the professor pleaded as he lifted a hand off his wound to wipe the tears and snot from his face. "They made me do it. I have a sickness."

"Undoubtedly. A level-five membership in The Circle. That's almost as high as it goes, from what I'm told."

"You don't understand."

Edgardo shook his head. How could anyone understand the vile group of creatures that Temmy had created and collected under The Circle program?

"Which step came first? Was it killing someone, or the bestiality?"

"I wasn't going to tell anyone." The professor slapped the floor with a loud smack. "The file, it's encrypted. No one can read it without the key. It was just an insurance policy in case they wouldn't listen."

"Wouldn't listen to what?"

"The process can't be controlled outside a lab. Whoever is paying for my work, they need to be told. The go-between refuses to listen. If they move forward, it could cause an extinction-level catastrophe."

"Yes, many people will die, but I'd hardly call it an extinction-level event. Mosquitoes only live about thirty days. They deliver the poison among the target group, and soon enough all the mosquitoes die."

"No, the synthetic virus is designed to be carried from one generation of mosquitoes to the next, so the outbreak spreads further with time."

"But it says here that you solved that problem through something called CRISPR doublesex."

"We did, yes. Clustered, regularly interspaced, short palindromic repeats."

"Forgive me, Professor, but... ?"

"That's what CRISPR stands for."

"I still don't understand."

"We used a gene drive that rapidly transmits a sterilizing mutation through the mosquito species," the professor explained. "Once the mutation spreads to enough female mosquitoes, the group eventually crashes because they can no longer produce offspring. The process takes about seven to eleven generations, about six months in the lab."

"Why so long? Why doesn't it work by the second generation?"

"If female mosquitoes are born with just one copy of the gene, the effects are benign," the professor said. "But if mosquitoes are born with two copies of the mutation, it will render them sterile."

"So, this process works? What's the problem? The pathogen spreads throughout the targeted region, and then in six months it's safe to return."

"Almost one hundred percent of the time," the professor replied. "But *only* almost. Female mosquitoes can lay a set of up to a hundred eggs every three nights. Laws of probability. It's a gamble, so to speak."

"Even if the outbreak spread out of control, you, of all people, were in the best position to obtain the vaccine and wait it out," Edgardo said. "Why would you take the risk of downloading the research and hiding it away on that file?"

"It's not just the danger posed by one of the payload pathogens mutating and finding a way to spread from human to human," the professor said. "You have to consider the possibility that the sterilizing gene could spread from insect to human by accident along the same path. The sterilizing gene was designed to spread as easily as possible."

"Yes. But why design it to spread easily?"

"I told you already—this is how we eliminate all of the mosquitoes after they deliver the payload. If the sterilizing gene itself ever made the jump into humans, it would be guaranteed to result in human-to-human spread. Humans have a much longer reproduction cycle. It would continue to spread for years before the effects started to materialize. By then it would be too late to stop it."

"You're a soulless worm," Edgardo said. "What do you care?"

"I do not."

"Then why create the file?"

"They have to know the truth."

"You are a level-five member of The Circle," Edgardo said. "If you obtain level six, you can gain eternal life. They will allow you to have your consciousness delivered from mortal human flesh into an eternal machine, and all without judgment."

"I know." The professor lowered his head. "I did believe once, strongly. I wanted it to be true. And I know there's a lot of scientific consensus... but it all just seems insane."

"The freedom to gorge yourself on every monstrous desire, unhindered by conscience or fear of death?"

"But it's all a lie," the professor said.

Edgardo tossed the folder onto the floor, the contents spilling out at the professor's feet. The professor looked down at the folder, then back at Edgardo in confusion.

"The whole fucking thing is a lie!" Edgardo shouted. "Suddenly, after all of the evil shit you've done, you care about what's true?"

"But aren't you... aren't you here... on behalf of... of The Circle?" the professor stammered.

"The Circle?" Edgardo winced, and he snarled his lip. "How much of an *estúpido hijo de puta* are you to believe in even level one of that *mierda*? *¡Eres un imbécil!*"

He drove the knife through the side of the professor's mouth, piercing it clear through to the other side, where it protruded from under his left cheekbone. He yanked the knife back out, and the man screamed and gurgled, spitting blood out over the cement floor. Edgardo stomped his heel down into the center of the professor's chest.

"Now you listen, and you listen well," he said as he leaned in over him. "You are going to tell me the name of each person who *knows* about this. *Todos*."

He folded his knife and watched as the professor frantically flopped around on the floor, clasping his hands over the bleeding holes in his face.

Edgardo knelt down and used a loose sheet of paper to wipe the blood off of his fingers. After returning the knife to his pocket, he leaned over to retrieve the folder. He plucked out a newspaper article and tossed it next to the professor's head.

Keeping his palms pressed tightly to his cheeks, the professor looked up at Edgardo in bewilderment.

Edgardo turned away, picked up his gas mask from the floor, and walked over to the steel door from where he'd entered.

The professor attempted to raise himself up into a sitting position by pushing off the floor with his elbow.

Edgardo rapped his knuckle against the door three times, the sound reverberating through the room.

The professor finally worked his way into a sitting position under the light and looked at the paper Edgardo had dropped there.

"No, no," the professor gurgled through the pool of blood that had drained into his mouth.

The door swung open. Edgardo slipped on his gas mask and watched the professor spit blood onto the newspaper, all over the headline:

21 STUDENTS DISAPPEAR IN TEGUCIGALPA
Drug Cartel Suspected in Kidnapping

"What is this?" the professor asked. "Why would the narcos want my students?"

Edgardo turned away in silence and stepped out the door.

REX NASH

The earth shook and rattled as if it were an airplane thrown about by turbulence, the explosion kicking up a dust cloud into the night. It drifted toward Rex Nash's position, where he and a handful of guys from his squad were tucked in behind a mound of dirt and rock on the edge of a small, isolated village, and settled in over his head. A burning sensation permeated his lungs and sinuses. He coughed and turned his head against a large boulder, tucking his mouth under his collar and breathing through his jacket to filter out the fine particles.

The discomfort brought by the dust was irritating but endurable. It blew in and then out in the same way, causing only a momentary condition of misery. What drove Rex to the edge of madness was the cold, persistent wind that crept in over the embankment. It felt as though someone had parked an air conditioner over his head and set it to freeze.

He adjusted and readjusted his posture in the dark for the better part of an hour, futilely trying to escape the chill. Finally, he pulled his arms in tight and tucked his hands inside the breast pockets of his jacket.

Rex transported his thoughts elsewhere, an essential skill for adapting to life under the military's "hurry-up-and-wait" ethos. Each layer of leadership wanted to make sure their guys were extra early and ready to go for any activity. If a regimental commander asked to have a formation somewhere at 09:00, the regimental command sergeant major would tell his guys to make sure people were there at 08:45, which would lead the squadron commanding officer to tell his guys to be there at 08:30, and so on it would go down the chain. The phenomenon transformed life in the military into a constant rush to get somewhere without a purpose, hurrying to wait around for hours in mind-numbing agony without the slightest idea of what was going on.

The ground rumbled again with the blast of another mortar. Rex pushed his hands deeper into his pockets, felt the rough plastic edge of the laminated photo he'd been carrying since basic training, and smiled. He often looked at it during periods of hurry-up-and-wait. The sensation that ran along his fingertips sparked his memory, bringing him back to a beach east of his home in the suburbs of Washington, D.C., during the summer of his sophomore year in college. After a three-mile jog along the beach, he had ducked under a large wave to cool off. Upon resurfacing, Jessica Roark, whom he hadn't seen in years, had been standing there waving to him from the edge of the water. They'd spent the next week together, the picture taken at some point during those seven unforgettable days.

"Nash!"

Rex reluctantly pulled his mind back into the moment. Back to the cold, the dark, the dust, the rocks, the mortars, the squad. "Hey, what's up, Stevens?"

"Man, can you believe this shit?" Stevens asked.

"What shit? When did you get here?"

"This wouldn't be happening if it weren't for those jerk-offs on the other side of the ridge that came in with all that heavy equipment," Stevens said. "They might as well have shot up a warning flare."

Rex shook his head. "What's the deal? I haven't heard a single word, other than we're supposed to stay put."

Stevens pointed in the direction of the village. "This engagement popped off two hours ago. We can't advance forward, and we can't turn backward. They want us to sit here and wait for one of those mortars to land on our heads."

"Command has to readjust and get everyone in place," Rex countered.

Stevens nodded toward the ridge. "Those idiots showed up two hours before they were supposed to."

"When did you get here?" Rex asked. He couldn't fully wrap his head around the idea that Stevens was back. It seemed impossible. "I thought you were injured."

"Injured?" Stevens replied, with a puzzled look.

Rex rubbed his eyes to make sure they were working right. "I saw you take a bullet to the face."

"Oh, that." Stevens turned his head to reveal a grisly scar stretching from above his eye to the corner of his mouth. "Just a flesh wound."

"Holy crap," Rex said. "You signed back up?"

"They couldn't keep me out of this fight. You know that."

An explosion thundered twenty yards in front of their position. Rex was thrown to the ground. Dirt and debris rained over him.

Stevens pulled Rex's arm, helping him up.

"Fuck this," Stevens said. "I'm going in."

"We have to hold."

Stevens shook his rifle in Rex's face. "I'm taking that mortar out. I don't give a shit."

"Don't be stupid."

Stevens closed his fist and blew on it. He let a middle finger fly and scrambled to the top mound of dirt and rock.

"Nash!" he called from the top. "Get my back, let's go."

"No way," Rex said. Though it was great to see Stevens back and he loved having the crazy son of a bitch around, he was out of control. "Get back down here!"

"Let's go," Stevens called out again.

Rex felt a cold shiver run through his body. "I have a bad feeling."

"Fuck your feelings!"

Rex shook his head and slammed the butt of his rifle into the dirt. Why did this seem so familiar? He looked to the top of the mound. Stevens had disappeared over the edge.

"Shit."

He hurried over the embankment and spotted a glimpse of Stevens just before his friend sprinted off toward the village a half mile ahead, vanishing into the darkness.

He followed and took up cover behind a torched pickup truck, searching for signs of Stevens through the night vision scope on his rifle. He caught a glimpse of someone ducking behind a bullet-ridden home that was missing large sections of its roof.

He made his way toward the house and peered into a blown-out window. The interior was eerily empty, lifeless. Rex climbed inside, broken glass crunching under his feet. Moonlight shone through the holes in the roof. A badly decomposed body clothed in women's attire lay on the ground near a door.

Rex felt nausea building and looked away. *She's not there. Ignore it; stay focused.*

Heavy footsteps sounded from further inside the home. Rex rushed past the body and through the door beside it, pointing his rifle at the nearest corner.

"Nash," a voice called from the other side of what had once been a living room. Rex turned to see Stevens sitting a foot back from the corner of a window. "Come here. I have him in my sights."

Rex crouched and darted to a post on the opposite side of the windowsill. He leaned back against the wall.

Stevens glanced up from his rifle and smiled at him. Seconds later, blood spray and skull fragments struck Rex's face. The sound had been so much smaller than Rex could have imagined, just a *pop!* as Stevens's head ripped open in front of him.

A light flashed, and Rex's heart jumped a beat. He shut his eyes and then opened them to extreme brightness. Squinting against it, he made out what looked to be a TV screen surrounded by blue leather. He felt the rough plastic of a seat-back tray table under his fingers and let out a deep sigh of relief.

Someone tapped him on the shoulder.

"Are you all right?"

He turned toward the woman's voice. Teresa, a colleague at the American Insurance Institute, was seated beside him. Regaining his bearings, he remembered that he was on a return flight to D.C. from Atlanta. A business trip.

"Yes, why?"

"You were mumbling something," she said. "And your arm started shaking."

"I must have dozed off for a moment," Rex replied. "A dream."

"You sure?"

"The air-conditioning gave me a shiver, maybe." Rex pointed up at the nozzle on the overhead console. "Pray I don't catch a cold."

It wasn't the A/C. He had suffered a rash of similar dreams since leaving the military eight years ago. He used to blame the nightmares on the long hours, stress, and exhaustion that came with the roller-coaster lifestyle of the political campaign trail. This, however, was the first incidence in the year since he'd begun working at this particular job.

"I never sleep on planes," Teresa said. "I saw on the news where this woman fell asleep and left her legs in the same position too long. The lack of circulation in her legs caused a blood clot to form." Her eyes widened and she placed a hand over her heart. "The poor woman stroked out and died right there on the plane."

"Well, who knows? I guess that could happen, but millions of people sleep on planes without any issue every day, so I think you'll be fine."

She shook her head. "I'm using two weeks of vacation to go to Paris with my husband at the end of the month. I don't want to chance dying, and it's a long time to stay awake."

"About eight hours, right?"

"Yes. Awful."

"Booze is usually free on international flights. Throw back a few cocktails and try not to think too much about it."

"Okay. I'll try that." She smiled. "You put in for any vacation time?"

"Not yet."

"Better hurry. You don't use it, you lose it."

Rex recalled the only good part of his dream—the moment he'd held the picture of Jessica. Though Jessica had long since moved away, her parents still had that beach house.

"I will," Rex said. "Definitely." Which week was it that her family used to vacation there? "The week of July 15."

EDGARDO BLADES

Tegucigalpa, Honduras
May 5

Edgardo waited at the foot of a stairwell leading to the loading area of the rotted-out industrial building. He knew it would be a dirty job, but a pair of slacks and a linen sport coat was about as dressed down as he was willing to go at this stage of his life. Though he'd packed the cheapest and oldest clothes in his wardrobe for the trip, he was still determined not to get anywhere near a single droplet of the foul mixture oozing out of those plastic tubs.

The cook had on full-body protective gear to shield his skin. The two men helping him wore high rubber boots and long rubber gloves that reached up to their elbows. Each also wore a gas mask.

There were twenty-two tubs in all. The cook was peering into one open tub from atop a stepladder, and another nineteen sealed ones were lined up in rows of five at the back of the room. Two empty ones sat next to Edgardo at the edge of the steps. He watched as the two helpers pulled the body of a young man off the ground and lifted it up the ladder. The kid had been broader at the shoulders than the others, so they'd had to cut his arms off. The cook clasped the kid's chin in a firm grip but struggled to grab the armless torso with his other hand. The body slipped a few inches, and the lower helper tumbled back a step as the weight shifted. He recovered quickly and held the torso up steady. Once the cook had a strong enough grasp, his helpers let go, and he guided the young man's body headfirst into the acid bath. While one helper held the ladder, the other retrieved the young man's arms from the ground.

"When you come back in two days, and this stuff has done its work, don't just open the drain valves and flush the contents into the field like last time," Edgardo said. "I want you to take each one of these tubs down to that stream in the back. You can pour any remaining sludge out there."

The cook acknowledged the directive with a nod as he dropped the arms into the tub, one after the other.

"*Jefe!*" a voice called from deeper inside the building.

"Over here," Edgardo replied.

"We brought the last kid out and tied him to a chair, like you asked. Left him outside the storage room."

#

"Bring him over here." Edgardo pointed to the lit area in the center of the storage room. He pulled off his gas mask and directed the two henchmen to place the weighty desk chair under the light next to the professor. Excessive layers of rope and tape had been wrapped around the college student's legs, stomach, and arms.

"Ivan!" the professor cried.

Edgardo waved the two guards out. "What's the matter, Professor?"

"He doesn't know anything."

"Entrusted the file to your little teacher's pet, did you?" Edgardo pulled his knife out of his pocket and flicked it open.

"I never told him what was on it, just that it was important."

"Important?" Edgardo ripped the duct tape from Ivan's mouth.

"He's right," Ivan said. "It's true, I swear. He gave it to me to hold in case something happened to him."

"So you never looked at it." Edgardo pointed the knife at Ivan.

"Well, yeah, maybe. But it was encrypted."

He swung the knife back to the professor.

"Who else knows about it?"

"Ivan is the only one I told. Why would I risk telling anyone else?"

Edgardo turned to Ivan and placed the point of the knife just below the duct tape on the kid's stomach.

"You know what? I believe the professor."

Edgardo pushed the knife deep into Ivan's gut. The kid screamed. He tried to struggle, but his movement was restrained by tape.

"The only reason we know anything is because Ivan here told someone," Edgardo said. "Another student."

He held the knife steady, taking care not to let it slip in either direction.

"Now, Ivan, I'm going to turn this knife with every second that you don't tell me exactly who has that file."

"Hector Lopez."

Edgardo's grip tightened on the knife.

"My cousin works for him."

"*The* Hector Lopez?"

"I only talked to my cousin—that was it."

Edgardo shook his head and turned the knife ever so slightly.

"No! Please don't. I've told you everything I know. Take the fucking knife out. I only asked if he knew anyone that could help with encryption, that's all."

"This is who you ask for *help?*"

"My cousin is a low-level nobody," Ivan replied. "He's never even met Hector. I thought my cousin might ask around, or whatever. How was I supposed to know Hector's sister was some kind of encryption expert?"

"Hector's sister. What's her name?"

"I don't know. My cousin mentioned it to somebody up the chain. Next thing I know, my cousin comes back with a bunch of people. They took everything. My computer, my phone, everything."

Edgardo stared at Ivan in disbelief and gave the knife a slight twist. The kid screamed and twitched.

"Nooo onnnne else has it!" the professor shouted.

"Only Hector the Mexicano." Edgardo jerked his wrist to the right, slicing Ivan's belly wide open and spilling his intestines onto the floor.

Edgardo walked to the steel door and knocked three times.

"Wait!" the professor yelled. "I gave you everything I knew."

Edgardo gazed at him for a moment before the door swung open.

"You said you had the power to let me out!"

Edgardo stepped out into the hall, as the professor babbled behind him.

"Didn't you get what you wanted?"

"Shoot him," Edgardo said, as he walked past the two henchmen in the hall.

He pulled a phone from his sport coat pocket and dialed.

The henchmen went into the storage room.

"Armando, sorry it took so long to get back to you," Edgardo said. "It's been a busy morning... Yes, yes, all thanks to Temmy, of course. I'm stuck in a highly uncomfortable location, which I would have preferred to never have visited."

Pop! Edgardo winced slightly and put his hand over his ear.

"Oh, that?"

Two more gunshots rang out from the storage room, echoing through the hall.

"Nothing to worry about," Edgardo assured Armando as he found his way to the exit.

"What were you saying again? Okay... Yes, yes... Vasquez could be a real problem, but he's a long shot, right? Wait until I get back to Panama. We can talk all things politics over a bottle of that dark rum Temmy likes."

RAUL VASQUEZ

June 25
Comarca Indígena Guna Yala, Panama

Did the Guna even vote?

This was among the many doubts that crept into Raul Vasquez's mind on the boat en route to an island in an indigenous province known as Guna Yala.

The visit he and his wife were making to the Guna people, known as the Kuna before a spelling change in 2010, would be his third campaign stop today on one of the fifty-nine small islands they inhabited along the eastern Caribbean coast of Panama, just above the Colombian border. The trip hadn't been in the plans at all until a glowing news story had broken about President Martinez's recent visit and the celebratory reception that the Guna had offered him, and Vasquez hoped that it was worth it. The images of villagers carrying "Vote Martinez" signs and scores of cheering kids dancing in the streets, all wearing the colors of the Partido Popular—white T-shirts with a green star emblem—had sent Vasquez's campaign into a panic. He himself had begun to wonder privately if it was possible to beat such a man if even voters at the furthest reaches of human civilization, according to the news coverage, had rallied to Martinez's side.

Vasquez's confidence had been rejuvenated, however, as he'd entered the first village of the day. Only a month after the president's visit, the Guna had greeted Vasquez with overwhelming support.

At the second village, Vasquez had again received energetic support and praise. His campaign signs were everywhere, some tied to the bamboo walls of the people's simple huts. Still more were fixed on top of the small roofs made of dried palm tree fronds.

He had rejoiced in his achievement, starting to believe the trip would mark the start of a new beginning for his campaign, until the moment he'd begun his second speech of the day. Looking out past the edge of the crowd, he'd spotted a man standing next to the village's only concrete building—a dual convenience store and pub—holding a paint bucket and brush. At first glance, Vasquez was pleased to see that the building had been painted in the red and yellow colors of his political party, the Molirena. But then he noticed a few splotches of white where the man had yet to paint. Staring more closely, he detected the outline of a green star. Though he was glad to have won the man over, he couldn't get over how last minute the conversion appeared.

The image played over and over in Vasquez's head as the boat approached the third village.

Was the Guna's support real? Or was it all just for show?

He gazed out over the water and spotted two white corrugated plastic signs bobbing in the waves. He pointed them out to his wife as they floated past the boat into the wake.

"See the green stars on them?" Vasquez said.

"Oh, the Guna," she said, with a sigh and frown. "Do they throw everything in the water?"

"That's all they can do with their garbage out here, mi amor."

"Martinez was here over a month ago," she said. "Why are they all still floating so close to shore?"

She stopped, apparently realizing the answer, and quickly changed the topic by opening a text message on her phone.

"Looks like I missed this," she said, showing him the phone. "From a Padre Abasolo?"

"Who?"

"He says your mother asked him to contact you."

"Oh yes. That's her priest friend," he said. "A few months ago, she was pestering me about meeting him."

The boat's captain cut the motor as they approached the dock. The quick reduction in speed knocked Vasquez forward, and he fumbled his wife's phone.

"Watch it," she cautioned.

"I have it," he said, still juggling it under control.

The boat docked, and the deck hands tossed ropes down to help the captain tie on.

"Mamá suggested I play golf with this priest guy next time I come to visit her."

"Aww, you should."

"When was the last time I played golf?"

The captain waved for them to climb onto the dock.

"He went through the trouble to text me just to get a hold of you. What if it's something serious?"

"Mi amor, this is my mother we are talking about here. She is always scheming up some way or another to get me to leave the city and go visit her way out there in the interior."

His wife smiled. "She misses you."

Vasquez stepped up the dock ladder. The scent of salty sea air mingled with smoke from the village's cooking fires. "We won't be anywhere in range of a cell tower until we get back to Panama City tonight."

"I must have received the text this morning as we were getting on the helicopter," she responded.

Vasquez knelt and extended his hand over the dock to help his wife up. "I will try to call him in the morning."

Several young children approached them, all wearing red and yellow T-shirts. One asked Vasquez if he was going to become president. As he gave the kid a hug and a twenty-dollar bill, he noticed what appeared to be a green star emblem that was showing underneath a wet spot on the kid's Vasquez T-shirt.

"I like this new shirt on you, kid," Vasquez said with a smile. He patted the kid on the head. "It's much better than that other one."

On a grassy clearing next to the village, a group of fifty Guna cheered as he made his way off the dock. The kids followed along, clapping and dancing. Vasquez went straight into the crowd and began shaking hands and giving out hugs. The men wore modern shorts and T-shirts. The women wore handmade dresses in bright colors and traditional patterns they called *molas*. They also displayed distinctive jewelry around their necks and multicolored beaded bracelets on their arms and legs as protection against bad spirits.

The crowd walked with Vasquez and his wife into the densely assembled hut village. They slowly paraded through the narrow dirt streets as he kissed babies and posed for pictures. Halfway through, he stopped and asked the photographer to show him a few of the pictures. The photographer pulled up his favorites of the day on the camera's display screen. The first was an endearing shot of Vasquez hugging an elderly Guna woman with a brightly colored scarf.

"This is good," Vasquez said, pointing to the scarf. "Look at that mola—beautiful picture. Let's get that on the website."

"Yes, for sure," the photographer replied as he pulled up the next photo.

This one was of Vasquez and the village leaders standing with their arms resting over each other's shoulders in front of a multitude of red and yellow flags.

"Joder esto es malo," Vasquez cursed. He pointed at the tribal flags mixed in with his own. The sight of the two similarly colored red and yellow flags placed in such close proximity lent the appearance of their being unified under the same party. The only noticeable difference was that while his Molirena party flag bore the symbol of a proud rooster, the Guna flag featured a large black swastika in the center.

Vasquez waved his hand under his chin in a cutting motion. "No more."

He remembered seeing that flag during a high school Panamanian history class. It harkened back to a revolt by the Guna in 1925, and he was shocked to see it still flying proudly from atop the village huts. His history teacher had rationalized the swastika away by explaining that World War II had not started until 1939, and therefore the Guna had had the symbol first. Supposedly it was an ancient symbol depicting the four sides of the world, as well as the point of origin from which the peoples of the world had emerged. Vasquez had never fully bought that explanation. He had learned in still another history class that Hitler had started using the symbol in 1920, five years before the Guna revolt.

"Erase what you have. Put the camera away."

As Vasquez toured the rest of the village, he mentally prepared himself to deliver his speech. He knew it by heart and had delivered it to great effect in Panama City the week before. When he'd first put together the trip, his intention had been to tailor the speech more specifically to the Guna audience. Amidst the frantic pace to get things organized, though, he'd forgotten to make the changes. His standard stump speech was a firebrand populist address about poverty, injustice, and corruption. Fortunately, the Guna in each of the villages he had visited so far seemed to like it, though he wasn't sure why the speech was so enthusiastically received.

Maybe the Guna simply liked hearing about the problems of the outside world because they served as reaffirmation of the Guna's choice to continue living the traditional lifestyle of their ancestors. The anti-corruption thread appeared to work particularly well.

The crowd had grown to several hundred Guna as he began to speak. Even a few tourists watched from a distance. This time through, though, in the middle of the speech, he decided to double down and expand on the anti-corruption theme. He had pulled certain lines out in Panama City, concerned that they could be too dangerous. But here on the edge of civilization, out of sight from the rest of the world, he felt more comfortable speaking from his heart.

"It is not enough to simply shuffle around the same cast of characters among positions of power within our government," he told the crowd. "We must vote to break free of the corrupt powers that have foisted these villains upon us. We must not accept the option of choosing between the lesser of two independently evil personalities when we know their souls are owned by the same man." The Guna clapped and cheered. Vasquez was emboldened to see that his metaphorical language had struck such a chord. He wondered, though, if the Guna knew which devil or demon he was referring to. Were they excited because they understood what he was saying? Or did they hope he was promising to free their village from some kind of actual *chupacabra* living out in the forest? He decided to elaborate on the point.

"If you support me in this election, know that I will never back down and submit to the hidden powers lurking in the shadows. Powers such as the likes of the billionaire Armando Delgado."

The Guna went quiet, gazing back at Vasquez with blank expressions. For a people whose official currency had been coconuts as late as the 1990s, the very concept of a billionaire had to be difficult to imagine. They looked at one another to see how to react, perhaps wondering if anyone among them knew of this man who owned so many coconuts.

The flickering of a gold watch in the afternoon sunlight caught Vasquez's attention. It was attached to the wrist of a tall dark-haired man in tourist clothing at the periphery of the gathering. The man was glaring at him. Apparently, there was one person for whom the name Armando Delgado meant something. Vasquez paused and squinted to get a better look at him. The man turned his back and walked away.

REX NASH

July 15
Fenwick Island, Delaware

Early that morning, Rex had found the beach house owned by Jessica's parents. Although there hadn't been any noise coming from inside the house, and the driveway was empty, he'd decided to go to the door and give it a knock anyway. No answer.

He'd lowered his head, walked back into the street, and kept going until he'd reached the top of the sand dune that separated the end of the road from the beach. He'd looked back at the house. Still no sign of anyone.

After taking off his shoes and continuing over the dune, he walked along the beach for what must have been miles before he stopped to wade his toes in the cool water. The sea rushed over his feet and rose up to his knees before flowing back into the ocean again, leaving behind only isolated puddles until the return of the next big wave. He stared at the water and wondered if he would ever see Jessica again. Suddenly, he heard an unmistakable voice cry out to him. Was his mind playing a trick? Was that really her?

He turned to see a woman sprinting along the sand. Rex rubbed his eyes. There she was, all grins, as if no time at all had passed. Seeing her lit him up, sparking emotions long dormant.

He hadn't seen those eyes for almost ten years, and it was in this very place that he'd last gazed upon them. It was also not lost on him that it was here he and Jessica had spent their last night in each other's arms.

"Hey, Rex... where have you been?" Jessica asked as she hugged him.

"I can't believe it's you," Rex said, leaning his chin on her forehead. He tightly held onto her embrace as his emotions swung wildly back and forth between overwhelming joy and an overbearing sorrow. Such intense happiness had eluded Rex in every relationship since he'd last seen her. The feeling triggered a sense of loss, like that of a prisoner being set free and returning to the real world only to be reminded of everything that he'd forfeited. He knew without question in this moment that he needed to marry this woman.

Jessica looked up at him with that beautiful smile. It reminded him of those days of their youth when there had been nothing but possibilities, and all roads had been wide open. They'd grown up in the same D.C. suburb and gone to school together until her parents transferred her to a private school. After that, they only saw each other on occasion, mostly by chance, but there had always been a mutual sense that they would inevitably find their way back to each other. It had never seemed possible that they'd run out of summers or that so much time could pass by.

Despite a decade of what had to have involved at least as many misadventures and failed relationships as his own journey, she looked barely a day older than how he remembered her. This time, however, the fantasy of never-ending youth was gone, replaced by an unrelenting force, much like gravity, pulling the doors closed on the future.

They spent the rest of the day together, catching up and revisiting the nostalgic pubs, mini golf courses, and beach shops of their youth. They even snuck in a game of Ping-Pong after lunch at the ultra-cheesy Bad Ass Café on the boardwalk in nearby Ocean City, Maryland. They took goofy pictures in front of the hardwood sign on the ocean-facing patio. It featured a purple donkey and the slogan "Where the Celebrities Hang Out." As the afternoon grew late, they returned to the Fenwick seashore.

"So, you want to know why I left politics?" he asked as the sun began to set.

Jessica shaded her deep, dark-brown eyes with one hand and smiled. "I was actually wondering why you entered politics in the first place."

Rex raised his eyebrows and responded with an exaggerated shrug. "A myriad of motivations drove the decision."

"I remember all of your passions to save the world," Jessica replied. "But politics?"

Rex just sighed.

"Well, you must have been good at your job, I guess," she said, raising her body up into a sitting position on the beach blanket they had laid out. She opened the Styrofoam cooler they had picked up at Anthony's Liquors on 33rd Street. It was filled to the brim with ice and wine. "I mean, you got Senator Sheehan elected. My parents were very impressed when they heard you managed that campaign."

"They were?"

"Yes. They said it was a big upset when she won." Jessica poured a splash of prosecco into a plastic wineglass. "How could you walk away from running campaigns after a big win like that?"

"Here, give me your glass for a second," Rex said. "I want to show you something." He placed the plastic wineglass down on the sand. "Cup your hands. Okay, good. Press your thumbs together until there is only a pinpoint opening in the gap over where your thumbs meet. Now tilt your hands back slightly."

Jessica placed her hands together but couldn't quite mimic the position.

"Like this." Rex wrapped his arms around her and cupped her suntanned hands with his own. He could smell the sunscreen on her skin. It felt warm and moist against his.

"Place one eye up to that tiny opening and try to look through," Rex said. "What do you see?"

"Wow, it feels like I can see the whole ocean."

"Now imagine it as the perspective you see through at all times," Rex said. "Based only on what you see, where would you figure that you are right now?"

"Ahh, I guess it looks like I'm in the middle of the ocean." Jessica laughed.

"But you're not," Rex said. "You're here on the beach. So, from your perspective, what you're seeing is a lie. Now hold still."

He plucked a small lump of sand from the beach and placed it in the opening between her thumbs. "Now what do you see?"

"A clump of sand and nothing else," she said.

"If that were your only perspective, then where would we be right now?"

"The beach," Jessica said.

"Which brings up a famous ancient saying I just invented."

"Which is?" Jessica asked.

"A grain of truth can conceal an ocean of lies," he replied.

"So grains of sand are not to be trusted?" Jessica teased. "I knew it; I was always suspicious of them. The way they just sneak in between my toes on the beach and jump onto my hair and hop all over my clothes like ninjas. Then, when I'm inside the house, they leap out and make a mess."

Rex smiled. "That too."

"What does all of this have to do with you and politics?" Jessica asked.

"When you're constantly working yourself to death for one cause or another, there's not much time for reflection," Rex said. "If you look at the larger picture, sometimes you end up realizing that even your most strenuous efforts are actually self-defeating."

"I'm sure there was plenty of time for you to reflect when you were cashing those paychecks," Jessica said. "Don't you think you're making perfect the enemy of the good here?"

"True, but we all operate with skewed perspectives. And I'm certainly no different."

"See, you're way too idealistic for politics. Plus, I know you, and you hate politicians."

Rex smiled. *She knows me better than I know myself.* He reached into the cooler and plucked out a cheese cube, then tossed it to a group of seagulls scavenging along the sand in front of them. "But I love to help get them out of office."

He watched as the seagulls huddled around the point in the sand where the cheese had landed. One lucky bird emerged from the group and shot skyward, flying over the ocean with its prize clenched securely in its beak.

"Also, it was easier to survive as a long shot. The sharks don't care about you when you're still small. But after Sheehan's win, it was as if I'd poured blood into the water."

"It's kind of a one-eighty to turn around and work for the insurance lobby, though," Jessica said. "Sounds like the least exciting job ever."

"Oh, it is. But before this I lived in six states in the last eight years," Rex said. "At some point, even I'll need a sense of home." Their gazes met, and he wondered if she understood what he really meant.

He felt torn between a boiling desire to let loose and express every detail of his longing for her, and the pull of his rational mind dragging him back from the edge of disaster. Unfortunately, as great of a gift as he had with words, he didn't know how to tell her outright.

Jessica plucked a handful of sand and flicked it onto Rex's chest. I still can't believe that you won at Ping-Pong earlier," she teased.

Rex grinned, glad for the distraction. "Oh, that was a close one. We can go back to the Bad Ass Café tomorrow if you really want to get beat again."

"Did you absolutely have to win?"

"Of course."

"But it was double match point!"

"We had quite the crowd of barflies looking on," Rex said, in mock outrage. "They were rooting for me. I couldn't let them down."

"I believe they were rooting for *me*."

"I know," he said. "Which is why I really *did* have to win."

They both laughed.

She planted her palm down on the beach blanket, her moist forearm pressing against his chest, and leaned in. Her hair dangled over him. Rex gently pushed a strand out of her face and put an arm around her as he brought his legs into a sitting position. He kissed her, then pulled her in near his cheek and stared out over the water.

"I miss this place," Rex said. "I miss you."

He felt happier than he could ever remember. How could he have let her slip away from him all those years ago?

"You're the one that disappeared," Jessica said.

"I know."

"The last thing I heard of you, my parents saw your mom at the grocery store one day. She told them you were overseas, in the war."

Rex lowered his head. In Jessica's world, everyone had parents that would foot the bill for college, or surely there'd be some scholarship or grant to cover those who didn't. At the time it would have been great to tell her a heroic tale about signing onto an ROTC commitment for altruistic and patriotic reasons. The truth? It had been about money, simple as that. "I never thought we would still be at war by the time I graduated."

"What happened over there?"

"Let's talk about something else."

"Fine then, since Rex Nash is done with war and politics, what's keeping him from leaving D.C.?"

"I am done with politics," Rex said. "Politics on the road, at least. And you're right. I guess I don't really need to be in D.C."

"Well, the time apart only makes the right now that much better," Jessica said. "You know, the weather's really nice in North Carolina," she added. "We never get snowstorms, and the traffic isn't bad."

"Tempting," Rex said, leaning in again.

Jessica kissed him back. "Think about it."

MARCO

July 16
Panama City, Panama

Not far from ATLAPA Convention Center, in a central residential district of Panama City known as San Francisco, Marco sat at a familiar table in a private backroom of the Los Años Locos steakhouse. He wore a gold Panerai watch, Italian brown leather shoes, khakis, and a polo shirt. Tall, dark-haired, and thirty-five years old, he knew he was good-looking. Still, he didn't want to rest on his bone structure alone.

The face of the gentleman sitting across from him was unfamiliar. Though Marco knew of him by reputation, they'd never met. From the way his impeccably tailored linen suit fit, he appeared much younger than a man who was supposed to be in his sixties. Was this really *the* Edgardo Blades?

"The meeting will take place this October, right here in Panama," Edgardo said.

Their waiter placed a fresh plate of beef carpaccio on the table beside the half-finished plates of manchego-stuffed calamari, fried plantains, and perfectly cooked slices of New York strip.

Edgardo pulled the plate close and stuffed a heaping bite of carpaccio into his mouth. Part of it dangled from his lips before he slurped it in. A drop of raw blood dribbled down his chin.

"What if he does not show?" Marco asked.

The waiter replenished their glasses of Catena Zapata Malbec Argentino and left. "He will show," Edgardo said.

A large bodyguard with glazed, dead-looking eyes closed the door behind the waiter.

"That triple-*hijueputa mexicano* Hector—he will be here for the meeting. He has no other choice." Edgardo smiled and wiped the blood from his mouth.

"A lot can happen in a few months," Marco replied.

"Yes, so do not take any further chances with that sister of his," Edgardo said. "Her computer files, you have them, yes?"

"It's done," Marco said.

"Well, leave it at that," Edgardo said.

"*Claro.*"

Now, how can I trust this Vargas man of yours won't suddenly get cold feet?"

"Trust me, he won't lose heart," Marco responded. "He doesn't have one. The man is a pure zombie."

"You're going to put this in the hands of some brainless goon?"

"Vargas is very capable," Marco said. "He's extremely good at calculating his way through things."

"Maybe he is too smart for his own good?"

"What's important is that you can trust that this man is unflinching," Marco said. "What I meant by zombie is that if he ever had a soul, it left the building long ago. The man is all impulse, programmed to react logarithmically, without inner thoughts. Like some kind of machine."

"Ahh, yes," Edgardo said. "Very useful."

Marco shrugged. "Can be."

Edgardo took a long sip of red wine and placed his glass softly down on the table. He twirled the stem between his fingers and observed the glass as fine particles of sediment swirled up from the bottom. "I'm sure you have heard some of the stories that people tell about me."

"A couple, maybe," Marco said. "I doubt they are all true."

"True or not, they create a sort of image, yes?"

"To be sure," Marco said.

"An image meant to really scare the people, yes. But if they knew any better, they would be more concerned about *you*," Edgardo said. "I'm sure they would forget me entirely if they knew even half of the disturbing things you have been up to lately."

"Let's hope not," Marco responded.

"That would be unfortunate because I do like you, Marco."

Marco looked down at his watch. "Alexia will be here soon."

"I want this to be clean," Edgardo said. "You know what that looks like?"

"Yes, I will use only the natural elements of time, place, and situation," Marco said. "My specialty."

"So they say," Edgardo said.

Marco looked again at his watch. "It's been a pleasure, but I really must go. She is probably here by now."

"Yes, go." Edgardo waved.

Marco left him in the private room and crossed the dining area to the patio. He could see Alexia waiting at a table, sipping a cappuccino. As he stepped onto the terrace, she placed her cup down and smiled at him with wanting eyes.

He approached the table and leaned over to kiss her. He pulled up his chair, took her hand, and kept her gaze.

As she began to speak, he listened with a smile, sliding his thumb up and down her hand.

REX NASH

August 23
Washington, D.C.

On a sunny day, Washington traffic was a storm of unpredictable idiocy, but add so much as a drop of rain and it became a natural disaster. Rex had already inched past two car accidents that morning and was again at a standstill.

The rain had since stopped, but the streets, cars, sidewalks, and occasional patches of grass were still coated in moisture. Ground spray splattered his windshield with gray droplets that clung and stained and smeared. Jessica was right. North Carolina had to be better than this.

Rex's attention shifted to the maniac in the car to his left who kept screaming and pummeling his horn. Foam was forming at the edges of his mouth.

D.C. was a town of outsiders. A new bunch of people flooded in with every administration, and the old bunch headed back to wherever they came from. The annual freak-outs over the slightest dusting of snow each winter was one thing, but why did they flip out over rain? It rained everywhere. There had to be another reason. Maybe the city just attracted assholes. Nothing else could explain this insanity.

Rex pulled the bar behind the steering wheel, and blue wiper fluid bubbled up and sprayed across the windshield just as the sun broke free of the overcast. The dawn, immense and furious, blazed well beneath the reach of his visor. The brilliant, migraine-inducing light was intensified even more by the reflection from hundreds of cars.

Each of his limbs bore an awful tension. From his wrists to his shoulders, his arms felt like they were weighed down with rocks. His right foot, currently pressing the brake, was granite stiff. There was nothing he could do but sit, sardined, in the line of cars.

The screen on his dashboard lit up: an incoming call from Jessica Roark. The tension in his muscles loosened, and the previously obnoxious sunrise now seemed glorious and rosy. He couldn't help but to grin.

"Hello, Mr. Nash."

"Ah, Jessica, I can't thank you enough for distracting me from rush-hour misery."

"Hey, that's one more reason to move here to North Carolina," she said.

"There is that one little problem known as my job."

"Right, and what sort of job is that?"

Rex knew where she was going with this one. "The job I hate and complain about all the time. The one I can't wait to leave, but never do."

"You always have all these detailed plans in your head, but life has a way of prevailing," she responded. "You could die tomorrow."

"Come on, Jessica, don't be overdramatic."

"Well, what if you get fired? How can you know staying there is the only way?"

Rex jerked the steering wheel as he was suddenly cut off at the light. His car swerved just inches out of the way from being hit by the foaming maniac. The man raised his middle finger as he drove off. Rex mouthed the word *motherfucker*.

"What day are you back in D.C. for your birthday?" he asked to change the subject. Her parents still lived in the same house she'd grown up in on the outskirts of D.C.

"Tuesday. I can't wait to see you!"

Rex looked over at the passenger's seat, currently filled with store-wrapped presents. The one at the top of the pile was a small blue box.

"I did get a call from a pollster in your area," he said. "Charles Lee, a friend of a friend. He said if I was tempted to get back in the politics game, he might have something for me."

"See, there you go." Jessica sounded triumphant.

"It's an option."

Rex gazed out his left window at two oversized black Range Rovers that were pulling up alongside him at a traffic light. He peered into the pitch-black tinted windows. Who was hiding in there? Another bureaucrat or politician dutifully lavishing as much taxpayer money on themselves as humanly possible? A city full of assholes. Jessica was right to return here only a few times a year.

The pair of larger vehicles crept into the intersection as the light turned, blocking his view.

"Two months is too long," Rex said as he edged out into the intersection. "It's been killing me."

As the words left his mouth, a movement caught his eye just long enough before impact for him to understand the impossibility of escape. Time slowed around him as he leaned away from the steering wheel, braced his arms, and placed his thoughts with God as a huge gray Escalade smashed through the front of his car.

#

Rex opened his eyes. The smoke made them burn and water. He was dazed but intact: a few cuts and bruises along with a searing burn from the airbag.

He heard people talking outside his car.

"Ah, shit, son!" a voice called out. "Look at this bamma."

It didn't sound like EMS.

"He gots that need for speed." Rex heard what sounded like a bunch of high school teens laughing. "Speed kills, youngin." There was a burst of coughing and more juvenile laughter. "Man, look at them presents," an older voice said. "Santa wrecked his sleigh, and I been waiting to catch that dirty ass chimney creeping, reindeer beating mother fucker out in these streets."

Rex smelled pot. *What the hell were they going on about?* He looked at his bleeding hands, then around at the busted car interior. A jagged piece of metal protruded from the dash in his direction.

That was one close call.

An arm reached in through the passenger side from the street. A fireman?

As his eyes regained focus, Rex realized the grubby face leering at him did not belong to a first responder. The guy grabbed Rex's phone and the blue box off the seat, then stuffed the phone into his own pocket.

"What the fuck?" Rex shouted.

He shouldered the door, gave it a push, and stumbled out to stare down at the twisted, smoldering mess that once had been his car. The passenger-side door was open, hanging by a single hinge. Among the broken glass and debris was a single present, still neatly wrapped in pristine glossy white paper. *Where did he go? Where is the blue box?*

Spectators were gathering, whispering, and taking photos with their phones. A few put their hands to their mouths. Rex noticed a group of shady-looking characters hanging out on the steps of a nearby house. They seemed indifferent. Probably had been partying since last night.

One of them ripped open a present and tossed the wrapping paper into the street. Pissed, Rex stomped their way.

"Give me my stuff!" he shouted, closing in.

The older one stepped off the porch, dismissing him with a squint.

"Slow your roll, my guy."

Rex's eyes locked onto the little blue box in the man's hand. "Let me rephrase this," he fired back just a few steps away. "Get your hands the fuck off my stuff."

The older guy lurched forward, narrowing the distance between them. "Your stuff?"

The closer Rex got, the more certain he was that this might not end well. He tried to calm himself and said, in the most reasonable tone he could summon, "You just stole it out of my car."

He knew these guys had probably seen plenty of people that looked like him rotating in and out of the district. Cogs in the political machine, shipped in from Iowa, South Dakota, wherever. The types that thought they ran the world and said all kinds of stupid shit. He suspected that these guys had probably educated more Rexes than they could count. They didn't care what Congress member, what office, or what agency such people worked for. On this corner, this block of South Capitol Street, they were the ones who ran things.

"Santa Claus gave us this shit right here! It's mine now, so what you gonna do about it, biatch?"

Rex sprang forward and grabbed for the blue box in the guy's hand, but the thug jerked it away and stuffed his palm into Rex's face. A hard punch from one of the younger ones landed in his gut. Hunched over and coughing, Rex reached up with his left hand and grabbed the older guy's shirt.

He pulled himself up and swung around with a well-placed uppercut to the guy's chin. The thug's knees gave out, and he dropped. The blue box hit the ground, and a diamond ring tumbled out.

Rex looked up, expecting an onslaught of blows from the other two, only to find them running down the street with the other gifts. As he stood over the woozy older thug, he felt a sudden jolt in his back. He crashed hard into the ground, and a cop grabbed for his arms. Cold metal cuffs clamped onto his wrists.

#

It was almost surreal to see his old friend Ronnie from grade school wearing a police uniform and driving a squad car.

"Hey, sorry about all that back there," Ronnie said. "The officer who tackled you, he's actually a pretty good guy. He feels bad that you got stuck with that assault charge. There wasn't much he could do, though."

Rex nodded to him in the rearview mirror from the back seat. Ronnie was an odd mix. His military buzz cut had no business being matched with goofy pothead eyes and a surfer-dude facial expression. Then again, there was a lot about Officer Ronnie Beverly that was odd.

The first time Rex had met Ronnie was at the lunch table in fifth grade. Ronnie had randomly sat down next to him and begun peeling off the plastic wrap on a waterlogged peanut butter and jelly sandwich. A piece of jelly fell and splattered on his shirt. Ronnie had frowned and offered the sandwich to Rex.

"You want this?"

"Man, that's soggy," Rex had told him.

Ronnie had shrugged and flung the sandwich across the lunch table. When it landed squarely on the forehead of the biggest bully in school, a melee ensued. All three of them had spent the rest of the day in the principal's office. Rex and Ronnie had been friends from that point on.

"Ronnie, we have to speed up the pace here. I'm really late for work," Rex said.

Ronnie looked over at his partner sitting in the passenger seat and smiled.

"Sure, Nash, I'll speed things up!"

The other cop rolled his eyes.

Ronnie flipped on the police lights and slammed the pedal to the floor. He started weaving recklessly in and out of traffic, making use of his siren to speed through red lights.

"Oh shit, Ronnie, not that fast! I just got out of a major accident!" Rex yelled.

"Hey, I'm a professional here," Ronnie said.

"Okay, okay, it's coming up here on the right."

Ronnie slowed his speed, and his partner glanced at Rex in the rearview. "Yeah, that dirt bag you punched, I saw him in there yelling up and down about civil rights and pressing charges, the whole nine yards. Don't worry about it—it's not going anywhere. All you have to do is call and make an appointment at the DA's office. If you go in there and explain what happened, they'll probably drop it. Saves them money and they also like handing out favors for votes over there. If not, just plead self-defense. The whole thing will be thrown out. Trust me."

"This is it," Rex said, as they approached the front of a tall modern building. "Pull over here. Guys, thanks again for your help, and the ride and everything."

As he crossed the lobby that housed the American Insurance Association, a voice shouted, "Nash, hold up!"

The receptionist was waving him down. Rex, still boiling from the morning's events, snapped back, "What, Lamar?"

Lamar held up his hands in surrender, looking hurt.

"Why you got to be like that?" he asked. "I'm just trying to do my job. I don't know who you think you is."

"I apologize," Rex said. "A really difficult morning and I'm late. So what's the vital issue at hand?"

"You look like shit," Lamar replied.

"Is that what you stopped me for? To tell me I look like shit?"

"Oh, no. Mr. Jacobson said you were to see him first thing."

"That clown? Really?"

Lamar started to giggle. "I wouldn't say that if I were you. As of last night, Jacobson is the new department head."

Rex felt his stomach sink and his nerves tingled with a foreboding sense of anxiety. "How is that possible?"

"Since there won't be a new CEO 'til next month, Bob Ackers is temporarily in charge."

Rex clenched his jaw. Ackers was placed in the VP position as a figurehead. The board had never meant for him to make any decisions.

"He's promoting everybody on his team before the new guy shows up," Lamar said.

Rex shook his head. The old man would never have put up with this shit. Why had he needed to retire so abruptly? No warning, no transition, nothing. On his last day the old man had rambled off a few sparse words about his health and then he peaced out.

"Ridiculous," Rex said. "I mean, of all people, Bob Ackers decided to promote Jacobson?"

Lamar tapped his index finger to the bridge of his nose and smiled.

"The fraternal order of coke heads?"

Lamar murmured, "Um-hum."

Rex sighed. "Wonderful."

"Tough luck," Lamar said, with an exaggerated frown.

Rex forced a smile. "Guess so. Thanks."

He took the elevator up to the fifth floor and went to the men's room to clean himself up. He dabbed specks of blood splatter off his collar with a wet paper towel and pressed dried toilet paper around his hands to stop the blood from seeping out of the cuts on his fingers.

He walked down the hall toward Jacobson's office, hearing the chatter from meetings and the one-sided barking of employees on the phone. The AIA had been in business since 1866, but the practice of lobbying went back to the beginning of human governance. The courts of every kingdom had always been besieged by the different powered interests of their times. The world of mass media and corporate public relations, on the other hand, was something entirely new to the human experience. The rapid expansion of radio and film in the years following the First World War had altered the nature of human communications forever.

The AIA began to hire former journalists with the aim of leveraging these new technologies. Soon, PR experts at the AIA and other trade associations and corporations became a seamless part of the system. Major universities now had entire departments dedicated to teaching public relations, and more students were graduating with degrees in public relations than journalism.

Rex saw corporate PR men and political campaign managers as operating in similar ways. Having worked on campaigns for most of his twenties, he had learned to sell ideas, which had come in mighty handy during his time at AIA. He found corporate PR work less satisfying, however, because it relied mostly on the power of message complexity, rather than on advocacy. Whether called jargon or

Fed speak, it had an underhanded purpose: to create obscurity and undermine a clear perception of the facts. That purpose, and the whole PR world, had always rubbed him the wrong way.

Rex strode into Jacobson's office. His new boss didn't bother to look up, his focus on his laptop screen. Thirty-five with thinning brown hair, Jacobson wore a sloppy untucked polo shirt that revealed a patchy red sunburn at the collar. As Rex neared Jacobson's desk, he noticed small pieces of dried skin peeling off around his cheekbones.

Jacobson finally glanced up and raised his palm in the air. "Hold on, give me a second to finish this."

Rex leaned in to peek over Jacobson's desk. His computer screen was open to a social media site filled with vulgar memes. Rex couldn't quite figure out the exact message being conveyed, but from the images, he could clearly see that the discussion had something to do with penises.

"Are you sure you don't want me to return later?" Rex asked. "Once you finish, um, this important activity?"

Jacobson slammed his laptop closed. "What happened to you this morning?"

"I was in a car accident."

"All I know is, you're late."

"Thanks for the concern. Lamar said you wanted to see me?"

"You're already off to a very bad start in this new era," Jacobson said. "Did you remember to call and inform me, as required by our new company guidelines, that you would be delayed after this so-called accident?"

"My phone was stolen. I went above and beyond by heading straight here. The cops gave me a ride."

"Well, it doesn't matter anyway because I've already written this incident up in an amendment to your performance report."

"Then unwrite it."

"Well, Rex, I don't think I can do that. If you want to keep your job, sign here and admit you violated the policy."

Rex took the forms and stared at them. "You know, I hadn't planned on quitting when I woke up this morning. But yeah, I'm going to go ahead and say, I quit, a hundred percent. Take these forms and eat a dick." He tossed the papers on Jacobson's desk and walked out without waiting for a rebuttal.

"You can't quit—because you're fired, buddy!" Jacobson yelled from behind the door.

Rex headed straight to his own office, collected his personal items in a cardboard file box, and took the elevator down to the ground floor. He quietly walked back across the lobby.

Lamar snickered as he pushed open the lobby door. "Uhmmm, Naaaaash."

Rex paused and held his tongue for a second. He was still pissed from the encounter with Jacobson, but he reminded himself to be nice. "What's up, Lamar?"

The receptionist's wide white smile made him look as if he were holding back a secret. He let the receiver dangle from his fingertips. "You have a phone caaall."

"On the main line? Who?"

Lamar lowered his voice. "It's *yo* mom." Clearly amused, he handed Rex the receiver.

"Hey, Mom," Rex mumbled.

"Rex, there's something I need to tell you."

"Can it wait, Mom?"

"Your grandma passed away last night."

"Oh no. What happened?"

Rex lowered his head and took a deep breath. What would happen next? He didn't know how his mom could take another loss like this so soon after his dad.

"Mom, I'm really sorry. I'll come straight to the house. Let me take care of the plane tickets, and we'll make sure to get everybody up to Grandma's as soon as possible."

"What about your job?"

"I'm going to be there, Mom. I'm one hundred percent certain that it won't be an issue to get out of work."

The funeral would be one day before Jessica's birthday. He asked Lamar to dial her number on the front desk phone so he could break the news that he wouldn't be able to spend it with her.

RAUL VASQUEZ

August 29
Boquete (Province of Chiriquí), Panama

The early-morning orange light glowed in the spaces between the window shades just as it had yesterday, when Raul Vasquez had, like today, met the dawn at his mother's bedside. The hospice nurse seated on the other side of the bed was drowsy. She stood, wiggled her foot, and massaged her calf. Then she straightened and looked at her watch. Her replacement appeared at the door, and she stepped outside into the hall to talk to her.

Vasquez was quiet as he watched his mother. Her eyes were open, but just a little, and she strained for breath. She turned her head toward him and pressed it into the pillow. Vasquez grabbed her hand and held it.

"*Mi hijo,*" she whispered. A tear fell from Vasquez's cheek, and then another. They continued until he had to bring his sleeve to his face.

Feeling a pat on his shoulder, he pulled his hand from his eyes, wiped it on his leg, and looked up at the man in a black shirt and white collar who stood next to him.

"*Gracias, Padre,*" Vasquez said.

"Señor Vasquez, your mother has spoken much of you these past few months," Rev. Abasolo said.

"It had been so long since I saw her, and then this happened," Vasquez said.

"She told me," Rev. Abasolo said.

"Why did I not come to see her, Padre?" Vasquez asked. "I acquiesced to the pressures of running the company. And for what? I already had more money than I knew what to do with. When my father passed away, I was on a failed business trip that meant nothing."

"And now it's politics," Rev. Abasolo said.

"Why?" Vasquez asked. "So I can brag about how popular I am? To make more women chase after me and piss off my wife? Pressure on all sides, pulling me toward bullshit in every direction. And now I'm losing my mother."

"Clarity in life is best found looking inward, my son, not outward. The world is awash in deception."

"I want to get it right, Padre, but—"

"Trust in logic, faith, and your own mind," Rev. Abasolo said. "Tragedy can create opportunities for clarity, or you can allow it to intensify anxiety and fear of the truth." Vasquez looked down at the floor and quietly nodded. The reverend waved his hand over the bed and made the sign of the cross. "It's because you love this woman, your mother, that distraction fades and you begin to see."

Vasquez raised his head and looked into his mother's eyes.

REX NASH

September 11
Asheville, North Carolina

Rex watched as Charles, phone pressed to his ear, placed his custom-made cowboy boots atop his mahogany desk. There were several old leather chairs in the office, all of which looked expensive. The walls were lined with hunting rifles. The room boasted a fireplace, a humidor, and a small but well-stocked bar.

Rex sat in one of the leather chairs and stared at those black ostrich-toed boots with rusted brown leather calves, intrigued by the distinctive pattern of bumps in the ostrich skin where the feathers had been plucked. Charles, a slick, tall man in his early fifties, looked more like a southern lawyer than a genius in the polling business. This, to Rex, was a good thing—the typical polling wizards dressed like number-crunching nerds, but half of them couldn't do math to save their lives. The reason guys like that got business was because of how they looked, not their qualifications. Rex could tell Charles Lee was different, and not just because he had one of those *Magnum, P.I.* mustaches that had gone out of style in the eighties. He dripped confidence and gave the sense that he wasn't out to impress anyone.

Rex wondered what had brought Charles to work way out in Asheville. Strangest city, Asheville. It seemed to have sprung up spontaneously, an anomalous city in the vastness between the Blue Ridge and Appalachian Mountains. Rex knew Charles was the furthest thing from an Asheville native. He'd grown up a pure Yankee in Massachusetts, and the statistics degree on the wall was from Boston College.

Charles pulled the phone away from his ear, mouthing, "One more minute."

Rex nodded.

"The campaign season is in full swing," Charles said into the phone. "Finding an uncommitted manager is darn near impossible."

Why didn't he just work out of his company headquarters in Old Town Alexandria, on the edge of D.C.? Why way out here? Maybe Charles just got a kick out of the way rednecks and hippies clashed and commingled in the city. Asheville boasted people of many types: hillbillies, hipsters, deer hunters, vegans, retired golfers, nudist colony members, military mercenaries, and evangelists... after all, it was the site of The Cove, a colossal retreat and training center built by the legendary evangelist Billy Graham.

"Okay, will do," Charles said finally. He pulled his boots off the desk and hung up. "Sorry, Rex, that's my Panama campaign: Raul Vasquez for President. He's running as a challenger. It's nuts."

"An opposition candidate in Latin America?" Rex asked. "Good luck on that one."

Charles let out a chuckle and sank back in his chair. "Yeah, no kidding."

"Where did you get those boots?"

"Rios of Mercedes in Texas," Charles replied. "I received them as a thank-you for helping a congressman win his seat in Tyler a few years back."

"Texas?" Rex said with a raised eyebrow. "I heard you were an East Coast guy."

"Oh, I am," Charles said. "And yes, I never really wore cowboy boots before these, but they fit well, and they look pretty good."

"They do," Rex replied. "Different, but nice."

"They even make me a little taller. Best thing is, they're a conversation piece. People ask about them all the time, and it's a great excuse to tell them about that congressman from Tyler and how I helped him win."

"Always an angle with you."

"I even had a replica pair made for when these wear out."

Rex smiled and delivered a nod of respect.

"Well, I'm glad to see you here," Charles said. "It's a lot tougher to find a good campaign manager these days. Gerrymandering of congressional districts has exploded, and the national committees are dumping all their money into shoring up incumbents against primary challengers. It's a crime, really. They're defrauding the donors."

If anyone understood the operations of the Democrat and Republican national committees, it was Charles. He'd been around for ages, earning an almost legendary reputation among campaign insiders. He'd managed to become the political director of our party's national committee by age thirty and used the connections from the job to open a polling firm in secret. He'd pressured candidates into hiring his firm and directed the committee to do the same as they poured money into nationwide independent polling expenditures. Soon his company had garnered millions of dollars a year in contracts. At the end of his term, he'd publicly joined the firm, which by that point had become the largest in the country.

"There just aren't that many competitive campaigns anymore," Charles said. "Makes it tough to find anyone with real experience. You've worked some much bigger races than our man Bob Haskins, though. Heck, I handled the polling for Senator Sheehan's opponent. To this day, I still don't understand how you pulled it off. We polled every month, and you guys were never even on the radar. That last month, though—it's like you flicked a switch and we were neck and neck. Impressive. Anyway, what attracted you here?"

"More than one reason," Rex said.

"Ah yes, the girl," Charles said. "She must be something. Win the campaign, get the girl. That's a good plan."

"You got it," Rex replied.

"Well, Haskins wasted no time on pulling the trigger to get you here," Charles said. "Now, he did balk for a second when he heard about that recent assault charge of yours."

Rex felt a rush of anxiety shoot through his body. He took a long deep breath and attempted to contain the fury that was boiling up inside of him.

"Hey, what can I say on that one? Knocked out a mugger." Rex shrugged. "I'm just glad the punch connected the way that it did. Otherwise, I would have been short out of luck."

"Tough-as-nails campaign managers are what you need if you want to win. At least, that's what I told Haskins," said Charles. "A pussy manager is a losing proposition. Now he says it's the main reason he hired you."

"Good man!" Rex laughed.

The door opened behind him, and an elderly man in a sharp navy blazer and khakis strolled in with an elegant, relaxed gait.

Charles stood up from his desk. "Congressman Potts! How are you?"

"Oh, fine, making the best of my forced retirement," Potts replied.

"I want you to meet Rex Nash," Charles said, gesturing. "He's our new campaign manager. The guy who's going to get that scoundrel Dumfries out of your old seat."

"Well, I'll do anything you need me to do. I hate that son of a bitch."

Charles's cell phone pinged. "All right, guys, looks like the candidate is downstairs," he announced.

They walked downstairs and out of the building to where a big black Buick idled in the parking lot. Bob Haskins, tall, gray-haired, and fifty-five years old, stepped from the car's passenger side and extended his hand to Rex. He looked like a true southern good ol' boy, with an unaffected "aw-shucks" grin.

"Bob, this is Rex Nash. Rex is gonna help put this thing over the top for us," Charles said.

"Good to finally meet you in person, Bob," Rex said, giving him a firm handshake. The candidate looked Rex in the eye, unblinking.

Bob squeezed harder, and Rex matched his grip. *Is this how they do it in the South?* Rex wondered as Bob gripped even tighter. Thrown off by the overly extended pissing contest, Rex broke free of the handshake.

"Good, strong politician's handshake you got there, Bob," Rex told him. "That's what I like to see."

"We're very excited to finally get you on the ground here," Bob said. "I think you will enjoy Asheville. Full of some very interesting characters."

"I think I saw a few on my way in," Rex said.

"Oh, you ain't seen nothin'," Bob said. "Here, hop in."

Rex, Charles, and James Potts piled into the back of the car, and Bob returned to the passenger seat.

"Let's take him on a tour, guys. He oughta see the drum circle before we show him the campaign offices," Bob suggested.

"You mean, let him know what he's in for," James Potts said.

"You can't be serious," Rex said.

"Oh, it's a real, literal drum circle," Charles said.

"Is there some kind of hippie festival?" Rex asked.

"Unfortunately, no. This is Asheville all year round," said Charles.

Bob pointed out the window. "Hey, Rex, you see those young bums over there on that park bench?"

"Yeah, I see the two people sitting there."

"Two bums."

"Yes, of course."

"Our bums are unlike what you may be used to up there in Washington, D.C. In fact, I bet you that those two vagrants on the bench have more money in the bank than all of us combined. Except James, 'cause no one has more money than he does."

As they passed a solitary skyscraper, Bob said, "Hell, there's one of James's buildings right there. He owns half the town."

Rolling along Patton Avenue, they passed Pritchard Park.

"There you go," James said. "The drum circle, as promised."

People of all persuasions were packed in a circle, beating on conga drums and tambourines, or just clapping. A cloud of what certainly wasn't tobacco smoke hung like fog over the gathering. A few tourists stood apart, taking pictures.

Several dreadlocked hippies danced in a trancelike state, one of them shirtless and body-painted, as a chant rose from the crowd.

"Interesting," Rex said.

"I told you it was real," Charles bragged.

The brakes suddenly slammed. Rex threw his hands up, bracing for another crash. When he realized he was the only one to overreact, he slid his hands back into his pockets. Still on edge, he peered over the driver's shoulder and out the front windshield. A man on a unicycle was stopped in front of their car. His head was bald, save for two purple-and-green Elvis-sized sideburns. The man crossed his arms, huffed, and gave them a *who-do-you-think-you-are* stare. He took his time pedaling away.

"Wow," Rex said. "Just when you think you've seen it all."

"All right, enough sightseeing," Haskins said. "Let's get out of here."

"James donated some office space to us in a couple of his buildings. Why don't we take a look?" Charles said. "Nash, you can let us know which works best on a strategic and functional level. We couldn't find a decent apartment for you, so James has a house you can use. After we look at office space and pick up the key, we'll take you there to get yourself situated."

"Sounds good," Rex replied.

A few hours later, they drove up to a big manor with a spacious shaded porch dating back to the days before air-conditioning, when rocking chairs and lemonade were the only reprieve from the Carolina heat.

"It's an old house, Rex. Probably close to a century," James said as they walked to the front door. "But charming, I hope. This is where I lived when I was in Congress. We even ran the last campaign from here. After we lost, though, I just didn't want to come back. There's a lot of stuff still piled up on the first floor, I'm afraid. You're probably best off keeping most of your activities to the upstairs."

"Is everything still working?" Rex asked.

"Oh, yeah. Came in here the other day with the gas company, electric, and all the rest," James explained. "Though you're gonna have to call the cable company on your own. I refuse to deal with such people."

"Thanks. The place should work out just fine."

After the others left, Rex was struck by how cluttered the first floor really was. James hadn't been kidding. Empty boxes and campaign material were piled on old furniture. The dust everywhere was as thick as the pot fog at the drum circle, and cobwebs clung to every corner of the ceiling.

On his way upstairs, he noticed a series of framed political cartoons on the wall. Every one of them referenced James Potts with jokes about his corrupt nature. In one, he was rendered as an enormous vampire, crouching over the town and sucking its blood. In another, he appeared as Doctor Faustus, making a deal with the devil.

Rex picked a bedroom and set down his bag. Exhausted, he fell on the bed and rolled onto his back. He'd only planned to rest for a second, but immediately found his eyes growing heavy. Just before they closed, he spotted a cat-shaped clock on a nearby bookshelf. The cat's narrow yellow pupils seemed to watch him. He wondered what the cat's intentions were. *Ridiculous*, Rex thought, and fell asleep.

ALFANZO

October 15
Panama City, Panama

Alfanzo drifted in and out of sleep, his feet dangling over the edge of his dirty twin mattress. The air-conditioning unit wheezed and buzzed and labored, but it barely diminished the heat of Panama City in the late afternoon.

He felt a tug at his shirt. He swatted at it with his arm and turned his face into the damp pillow. The fact that his cousin Yolma, her boyfriend, and their two kids also lived in this cramped apartment made sleep nearly impossible.

Alfanzo directed his thoughts back to a time when life had been more comfortable and sleep easier to come by. When he was about three years old, his mother had moved the family to their first house in Panama City. He fondly recalled the way the sun shone, warm and golden, through the windows of the living room, and how the skyline blackened in silhouette as it set. Those buildings looked huge, mythic, inaccessible.

One day, his mother sat him down. He was afraid when he saw the tears in her eyes and was startled by the tightness with which she hugged him. Struggling to steady her voice, she explained that they would be moving again.

They moved to a filthy, ramshackle place with some of his mother's old friends who had recently arrived in Panama City from their hometown of Colón on the Caribbean side of the country. Alfanzo and his mom had to live as squatters on a piece of neglected farmland, in an area known as Currundú. The place was filled with migrants, poor agriculture workers from the interior of the country, and indigenous Indians from the province of Darién. Others came from Colombia. The squatters built shacks out of wood, tin, cardboard, and zinc.

It was the poorest, least sanitary, and most dangerous sector of the city. Mounds of rotting food and other garbage piled up between the shacks, and there was no way to dispose of human waste. Alfanzo had never forgotten the stench.

After enough outcry and prodding from Christian movements in the city, the government had intervened, constructing thousands of low-income apartments, all in four-story complexes equipped with electricity, drinkable water, and plumbing.

The new housing was certainly more pleasing to the eye. The colors were well matched and vibrant: whites, yellows, pinks, and powder blues. Politicians of all stripes showed up to the opening, running over each other to take credit. The project, which employed construction workers from the neighborhood, didn't end with apartments. There was an amphitheater, and even new soccer fields.

Alfanzo's mother passed away shortly before the rebuilding of Currundú was complete. And before she passed, Alfanzo's cousin Yolma had come to live with them.

Life became better in the community, but scars remained. Those who had learned to live hard, to survive through violence and crime, didn't forget their old ways easily.

Now Alfanzo felt the imprint of small fingers pushing on his shoulder.

"Alfanzo, get up. You promised," Yolma's eight-year-old, Pablo, pleaded.

Alfanzo ran a hand over his fade hairstyle.

"Let's play soccer," Pablo said. "It's almost six, and Mamá won't let me go over there if it gets too late."

Alfanzo ground his fist into his right eye and wiped the sleep away. "All right, all right, be quiet," he said, swinging his legs over the side of the bed and pressing his feet to the tile floor.

"Why don't you take that boy out to the soccer field?" Yolma called from the other room. "He's been driving me crazy!"

Alfanzo shuffled out of his bedroom and into the combined kitchen and living room area. He ignored Yolma as he pulled a soda out of the fridge. The cool air washed over him, and he reluctantly closed the door.

His cousin, wearing a purple tank top and jean shorts, smacked her lips at Alfanzo as he drank his soda. She was painting her nails on the couch while a girlfriend braided her hair. When he finally looked over, she put her nail polish bottle on the table and gave him an evil stare. "Well?" she prompted.

"Okay, okay," Alfanzo replied. "*Niño, ir a buscar la pelota.*"

Pablo sprinted back into Alfanzo's room.

Yolma's friend gave Alfanzo a good looking-over and smiled. "Hey, Alfanzo," she said, "what you doing for the game tonight?"

"I have to work with Ruben."

"During a World Cup qualifier?" Yolma asked. "I don't know why you mess around with those people."

"We have to get the new flyers and T-shirts out to each of the party offices before Vasquez gets here," Alfanzo said. "He's going to change Panama, you wait."

Pablo returned from his room with the soccer ball.

"All right, kid," Alfanzo said. "Let's play." On his way out the door, he added over his shoulder, "If Ruben shows up before I get back, call me, please."

#

Alfanzo fell onto the artificial grass—pretending, of course, but he hoped Pablo didn't realize that. The kid seemed intent on winning honestly, and he'd voiced suspicion about his winning streaks before. Yet every time he bolted past Alfanzo to score, Pablo seemed to forget.

This time, though, the kid also forgot to aim. The ball sailed toward the goal but smacked the left goalpost and bounced back in their direction.

Alfanzo ran up behind him and took the ball away. Rushing down the field at full speed, he pulled his leg back for an improbable shot. From just past the half-line, he sank it hard into the right corner of the net. Then he leaped up and yelled, "*Goaaall!* Panama!"

"No fair! No fair!" Pablo screamed.

As he caught his breath, Alfanzo spotted a police officer on the sidewalk just past the field. He wore a military-style uniform and a machine gun over his shoulder. His manner seemed aggressive, but he grinned at Alfanzo, impressed with his shot, before going on his way. Alfanzo tossed the ball back to Pablo. "Maybe you could be the goalie and I could try a penalty kick," the kid said, but Alfanzo ignored him. Something else had caught his eye: a group of people on their way toward them. At the front of the pack was a tall, slender guy about twenty years old with his hair buzzed so high that it almost looked like a Mohawk. He wore expensive-looking jeans and thick, dark shades. Alfanzo recognized him immediately.

"All right, it's time to go," Alfanzo said to Pablo.

"But why?" Pablo whined.

"Just give me the ball and do what I tell you." Alfanzo grabbed it and shoved it into his backpack. "Let's go."

"Alfanzo!" the man with the shades called out. Alfanzo put his head down, pretending not to hear, and kept walking.

"I know you can hear me!" the man yelled again.

A knot formed in the pit of Alfanzo's stomach: part rage, part hopelessness. He stopped and gulped. *Deep breaths*, he thought. He tried, but it didn't work.

"*Que so pa?*" he said reluctantly.

"Hey, I need you to do something for me," said the man in the sunglasses, walking right up to Alfanzo.

"I have to meet Ruben in a few minutes."

"Don't worry about any of that. It's no big deal."

Alfanzo knew very well that it would be a big deal. It was always a big deal with this guy. He had seen him gun down two people in broad daylight and walk around the next day like nothing had happened. No one ever said a word to him about it; they were afraid to. A few times he had handed money to Alfanzo, a couple of years his junior, and had asked him to do small jobs. But Alfanzo had a real job now, working with Ruben on the campaign. He didn't want any more to do with this thug.

"I need you to keep this in your house for a little bit." The man pulled an item covered in a red bandanna from his pocket.

"Come on, man."

"Just put it in your backpack. No big deal."

He grabbed Alfanzo's shoulder and unzipped his backpack. He pulled out the soccer ball and stuffed the package inside.

"Thanks for the ball, Alfanzo."

Pablo's eyes welled.

Alfanzo delivered a pleading stare at the man and pointed to Pablo's sad face in hopes of sympathy, but the man turned and walked away with the ball.

"But, Alfanzo, the ball!" Pablo cried.

Alfanzo grabbed his arm hard and yanked him forward.

"Come on, Pablo, let's go."

Back at the apartment, Ruben, who at thirty years old had been Vasquez's longtime personal assistant since well before Vasquez had started his run for president, was waiting on the couch. Ruben didn't have any specialized training, but he was versatile and dependable. Trust was important, and rare, in politics, and Ruben was definitely someone Vasquez trusted. He'd even worked for the Vasquez Coffee Company right out of high school.

Right now, he had his arm around Yolma's friend. He quickly removed it, smashed his cigarette into a nearby ashtray, and tried to seem like he was in a hurry. "Come on. Let's go," he said.

"Just a second. I have to get something," Alfanzo responded.

"Ruben, you need to relax," Yolma's friend said. "Why don't you stick around and watch the game?"

"I've been running around with Vasquez all day. Believe me, I want to kick back and watch the game more than anyone, but we have to get this done tonight."

Alfanzo went into his room and knelt by his bed, unzipping the backpack. He unfolded the red handkerchief to find a revolver.

Ruben popped the door open behind him. "Alfanzo! *Vamos!*"

Alfanzo dropped the gun back in the bag and threw it under his bed.

"*Tranquilo*, Ruben."

"Just messing with you, man. Take your time. Besides, you smell. Take a shower or something. I can keep your cousin's friend company a while."

REX NASH

October 15
Asheville, North Carolina

It was nine thirty at night, and Rex was on his eighth cup of coffee for the day. He knew that once again he'd be staring up at the ceiling later, cursing himself for every cup. All the caffeine did was make him too sleepy to work and too wired to fall asleep.

He'd only been running Haskins's campaign for a month, but he was already back to the same old lifestyle: manic workflow, sleeplessness, neglecting personal relationships.

Rex loved the battle of politics. He loved the primal challenge of a zero-sum, winner-take-all competition. He was never afraid of a fight. He'd grown up in a tough neighborhood and had learned very early how it felt to be on either side of an ass kicking.

Those experiences had taught Rex to thrive in the heat of battle. During the most intense situations on the campaign trail, he was a rock. When everyone else was pulling their hair out, clamoring for the panic button, he remained calm.

Maybe I like the fight too much, he thought. *Maybe that's a problem. I came out here to spend more time with Jessica, but I haven't visited her all month. What happened to "Rex Nash is done with politics"?* Jessica's warning that he was too idealistic for politics kept echoing in his head.

At least, he told himself, Haskins was a better man for the seat than Dumfries. Hopefully. Rex didn't really know. It probably wouldn't make a bit of difference anyway.

Rex remembered his first meeting with Charles and how he had complained that there weren't many competitive campaigns anymore. Outside of a few truly tight races, most of these supposed contests had become something much closer to professional wrestling. Maybe the golden age of American democracy had passed.

Or perhaps it was just a bottoming out before an inevitable revival. People were dumber and more crooked than they'd ever been, creating fertile ground for the philosophy of Machiavelli to grow unrestrained like a noxious weed. Or maybe people weren't more crooked these days—they'd always been pretty corrupt— but this age had to be setting a record for stupidity.

Machiavelli's whole worldview could be summed up in one simple sentence: *Think of what an asshole would do in any given situation, then do that.*

This realization was probably one of the keys to Rex's winning streak. He held the strong opinion that most politicians were assholes. It was in no short measure due to this view that Rex had developed a nearly clairvoyant knack for anticipating an opponent's moves.

With a fair playing field, he could easily guide Haskins's campaign to another victory. But it wasn't a fair playing field, he reminded himself. It was basically war. And war—no matter what treaty you signed, or which human rights views you espoused— didn't have any rules. Fairness didn't even factor in. He wondered if a bunch of hicks from North Carolina would have the gall to steal an election. Yes, they most certainly would.

The air was humid, fragrant as Rex walked alone in the dark through the streets of downtown. A mist began to fall. He didn't mind—it was cold against the coffee in his belly.

The dead were going to rise on election day, as they did every election day. And they were going to cast votes for the other guy. Though the dearly departed were the most dependable voters in the system, he reassured himself that those voters barely made a dent.

Maybe if things came down to a few hundred votes—but it was hardly ever that close. More often than not, such razor-thin elections were decided in the shadiest of ways: Some random ballot box would turn up late in the evening in an isolated spot, such as an Indian reservation or an unincorporated township in the middle of nowhere. There'd be a hundred-percent turnout for the precinct, every ballot would be cast for the same candidate, and there would be just enough votes to tip the balance.

When you had multiple parties, as in most general elections, the counting was pretty reliable. There tended to be enough competing interests in the room to watch important elections carefully. Primaries, though, were a whole other story. The vote-counting game was run by the powers that be, who tended to favor incumbents. But for this election, redistricting had shaken things up, and no one had had time to develop the infrastructure needed to steal a victory.

Rex found his way inside to the Thirsty Monk Pub, an eclectic dive bar with cluttered walls and high-end micro brews. His hair was a bit soggy from the rain, but he didn't care enough to deal with it.

He spotted Charles Lee and Bill Casey, his team's TV ad producer, at a table and joined them. Bill was a huge guy, a former linebacker for the University of Nebraska. He'd taken his first real job working on one of Rex's campaigns, and they'd remained friends ever since. Bill worked with the same intensity he'd demonstrated playing football, and only a few years later he had become one of the best in the business.

Rex stood to greet the next arrival. Dan Greener was a skinny guy with tight white curls of hair and orange leathery skin from too many days on the golf course. A pioneer in the direct mail business, he was an expert in targeting and persuading primary voters.

"Dan, thanks for flying in so quickly and for coming out tonight," Rex said. "This is Charles, our pollster, and Bill Casey. Bill runs our media spots."

"No problem, happy to be here," Dan replied, shaking hands.

They sat, and Bill waved a waitress over. After he asked what everybody wanted, Rex got things rolling.

"We took a gamble by going aggressive early, but Dan has come through big with some top-notch mail that's scaring the crap out of the competition right now. And, Bill, your radio blitz is generating a ton of responses on Twitter, so it's having an effect."

"Damn right," Bill said, smiling.

"We also picked off some major donors from our primary opponents," Rex continued. "Even more significant, rumor has it that Congressman Dumfries pulled together his advisors and donors late last night to decide whether he'll even run again. I doubt we will be so lucky, but the fact that he's even asking the question is a positive for us."

"The gerrymandering of the new district is absurd," said Charles. "Dumfries is good, but he has to know this could be a bridge too far, even for him. If he sees us make a few big moves, he will think twice about running. But they have absolutely no one else to fill his spot. If he drops out, the general election is a done deal."

"Let's double down on the frontloaded strategy and push these fuckers out," Rex said.

"Agreed!" Bill said.

"Dan, I sent over final edits on the next generic pieces last night. Haskins already approved them, so pull the trigger."

"Already at the printer," Dan said.

"Perfect," Rex said. "We should have voter ID data in by week's end. Over the next three weeks, let's get three issue-ID pieces to the full universe of people in the voter file who cast a ballot in the past two primaries."

"I'll get the price quotes and drafts to you by this weekend," Dan said.

Rex turned to Bill, who put his oversized beer down as if he'd just been busted for something. "I love the media plan and rapid-response prep, but it's anticipating too much from the enemy here," he said. "This is not a presidential campaign. We're dealing with a bunch of jokers in a backwoods Carolina primary here. Delaying our TV ad production to try and outfox these idiots is totally unnecessary. Just run high quality out of the gate and steamroll these clowns. Doesn't matter what they respond with—they won't have enough time or money to catch up."

"We can do that, but we're going to need a benchmark poll first," Bill said.

"You have to love TV," Charles said. "We can say whatever wild shit we choose, and no one can question it or answer back. Yell at the tube all you want—it can't hear you."

"The media is ten times worse," Bill retorted. "At least with ads, you know what you're getting. All these hundreds of cable channels, yet they all suck. It's a mirage. They're all owned by the same handful of people."

"It's fucked up," Rex said. "Winning campaigns is all about time, money, and message. But today's voters are being hit with an outlandish barrage of useless info: tablets, cell phones, wearables, cable, whatever. It's tough for a message to get through that level of mental pollution."

"People can't concentrate under that kind of an onslaught. It really supercharges the effect of distorted reality," Charles said.

"We have a benchmark in the field right now," Rex said.

"Yep," Charles replied. "We should get top lines off of the poll tonight."

"Once we have the results from the poll, I'll draft up some scripts. Bill, let's plan to start filming next week," Rex said. "Four ads over the next eight weeks at five-hundred-fifty points per week, capping each at a thousand total per message. Bump it to a thousand points per week down the stretch."

Charles looked down at his pinging phone. "Here we go," he said. "Top lines are in, and wow. Forty-five percent Haskins, eighteen percent Murphy. Look at this: fifty-five percent Haskins over thirty-eight percent Dumfries, the fucking incumbent!"

"Holy win bonuses," Bill yelped. "This is good!"

"Yes, and it's an absolute catastrophe for the enemy," Charles said. "The trustafarians of Asheville are going to go batshit crazy when they see this."

"Wait, who are the trustafarians?" Rex asked.

"Oh, they're a unique novelty of the city," Charles said, chuckling. "Can't believe you haven't heard about them yet. Here, watch this." He tapped a passing waiter on the shoulder. "My friend here is still a bit new to Asheville," he said. "Could you explain to him what a trustafarian is?"

"Sure," the waiter said, grinning at Rex. "You see those two hippie types over there in the corner? Dirty clothes and dreadlocks?"

"Yeah, so you mean like Rastafarians, but white? So they're basically just vagabond hippies?" Rex asked.

"Not really," said the waiter. "At first glance, that girl there, she looks like a bum without money for shampoo or clean clothes, right? But notice those seven-hundred-dollar phones they're rocking. Can you afford those? There's a good chance she's Steve Jobs's daughter or something. Trust funds, my friend."

"That doesn't make any sense," Rex replied.

"Nash, it's something about the city of Asheville and the college," Charles said. "They flock from all around the country. It's like Muslims fulfilling a requirement to visit Mecca at least once in their lifetime. Asheville is the trustafarian's Mecca. But instead of pilgrimages for prayer, they come here, do heroin, and fornicate in the woods. It's been this way as long as I've lived here."

"Yeah, it's just the way it is," the waiter said before leaving the table.

"How charming," Rex said. He lifted up his phone and opened a text.

"Charles, does the candidate know the results?" Bill asked, after the waiter left.

"I'll send Haskins the top lines tonight and sit him down with the analysis tomorrow," Charles said. "Hey, Nash, you with us?"

Rex looked up from his phone. "Yep."

"Round of shots!" Bill yelled suddenly. "We're going to win this thing."

"All right, then. Get off the phone with your boyfriend," Dan scolded.

"Just a text from a girl," Rex replied.

"Let's drink," Bill said.

"Hey, Nash, you see me on the phone with my wife?" Dan asked. "This is supposed to be a business meeting, for crying out loud. Now put down the phone, and let's get fucked up."

"It's complex." Rex rose from the table. "Believe me, if it was just some random girl, I would not even think of attempting such an outrageous and grave atrocity to decorum. I'll be right back."

ALFANZO

October 15
Panama City, Panama

Alfanzo picked up a large box of campaign signs and heaved it into the back of Ruben's black Suburban. The engine was off, but the radio was on. Ruben sat in the driver's seat, listening intently to the Panama-Mexico game.

"Get up here," Ruben said. "We can finish up after the match. It's three-two, Mexico, five minutes left."

"No," Alfanzo said, tossing another box into the back. "Have to get these to the campaign office before nine. Just turn it up."

As soon as Ruben did so, cheers echoed from the condo buildings around them. "Goooooaal!" the radio howled.

"*Victoria!*" Ruben shouted. He jumped out of the car and picked Alfanzo up in a bear hug, then slammed him down on the pavement. Alfanzo threw out his arm to keep from landing too hard.

Ruben laughed. He ran into the street, jumping up and down and yelling, "Panama! Panama!"

Alfanzo raced after him.

"*Victoria!*" someone shouted from an apartment just above them. Alfanzo looked up and saw a drunk man in a Panama jersey waving a pack of lit firecrackers on the balcony. The guy threw it right at them. Alfanzo and Ruben scattered.

Ruben ran back to the sidewalk and hid behind the car. Alfanzo sprinted across the street as the firecrackers popped in his wake. As Alfanzo tried to catch his breath, a massive boom echoed across the sky. Lights exploded over the rooftops in a dazzling display of red and blue. As he stood in the middle of the street, looking up in awe, he heard a popping sound from inside a nearby apartment. Maybe they were lighting fireworks—but indoors? He jogged over to investigate.

#

High above Alfanzo and the black Suburban, Marco uncorked a wine bottle in the kitchen of a spacious, elegantly appointed modern condo that didn't belong to him. A whiff of the wine's fragrance, black fruits with subtle notes of dark chocolate and hints of green olive, verified its quality. Two glasses, two generous pours. He looked at his watch and then carried the drinks into the living room. Alexia stood waiting with a cute smile and a Team Panama Jersey. Four gentlemen sat on the sofas, her younger brother Hector among them, wearing Team Mexico jerseys and watching the game.

"Alexia. Take your glass," Marco said.

She did so just as the goalie for Panama made a critical stop with very little time left on the clock. Both Marco and Alexia breathed a sigh of relief.

"Marco!" Hector shouted from the sofa. "You and my sister need to take that Panama bullshit somewhere else. Time for you to support a real team. Alexia, how can you turn on your own country?"

"I have lived in Panama for twelve years, Hector," Alexia said. "Panama is my home now."

Panama scored a last-second goal.

"Panama!" Alexia screamed, while her brother and the other men cursed and pounded the arms of the sofa.

Fireworks erupted over the city.

"Let's go to the roof to watch," Marco suggested. She took his hand, and they climbed the stairs. Fireworks crackled as they stepped onto the roof.

#

Hector stared warily at Marco and Alexia as they left.

"*Puta maricón,*" he said, once they were completely out of sight.

Hector's friends responded with raised brows in a moment of shock that quickly turned to chuckles and applause. They conjured up their own rounds of insults aimed at Marco, each trying to out-do the other in echoing Hector.

Hector knew he was too protective of Alexia. As he listened to the others pile on, he immediately began to regret his momentary loss of control.

He thought of his sister's insistence that he not complain about Marco. She claimed that Hector distrusted everyone and said she didn't want to be infected with his paranoia. He knew she was right, but every single thing about Marco bothered Hector, right to his core. The guy shared too many of Alexia's interests—they followed the same fad diet, listened to the same stupid music, and Marco even championed the same causes of the month that Alexia did. Hector had never met such a fraud. He was certain the guy had five other girls he was stringing along. Hector tried to keep calm by reminding himself that only a lunatic would attempt to disrespect him. As much of a fraud as Marco seemed to be, he didn't seem like a lunatic.

He heard a loud rustling just outside and turned his gaze back to the door. Deep in his gut, he felt something was wrong. The door crashed open.

#

Alexia watched Marco take in the spectacle of fireworks splashing across the sky and waited, with a seductive smile, for the moment his attention would return to her. She could feel the echoes booming off the surrounding high-rises and shimmering through her feet, and her heart pounded with a rebellious furor. She dared not get overly affectionate with Marco in Hector's presence. The entire evening, she had waited in boiling expectation, hoping to finally obtain a moment alone.

When Hector had asked to visit, Alexia had made him promise not to embarrass her. She trusted that he'd at least *try*, but knew she needed to avoid provoking him. Marco looked down at her desirous eyes and smiled. He pulled her close and kissed her.

#

The SWAT team threw aside the battering ram and opened fire, scores of bullets spraying Hector's friends, ripping through the torsos of the nearest two and striking the other in the face. Hector tumbled backward, drew his handgun, and fired three rounds around the side of the sofa. Something was seeping through his shirt. He grasped his chest and tried to breathe.

He looked up and into the barrels of four assault rifles. He tried to raise his gun, but the pain of his wound had sapped his strength. He threw his gun across the tile floor and coughed.

The SWAT team gave way to a man wearing full tactical gear and a police badge hanging from a chain around his neck. Engraved on the badge was VARGAS. Hector stared up at the dark eyes behind the mask.

Vargas drew his revolver. "Puta!"

He squeezed the trigger.

#

As the fireworks began to fade, Alexia grabbed Marco's arm and looked up at him with concern.

"What was that sound?"

"Fireworks," Marco said.

"No." She gave a fearful look over the edge of the roof. "It sounded like it came from below."

"Below?" Marco gestured toward the ledge. "There's nothing down there but happy people."

Alexia peered down again cautiously, keeping her hand on Marco's forearm.

"See?" he asked, putting an arm around her back. "It's nothing."

She took a deep breath and nodded.

Marco tightened his grip around her neck and shoulders, stepped forward, and pushed her as hard he could. Alexia frantically reached back, grasping into the air, searching for Marco's hand. He leaned over the edge and stared at her as she descended.

#

Alfanzo saw the woman drop and heard an awful crack. He ran toward her and gagged at the sight. She lay on the pavement, her shoulders raised, her head buckled all the way behind and underneath her. Alfanzo looked up at the top of the building and saw a man staring down at him. They held each other's gaze for a second in the darkness. A bright firework exploded high above them, fully illuminating the man's face before he backed away from the ledge and disappeared from view.

REX NASH

October 15
Asheville, North Carolina

"I miss you too," Rex said as he paced along the sidewalk in front of the Thirsty Monk. "It just looks bad to leave town during my first month."

"All right, I'll come visit, then," Jessica said.

"Awesome," Rex replied. "You'll love it. We have a very cool fundraiser coming up."

"Rex, I think they just said something about your race here on the Charlotte news," Jessica said. "Yes, that's your race. Quick, find a TV!"

"I'll head back inside," Rex said. "The fundraiser is the Wednesday after next. Can you make it?"

"I'll be there. Can't wait." Jessica hung up.

As Rex walked back into the pub, Bill yelled, "Nash! Nash! Look! Dumfries is dropping out, man!" He gesticulated wildly toward the TV.

"Unbelievable," Rex said, returning to the table.

"We're going to win!" Bill cried. "I'm getting a new boat!"

Dan rubbed his fingers together. "Cash money."

Bill handed out shots as Rex stared at the TV, watching Dumfries deliver his speech. He raised his shot to what had to be the easiest win of his life.

EDGARDO BLADES

October 21
La Tablas, Panama

Edgardo focused on the three-way phone conversation as he prepared to exit Restaurante Los Faroles outside the rural town of Las Talbas, Panama.

"Claro," Marco said on the other end. "You're the ones who understand this communications world, propaganda, or whatever it is you call it. Me, I react to what I hear, what I am told."

"See, this is a guy who knows his role," Edgardo said. "Your people did well to find him. Marco, that last thing, I have to say, you handled it just right. *Perfecto.*"

"Quite the high-wire act from what I heard," the third man added. "A pristine performance though."

"Yes, very clean." Edgardo walked past a television on the wall near the door. "Vasquez of the Molirena party," a voice from the TV said.

Edgardo pulled his phone slightly away from his ear and glared over at the TV screen. It was cable news coverage of the presidential election in Panama. The anchor named the other top-tier candidates for the presidency: *Presidente* Martinez of the Partido Popular and Diego Dopazo of the PRD.

A pair of bodyguards trailed Edgardo out of the restaurant toward a line of three black SUVs parked in front. Armed guards snapped to attention as he passed. He took a seat in one of the cars and waved. *"Vamos,"* he told the driver before turning back to his phone conversation. "Okay, gentlemen, I appreciate what we are doing to isolate the voting public online. I get the self-contained silos thing, but the problem is TV. Both candidates hold big stakes in one network or another. It doesn't seem like we can drown them out entirely."

"Edgardo, Plan B isn't something we can slap together overnight," Marco said. "If we end up needing to adjust course, we must begin preparations before the fact. Otherwise, let's just try to win the thing by playing it straight."

"I agree with your man Marco," Edgardo said. "I think we prepare for all eventualities here."

REX NASH

November 8
Asheville, North Carolina

"Last one."

The campaign's field director tossed a door-to-door volunteer packet into a tall cardboard box that had been sitting on one of the six long folding tables in the main room of Bob Haskins's campaign office. The tables were piled high with manila envelopes overstuffed with walk lists and campaign flyers.

Rex rubbed his knuckles under his red eyes and pulled the box off the table. It had been a long day, and he had a contact buzz contracted from the stench of too many open blue permanent markers.

Rex had spent the day compiling data on precinct voting patterns and demographics. Using vote histories and consumer data purchased from credit card and social media companies, he'd calculated the probabilities for hot zones of undecided primary voters and which flyers would resonate with them. Once everything had been sorted, he huddled his staff together.

"Tomorrow will be the largest grassroots effort ever attempted in western North Carolina," Rex said. "I need everyone, regardless of position, to be fully committed. I know we are way up, but that's all the more reason to step on the gas right now and put these guys down for the count. See you in the morning."

Someone turned the lights off as the staffers left, and Rex walked back to his office in the dark. Polling binders and papers obscured the surface of his desk. Dozens of precinct maps covered the walls, and every free inch was peppered with calendars, graphs, and timelines. A deadly looking "beating stick" wrapped in campaign bumper stickers hung on the wall behind his desk.

As he sat down to check his email, his phone pinged with a text: *Hi.*

Rex typed, *Love the sound of the ping when I know it's you. Brings a smile every time.*

You're so sweet, Jessica replied.

Can't wait to see you at the fundraiser tomorrow, rocking a sexy cocktail dress. Everyone will be jealous.

Cocktail dress. That may be a problem.

Don't be crazy. You'll look amazing.

Not sure it will fit.

I'll buy you a new one.

I'm starting to show at this point.

Huh?

I'm 3 months pregnant.

Rex's throat swelled, and the blood in his head rushed down to his chest.

I know I should have told you in person.

Was it the last night we spent together?

No. You're not the father.

He stared at the phone, feeling terrified and helpless and broken. The phone seemed to weigh a thousand pounds. He tried to fight back tears but failed.

His name is Ben. He just moved in with me and we are both very excited about the baby. :)

Rex dropped the phone onto the desk and dug his nails into his cheeks. The room began to spin, and he scrambled to the trash can in the corner to puke. He gave a couple of heaves and rested his head against the wall, trying to catch his breath. Then he ran his sleeve across his forehead to wipe away the sweat and walked to the bathroom to throw some cold water on his face.

He called Jessica back as he headed to his car, phone in one hand and a cigarette in the other. Voicemail.

I don't understand, he texted. *Pick up the phone? I need to talk to you. This text stuff is crazy.*

Rex took a drag and tried her again. No answer.

I'm sorry, she wrote back. *Please don't call me again. It's for the best.*

He mashed the power button and watched it turn off. It was all he could do to keep from smashing the phone. He opened the door and threw it into the back seat as he got behind the wheel.

Still in shock, he stared out at the night sky through the windshield and tried to pray. *Lord, I'm at a loss here. Everything told me she was the one, and that I needed to be here. Do I stay? Go home? Was this all just about bringing me here to help Haskins win?*

How had this happened? Who was this Ben guy? Had Jessica ever loved him at all? At this point he had no idea. *Lord, let me know a direction, and I will follow. Am I on the right path, or am I falling down the mountain here?*

Rex felt a sudden wave of calm. He didn't hear an answer, but a peace, tangible and steady, came over him.

"All right, if that's what it has to be," he said out loud. "I'll do it."

REX NASH

November 28
Asheville, North Carolina

Rex sat behind his desk going through the tedious work of updating and appending vast sets of data to the registered voter file. It was the end of yet another fourteen-hour day—there had been a lot of those in the weeks since Jessica had left his life. The door to his office opened without a knock, and Bob Haskins walked in. Rex gestured for him to have a seat.

"Hey, Bob, how is it going?"

"Pretty good," Bob Haskins replied. "Do you have a second?"

"Sure," Rex said.

"I heard about the situation with your girlfriend," Bob said. "That's a tough one."

"Ah, no. Did Bill Casey tell you?" Rex asked.

One could never trust a TV ad maker to keep secrets. Retelling stories was what they did. As much as Bill was a friend and not the type to intentionally promulgate negative gossip, sometimes he just couldn't help it. If a story was mysterious or wild enough, rest assured, the second he sat down for a beer, the first thing out of his mouth would be that story.

"You know he can't keep anything to himself," Bob said.

"It happens," Rex said. "Kind of shook the ground beneath me a bit, but focusing on work helps."

"Do you mind if I record our meeting?" Bob asked. "It's impossible to keep track of all my notes."

"Good idea," Rex said. "Makes sense."

"So, I think we need to talk about our communication," Bob said.

Rex shifted uncomfortably. "The ads are working great."

"Not what I mean." Bob glared at him.

What was this all about? Rex hoped Bob wasn't one of those candidates that buckled under the pressure at the end of a winning race. He'd seen it happen to guys before. Suddenly they found themselves surrounded by scores of newfound high-profile friends, all of whom had wanted nothing to do with them earlier. Sometimes if a win looked too assured, it was hard for the candidate to focus on following through with the rest of the campaign plan. Their minds became obsessed with what they planned to do after being sworn in.

Attempting to play psychiatrist was a risky bet. The best thing a campaign manager could do was simply be a rock for the candidate to lean on. Be an example. Direct each unproductive conversation back onto how to win by the widest margin possible. Exude confidence in yourself, the campaign, and the candidate. Genuine confidence was contagious. Of course, whether any of that would help bring the candidate back to reality was largely dependent on how crazy they were to start with.

"I'm talking about the communication between you and me. We're just not clicking right."

What struck Rex even more than the stupidity of Bob's statement was the way he winced, pinching his brows together like a toddler eating a lemon. Something spun in the pit of Rex's stomach. It was the same fight-or-flight instinct that had risen inside him in his final moments at the American Insurance Association.

He stiffened his resolve, lifted his chin, and prepared himself for another punch.

"What are you trying to say here, Bob?"

"Well, Nash, I think it's time that we part ways."

"Wow." Rex sat back as if struck.

"Thing is, it's just not working," Bob said, as if that were somehow an adequate explanation.

Rex recognized Bob's bullshit for what it was. The natural balance of power between candidate and campaign manager had shifted. The numbers had moved too far out ahead.

"I get that we have the win locked up," Rex replied. "Maybe we settle up early, if that's what you want, but there are better ways to go about it, Bob."

"What do you mean?"

"In three weeks we win, so I assume you have my win bonus check ready to go?" Rex answered.

"Your win bonus clause doesn't apply to a failure to perform," Bob countered. "The way I see it, getting rid of you is what will make us win."

"Okay, so what you're really saying is you want me to kick your ass," Rex said. "Because if you don't cut me my check, that's exactly what's going to happen."

"Watch the threats, Rex," Bob warned. "I'm recording this conversation."

"Well, good, bring it to court."

"My lawyer will call you tomorrow to work out the details. Just make sure you have all your stuff out by the end of the night," Bob said.

"My pleasure," Rex replied.

As Bob left the office, Rex grabbed the beating stick off the wall above his desk. He looked at it for a second, wondering if he should put it to use. He chucked it across the room, and it toppled a stack of boxes. Campaign stickers, T-shirts, and hats spilled across the floor.

CHARLES LEE

November 29
Panama City, Panama
(161 days prior to Panama's election)

Charles Lee worked furiously behind a desk in Vasquez's headquarters. The red-eye flight from Asheville had left his mind foggy and deprived of sleep. He fought to remain awake as his fingers hurried over his laptop keys, plugging in polling data. Occasional chants drifted up from the street vendors outside—from the squeegee guys to the valets to the hot dog sellers.

"¡Se siente, se siente! Vasquez Presidente!"

Ruben, Vasquez's personal assistant and head of logistics, had paid them a hundred dollars apiece to go wild every time Vasquez neared the office.

That morning, Charles had asked his people in Old Town to produce some new data tables. He'd received this crucial information only a few minutes earlier. Ignoring the noise outside, he plotted out a graph with the new data on voters who had recently adopted a more negative attitude toward Martinez, the current president, and how they viewed Diego Dopazo, a new challenger in the race.

Charles printed the graphs and updated the crosstab binders. Each binder was four inches thick, filled with endless rows and columns of data. The crosstabs ran each of the poll's sixty-five questions and twenty-five subgroups of voter file data through a series of segmentation combinations: "Of voters registered in Party X who live in Geographic Location Y, who believe crime is a number one issue and who initially expressed a favorable opinion of both candidates, forty-two percent of them now express a negative opinion of the opponent after being read a specific set of negative statements about each candidate." The crosstabs were really supposed to be analyzed on a computer, but if a pollster failed to print them out in physical form, candidates sometimes had trouble seeing the work as real.

Candidates loved the binders. Most didn't read them; they just carried them around so they could have something to point to as they bragged about how well they were doing. Candidates could request whatever data they wanted, but in Charles's experience, they were usually too caught up in the horse race numbers—who was winning, who was losing, and by what percent—to bother. The real reason this polling was valuable was that because without it Charles wouldn't be able to prepare the summary report he was working on right now.

"*Rauuuuuuuuul Vaaaaaasqueeeeezzz! Ganar por Panama!*"

His time was up. Charles needed to move to the boardroom fast.

Not perfect, but as good as it's going to get, he thought as he hit the save button. Just then, his phone rang. It was Roberto Marcelli, a legislator from Vasquez's party who had been actively helping the campaign.

"Roberto, what's going on?"

"Charles, sorry to be late. A few minutes, and I'll be there. I need your help on something, though. It's important."

"Sure, but I think Vasquez is already here," Charles said.

"Martinez... he put his security team after me," Roberto said. "They were following me. There's a tape."

"What tape?" Charles said.

"They put it on the internet," Roberto said. "This you must... please, you have to make it go away."

"Does it involve Vasquez?" Charles asked.

"No, it's something personal," Roberto said. "But you can't tell Vasquez anything."

"Roberto, I'm just a pollster." Charles gathered binders under one arm, trying not to let his phone slip off his shoulder. "I'm not sure what I can do for you. If you want to hire me, that's one thing. Maybe I can get you set up with a team to help you out. What is this about?"

"No, not over the phone. I'll be there in a few minutes," Roberto said and hung up.

Charles stepped into the main office and smiled at the two secretaries.

"¿Es el jefe aquí?" he asked.

"*Sí, él está allí,*" one replied.

Ruben was waiting just inside the conference room.

"Is the TV ready to go?" Charles asked.

"Plug the laptop in. Here is good," Ruben said.

"Thanks."

Ruben raised his eyebrows and pointed at Charles's black ostrich cowboy boots. "Nice. Where'd you get them?"

"Oh, these? A victory present from a congressman I helped win in Texas."

"Cool," Ruben said.

Charles looked across the room. Freddy Ramos, the chairman of Vasquez's party, the Molirena, rose from his seat to greet him.

"Good to see you, Charles," Freddy said. "So, what kind of numbers do you have for us? Please tell me they're good."

"Sorry, Freddy. It's going to be just like last time," Charles said. "All the horse race stuff toward the end. It's the only way to keep you guys engaged for the entire presentation."

"You know me too well, Charles." Freddy chuckled.

Vasquez finished a phone call and stood. He was wearing a dark suit with a red-and-yellow tie. "Charles," he said. He motioned to his laptop. "Unbelievable! Come take a look at this. Freddy, you too."

They gathered around the computer. Vasquez's laptop displayed a YouTube video of a car pulling up to a residential home.

"Recognize this car?" Vasquez pointed to the screen.

"It looks familiar," Freddy said.

"Not the car, but that looks a lot like Roberto Marcelli getting out of it," Charles said.

"Oh, it is him," Vasquez confirmed.

"What an asshole!" Freddy said.

"I don't get it," Charles said. "What's so bad? He walks up to the door and meets his wife at the front of his house?"

"That's not his wife," Vasquez said.

The boardroom door swung open behind them, and Roberto Marcelli walked in. He was a short, chubby man—not exactly fat, but round. He had been a star athlete in high school and had attended college in America, where he'd started for Wake Forest's soccer team as a right halfback. Now he was in his late thirties, and booze had aged him further.

"Buenas tardes," Roberto said. "Sorry I'm late."

Vasquez slammed the laptop shut. The room went silent. He looked to Charles, then diverted his eyes to an empty corner of the room. Freddy lowered his head and stared at the ground. Ruben fumbled for his phone, finally grabbing it and raising it to his face. Roberto, rosy cheeks and flushed skin, gave a nervous glance around the room.

Charles moved quickly to break the awkwardness. "All right. Well, let's get started!" After everyone was seated, he ran through issue testing and how it broke down into each subgroup. "A sixty-question poll allows you to cover a lot of ground on issues. Plenty of room for demographic stuff, too, such as marital status and education level. There were some questions, however, that just don't work in interviews, such as 'What is your sexual orientation?' or 'Do you or an immediate family member have a life-threatening illness?' The form one fills out when registering to vote identifies one's age, race, and party affiliation, but not much else."

They seemed to be following him, so he continued. "To overcome these limitations, we acquired enough social media and credit card purchase data to identify these tougher-to-find subgroups of voters. It didn't provide enough data to run crosstabs across all regions, but it was at least enough for a reliable polling sample for the country in general."

For well over an hour, Charles lectured the team on how to best tailor Vasquez's message to various groups. When their eyes began to glaze, he brought up the top-line numbers to shake them back to life.

"All right, here we go, top-lines: Vasquez, thirty-five percent; Martinez, forty-five percent; Dopazo, twenty-five percent," Charles declared.

"What's happening? We lost ten points?" Freddy asked.

"This is a disaster," Vasquez said.

"Guys, the top-line number is not very important this far out. What's important is whether we are accomplishing our objectives. We set out to drive down Martinez's numbers. These numbers show that we've succeeded. Martinez's favorable-unfavorable has tanked twenty percent since we started hitting him with the ads two months ago."

"I don't know, Charles. In Panama, the horse race thing's pretty important. We have to show that we are winning," Ruben said.

"Yeah. I mean, how am I supposed to raise the money to pay for any more of these stupid ads if everyone thinks we are going to lose?" Vasquez asked.

"Dopazo at twenty-five percent. *Mierda*, nobody even knows this guy," Freddy said.

"Diego Dopazo is a clown," Vasquez said. "There is no way these numbers are right. I talked to a friend of mine over at the Telemetro TV station, and he said we were doing much better than this on their own poll."

"Well, if you want to hire a pollster to make up some fake top-line numbers so you can feel good about yourself, then hire the Telemetro guy," Charles said.

"Maybe I should. I feel terrible," Vasquez said.

"Look, the reality is, an incumbent can't be defeated unless you drive up their negatives. You have to provide voters a reason for deciding to make a change. Just claiming you can do things better is a nonstarter. Diego entering the race, however, is a big problem for us. The votes we were driving from Martinez to undecided are now flowing to Diego instead."

All eyes turned to Vasquez. "And what do you suggest?" he asked.

"You need a real campaign manager," Charles replied. "All due respect, but you can't rely on your cousin to run a winning campaign for you. That's how you lost the last time."

"Who, then?" Vasquez sat back and crossed his arms.

"I think I might have just the right guy," Charles said.

REX NASH

December 1st
Washington, D.C.

Rex sat at a D.C. dive bar with five pints of Guinness before him, surrounded by five sinister shots of Jameson and Baileys.

"The rules of this Car Bomb race are ironclad, sacred, and binding," the bartender announced to his audience. "Loser pays the tab, agreed?"

Rex, Ronnie, and three random women shouted out their uniform agreement. Each picked up a pint in their right hand and a shot in their left. They rested the shot glasses just at the rim of their pints and braced themselves.

"Ready, set, go!" the bartender yelled.

All five shots dropped into their respective pints of Guinness, and the race was on. Rex slammed his drink, but only barely ahead of one of the women. Rex turned to Ronnie, who moved quickly, but too quickly. His friend looked like he was drowning and suddenly pulled the glass away. Beer spilled all over his face. Rex looked over at the other two women and saw that they were way ahead of Ronnie.

"Oh, shit," Ronnie said. He tried to catch up, but couldn't get close. The bartender called the contest and handed Ronnie the bill.

The nearest of the women giggled. "Thanks, Ronnie!"

"You got beat by a girl," another one taunted.

"This is an outrage," Rex declared. "You ladies must be hardened alcoholics. Ringers!"

"Not our fault your friend can't hold his liquor," the third one said as they walked off.

"Man, Ronnie, you suck," Rex said.

"Hey, it just started going down the wrong pipe, and I choked," Ronnie said. "And those girls were flat-out problem drinkers."

Out of the corner of his eye, Rex saw Dave Barese walking toward them. Though he was clean cut and shunned displaying obvious projections of trouble, no scary tattoos or piercings, he always exuded a not-to-be-messed-with toughness.

"Uh-oh, look who's here," Rex said. "What's up, man? About time you showed up."

Dave was often funny and full of life, but for as long as Rex had known him, he'd sensed something darker churning beneath the humor. His eyes were hard, and his hands were scarred and calloused. In one of them he held a pack of Newports.

"Hey, Ronnie, have you met Dave Barese?" Rex asked. "He grew up right down the road from me."

"Yeah, at the beach one summer," Ronnie said.

"Sounds right," Dave said.

"How could I forget? Craziest person I ever met," Ronnie said. "And by crazy, I mean the best. Nash, I swear, your boy here rolled up to the beach house and started shooting lit joints across the room like a T-shirt cannon at an O's game."

"Ah, yeah. That night was pretty wild," Dave said.

"Aw man, it was the best," Ronnie said. "Hey, got any of that weed on you now?"

"Better watch out, Dave," Rex said. "Ronnie's a cop now."

"No way," Dave said. "Time to abuse your authori-tah, then. Wave your gun and badge around. Get some women over here."

"Word," Ronnie concurred. "So, upstanding business guy Rex here hangs out with a troublemaker PG County boy like you, Dave?"

"Oh, Rex was a bad motherfucker back in the day," Dave said. "Life changes, though."

"Hey, guys, I'm stepping out to get some cigarettes. I'll be back in a minute," Rex said.

#

Rex felt a vibration in his front pocket as he walked toward the convenience store at the end of the alley. He pulled out his phone as he drifted toward the neon light from the store and checked the caller ID. It was Charles.

"Sorry to hear that Bob decided to fire you."

"What can I say?" Rex replied. "Moving on. Good to hear from you. What's up?"

"I have something that may be of interest to you. An international gig."

Rex halted his stride. "I don't know if—"

"Well, it's pretty late in the campaign cycle here, and the next congressman from North Carolina is pissing all over your rep stateside," Charles said. "So think about it."

"Still, that's quite a leap. Carolina was one thing, but out of the country? That's a whole other level."

"Look, Nash. Right now you have no job and no girlfriend. Right?"

"True. Thanks for the reminder."

"So, what's stopping you? You could pick up and make the move tomorrow."

"Who's the candidate?"

"Raul Vasquez," Charles said. "A challenger candidate for president of Panama. He's right up your alley—a reformer, drain-the-swamp type."

"Interesting," Rex said.

"Come on, Nash. Maybe you'll meet some spicy Latina girl down there," Charles urged.

"So it's win the campaign, get a girl, and try to stay alive," Rex said.

"There you go," Charles said.

"Has the State Department voiced a position on the race?" Rex asked.

"Post–Cold War policy in Latin America is at best described as disinterested confusion," Charles said. "Predictably, lots of bad actors have been free to make moves across the board ever since. A Vasquez victory would help reverse that tide of corruption."

"I'll consider it."

"It's your best move. It would be a rare win for the U.S. and the region, but don't expect help."

REX NASH

February 21 (morning)
Panama City, Panama
(73 days prior to Panama's election)

Tropical sunlight bounced off Rex's forehead as he looked up at a set of modern skyscrapers.

Most of what he knew about Panama revolved around either the canal or the country's 1980s dictator, Manuel Noriega. He remembered hearing about the invasion, which occurred about a month after the fall of the Berlin Wall. At the time, it was the largest U.S. combat operation since Vietnam, with twenty-five thousand troops and full air support. Outside of that, he didn't know much else about the place.

Rex gazed at the screw-shaped F&F tower and the massive, sail-shaped Trump Ocean Club. Impressive city.

Democracy was a hell of a thing if you could hold on to it. Peaceful and legitimate democratic elections every five years since the invasion, and look how far this place had come. The economy had boomed, and the capital, Panama City, had grown into an immense metropolis.

As Rex strolled down the sidewalk, he took note of the traffic jam beside him, along with the frustrated looks on the drivers' faces as he passed them. He thought of his former life in D.C. and all the time he'd spent driving to that awful Insurance Association job. A buzz in his pocket broke into his reverie.

"Hi, Mom."

"Now that you've been there a couple of months, what's Panama really like?" she asked over the phone. "It has to be so exciting."

"It's been great, and the candidate is awesome. Absolutely the right guy to win this thing," Rex said.

"I mean, how is Panama itself?" his mom asked.

Across the street, a shirtless, rail-thin man was speed-walking down the sidewalk, dragging a red plastic crate by a dog leash. It was stuffed to the brim with stolen fruit. Papayas pulled off a balancing act, but a pineapple fell out and rolled beneath the tire of a stalled car.

"Oh, you definitely know you are in Panama," Rex said. "I'm going into a store. I'll call you later, okay?"

As he walked up to the convenience store, he noticed a large man with dark sunglasses and short, curly black hair taking a selfie in front of the door. Rex maneuvered around him and slipped inside. He grabbed a coffee and got in line behind a narrow-shouldered black Panamanian man in a faded red T-shirt. An elderly Chinese-Panamanian woman in a blue and white flowered dress sat behind the register. The man in the red shirt pointed to a cigarette display behind the counter. *"Chino, como pricios los Malboros?"*

"Chino?" The cashier grumbled as she folded her arms.

The man smacked his lips and waved his hand dismissively at her. *"Apurémonos, Chino."*

"Always Chinaman, Chinaman, Chinaman," the cashier said in Spanish. "My name is Sue, not Chinaman."

"Yes, it is too Chinaman," the man insisted.

"You Chocolate," the cashier shot back. "Five dollars, you pay now, Chocolate Man!"

Rex stared, dumbfounded at the casual manner in which they hurled racial epithets at each other. The man finally paid for his cigarettes and headed toward the exit. Rex approached the counter and glanced back over his shoulder. He shook his head, sympathetic to Sue's plight.

"Hola," Rex said.

"Buenos dias, gringo," she replied.

Three men were waiting when Rex walked into his office at the campaign headquarters: Ruben, Vasquez's personal assistant; Sergio, the finance director; along with someone new, a young black guy with a short fade haircut. Ruben was on the phone, as usual.

"*Que paso?*" Rex said.

"*Que so pa,*" the young man corrected.

"Hey, what's wrong with *que paso?*" Rex asked.

"Alfanzo is our man in Currundú," Ruben said. "He's the Molirena party's district captain there."

"He's right, Nash," Sergio said. "Never say *que paso* to someone from Currundú. In Currundú, it's *que so pa.*"

"Yes, you might get robbed if you say *que paso,*" Alfanzo said. "When you visit Currundú, you must learn *que so pa!*"

"*Mi gente,*" Ruben chimed in.

"Man, what?" Rex questioned.

"*Que paso* is *gringo talk.* 'What passes, guys?'" said Ruben. "In Currundú, it's '*Que so pa, mi gente?*' 'What is it, my peoples?'"

"Okay, *que so pa,*" said Rex. "*Mi gente!*"

Sergio chuckled, "*Perfecto!*"

"Yes, very good," Alfanzo said. "Now you can come to visit Currundú, my friend."

"I look forward to it, Alfanzo." Rex took his seat behind the desk. "Any sightings of this new attack ad?"

"No one has actually seen it yet, but I just spoke with the TV station," Sergio said. "The government placed a large ad buy last night. This thing is dropping on us today."

"Is Vasquez here yet?" Rex asked.

Sergio cracked the office door and peeked out. "He's here."

"You actually see him?" Rex asked.

"Trust me. He's either here or walking in right now," Sergio said. "I have a sense about these things." He pushed the door fully open.

It was pandemonium in the main room of the office. Dozens more people had flooded in. Everyone was running back and forth, waving papers and shouting. A television crew was setting up for something. A loud voice bellowed from the boardroom. Vasquez.

"Nash! Nash!" Vasquez yelled. "Come quick!"

"I can see the future, Nash," Sergio gloated.

"No kidding." Rex sighed.

He walked through the mayhem into the boardroom and closed the door. Vasquez stood in the center of the room, staring at a television on the wall.

"I can't believe the people's tax money is paying for this shit," Vasquez said.

The attack ad streaming across the TV featured Photoshopped images of Vasquez in exaggerated feminine poses, accompanied by absurd sound effects. Then came scary music, footage of starving citizens and collapsing buildings, and finally, a computer-generated depiction of Panama City in flames.

"This crazy guy Martinez," Vasquez said. "He goes too far, always."

"Was that the fucking government seal at the end of that ad?" Rex said in disbelief.

"We can't win," Vasquez said. "It's impossible. They have the power of the government. They will just spend whatever they want and drown us in shit. Did you see that stupid picture they used of me? Now everybody is going to think I'm some kind of faggot."

"You're right that we don't have the money to trade blows in an ad war. But we're going to win," Rex said. "We just need to make it too painful for the government to keep pulling this crap. I'll write up a press release, put some talking points together, and get them to our spokespeople. We'll rip these guys apart in the media tonight. This is a disgrace, and we need to change the conversation to high-light that."

"That's why I brought you here," Vasquez said. "Let's get him."

JUAN GONZALAS

February 21 (noon)
Panama City, Panama
(73 days left)

Juan Gonzalas, President Martinez's new chief of staff, walked quietly into a large room high above the courtyard on the top floor of the official presidential residence, known as Palacio de las Garzas, or Palace of the Herons. Though it had been built in 1673, its current name hadn't been coined until 1922, when a number of large African herons were gifted to the country and came to live on the property. Since then, the palace and the country had survived constant upheaval from democratic elections, military coups, and even a U.S. military takeover.

Through it all the herons had remained, competing with other, more questionable forms of life lurking in the courtyard: ambassadors, businessmen, lobbyists, lawyers, and even the occasional cockroach.

The hand-carved moldings ornamenting the room contained painted portraits of past Panamanian rulers. At the far end of the room, they wrapped around a corner and continued into a back office, where the most recent holders of the position had their place. One of the portraits showed a man in his early fifties with gray hair, a chubby face, and the smile of a mischievous fourth grader. Sitting at the desk directly below the portrait was a man with an equally chubby face, but whiter hair and a more tired expression. President Martinez looked up from his desk.

"Presidente," Juan greeted him, waving a green folder. Juan felt his Rick Perry eyeglasses slip down on his nose. He pressed his index finger on the bridge of the glasses and pushed them back into place as he approached the president's desk. Juan had started wearing them because he thought they might make him look younger, smarter, or more hip. The constant slippage, however, had often led him to wonder whether it was worth the trouble. In those moments of doubt, he reminded himself how the majesty of those spectacles had once turned things around for the former governor of Texas. If it worked for that guy then the sky was the limit for someone such as himself. He was a full five years older than Martinez, but he took pride in knowing that most people found it difficult to guess his true age.

Juan's hand trembled slightly as he opened the folder and laid the contents, a multi-page report, on the president's desk. Although Martinez had appointed him acting chief of staff two weeks prior, the public announcement was still a month away, so his position would be on shaky ground until then. Even if his promotion had immediately been made public, anxieties over the ill fate of his predecessor kept him on edge. Martinez had ordered that poor fellow to check himself into a mental institution.

Publicly, most major resignations were reported to be the result of "heart problems." Each of the recent major figures that had departed the administration had checked themselves into a hospital for a minimum of two weeks. The previous chief of staff, however, had been the first to have been sent to a mental institution. Martinez asked people to do such things mainly to entertain his own cruel and dark sense of humor. This was Panama.

Carved through the strip of land connecting Central America to South America, the famous canal leading from the Atlantic to the Pacific had made Panama one of the world's most important regions in terms of both military strategy and international trade. The country's agreement to use the U.S. dollar as legal tender and the lack of a central bank, along with a liberal tax and regulatory structure, had attracted a flood of large institutional banks, and Panama City was now a critical international banking hub. The stakes at hand powered an unbridled ruthlessness among those in the courtyard of the Palacio de las Garzas.

Even though Juan believed that President Martinez would never think of ordering any violent action against past employees, the insinuation was always beneath the surface. Should one of them turn on the president, it wouldn't be impossible to imagine such a person suffering a real heart attack soon afterward. Or maybe even, as in the case of the previous chief of staff, committing suicide upon release from the looney bin.

The first page of the report contained the transcription of a phone conversation, and the next bore a summary report. The other three pages contained photographs of Rex Nash.

"We just obtained these pictures of the new *gringo* on Vasquez's campaign," Juan said.

"From where?" Martinez asked.

"You know that internet security wizard guy my predecessor brought on a few months ago?" Juan said. "Big guy, curly black hair?"

"No. Name?"

"Rafi. He's been very useful. I sent him out to follow the *gringo* around. He used an access mod for a social media site to obtain facial recognition data. Name is Rex Nash. Rafi says that one of the guy's most frequent correspondences was with a woman named Jessica Roark, a schoolteacher. They appear to have had an intimate relationship. Strange thing, though. All communication between the two suddenly stopped shortly before Rex arrived here."

"Is she in Panama now?"

"No, we checked with her school in North Carolina," Juan said. "She's there today."

"What else?"

"He communicates often with an American police officer named Ronnie Beverly."

"So okay, what's this Rex guy doing here?" Martinez asked.

"It's odd, *señor*," Juan replied.

"Let's make sure this is not some FBI, CIA, DIA bullshit," Martinez said. "I want you to find out everything about him. Send someone to the States to talk to this Jessica and Ronnie."

He looked over the phone call transcript in the folder.

"That's a conversation Rafi picked up this morning," Juan said. "Between Rex and his mother. Not of interest, except for this one thing." He pointed to an underlined section.

Text transcript (page 5).

MOTHER
So what's it like in Panama? It has to be so exciting.
REX
It's been great, and the candidate is awesome. Absolutely the right guy to win this thing.
MOTHER
I mean, how is Panama itself?
REX
Oh, you definitely know you are in Panama. Hey, Mom, I'm walking into a store. I'll call you tomorrow, okay?

End call.

"We need to check this out," Martinez said. "Make sure this is really his mother and not some kind of code word. What does he mean by, 'Oh, you definitely know you are in Panama'?"

"Yep," Juan said. "More than anything in the transcript, this seems out of place."

"And who is the 'you' he refers to?" Martinez asked. "Who is he talking about? Are they in Panama right now? Find out!"

REX NASH AND OTHERS

February 21 (afternoon)
Panama City, Panama
(73 days prior to Panama's election)

Rex took a long sip from a fresh cup of coffee and put on his headset. He cranked up the volume until the music blocked out all office sounds and turned his attention to the laptop on his desk.

He had developed a coping ritual after spending years under pressure to deliver rapid media response campaigns on short deadlines. There wasn't any time for panic or writer's block—his candidate could lose if he froze. Rex knew what he had to do before launching into a project. First, he'd grab a cup of coffee and let his mind race as he poured it—the darker, the better, but always with three packets of sugar. He would add a splash of milk, but this cup was more about heated caffeine and sugar than anything. Then he would calmly walk back to his desk and sit down. He would take a deep breath, relax his muscles, and clear the anxiety from his mind as he exhaled. Once the music drowned out the outside world, he was finally in his element.

Thirty minutes for research, and thirty minutes to write. Then another sixty to get the piece approved by the candidate, prepare the surrogates, and drum up interest from reporters.

He reviewed the polling data on issues of corruption, good governance, and democracy. He looked through old files and searched the web for rhetorical examples in similar political situations. He called every campaign lawyer he knew for opinions on current laws, existing practices, and norms for government political propaganda.

How could he break this down into digestible pieces so anyone could understand? What did he need to let the audience know to establish the material's credibility? Why should voters care? What would they get out of it? How could he destroy Martinez in three pages? Three paragraphs? Three sentences? Three words?

The anxiety began to creep back in. Another cup of coffee.

#

Rex set his coffee next to his laptop now and pulled up one of his sock puppet Twitter accounts to check the field team's progress in drumming up opposition to the government's attack ad. They were hitting all the right reporters and pundits, but the results were partly cloudy at best. Every hit used the same wording, and all were posted by similarly blank profile accounts. He knew exactly what needed to be done to fix that, but he marveled at how much technology had changed yet the principles of his work always seemed to remain the same.

For six months of his freshman year in college, Rex had worked in the basement of the national committee, dialing for dollars. By the time June rolled around, he knew he didn't want to spend his summer doing the same thing.

He'd called in what few favors he had and finally got a meeting with the political director. The director only gave him five minutes, but in that time, Rex convinced him to let him intern somewhere more hands-on. Rex made clear he didn't care if it was in Alaska or on the moon, and the guy had laughed and said there might be something in Nebraska. Rex told him he'd take it—though he'd privately wondered if the moon might have been better.

At the time, a special election was being held to replace the congressman of Nebraska's third district, who'd died of a sudden heart attack in some shady motel. Though this didn't seem like a particularly important race, the national committees always tried to flex their muscles in off-year special elections, out of boredom or just a search for relevancy during the dry season.

Rex had been responsible for overseeing a grassroots program of sending letters to newspaper editors. Things started off great. He recruited about twenty volunteers who agreed to write letters each week. He wrote example letters to reflect the themes that the higher-ups in the campaign were pushing and encouraged his volunteers to stay as close to them as possible.

Rex learned from that experience that everyone had their own expert opinions when it came to politics. If the issue of the week was foreign policy, half the letters would come back focused on domestic issues, or worse yet, they would be on-topic but so far off-script and absurd that they were counterproductive. It even occurred to him that it might be better to write the letters himself and just ask the volunteers' permission to put their names on them. Some agreed, but most wanted to write their own. He contemplated making up names, but the newspapers had already caught on to such tactics, and started checking names and addresses in the voter file followed by calls to verify authenticity.

One day at Walmart, a revelation came to Rex in the form of a "2 for 1" sale sign above a rack of prepaid phones. He bought twenty.

Back at the campaign office, he labeled each one with its own fake name and asked twenty staff members to record voicemail greetings.

As technology evolved and mediums of communication transformed over time, so did the power of this original insight.

Alfanzo walked in. "Sergio said you wanted to see me."

Rex pulled the headset off. "I need you to check out the room for the rally tomorrow at the El Panama Hotel. TVN and Telemetro are heading over there at eight to do a production run-through. I want you to make sure they get whatever they need, okay?"

"This I do, my friend," Alfanzo said. "I need a ride, though."

Rex walked out into the main room of the office. "Oscar!" he called to the head of security.

Oscar Duran was slender and middle-aged, but tough as nails. "*¿Que so pa*, Rex?"

"*Dale un paseo*. Get Alfanzo to the El Panama Hotel. Ramirez and most of the other drivers are across town at the party headquarters with Vasquez."

"Okay. We brought on a new man, part-time." Oscar waved the guy over. "He's a cop. His name is Vargas."

#

Rex swiped his key at the field office downstairs. Ten cubicles lined the walls on either side of the large room, each with a headphoned staffer bent over a laptop, typing furiously.

In one corner, Ruben was talking to two young women, who looked annoyed. He'd pulled up a rolling chair and had one foot on the seat, his whole posture designed to show off the bulge of his penis.

"Ruben!" Rex called. "What the fuck? Can we get serious here?"

"*Tranquilo*, Rex," Ruben said, walking over.

"We need to light a fire under everybody tonight," Rex told him. "We've gotta push this stuff hard. Here are the talking points."

He handed Ruben a stack of copies. "Pass these around and translate for me."

Then he advanced to the center of the room. "*Escuchais, escuchais*," he announced.

Everyone pulled off their headsets and swiveled their chairs.

"Guys, we can't just spout off from accounts with no profile pics and zero followers and expect to get anywhere," Rex said in English.

Ruben repeated his words in Spanish. Everyone looked confused, but Rex continued anyway.

"Remember that we are not the only ones in the game. The people we are trying to reach know that the majority of comments on Twitter and forums are made by people who have been paid to post them—whether by a corporation, a campaign, or a government. How many times a day do you come across posts from President Martinez's government? You can spot them from a mile away, right?"

The staffers smiled and smirked and nodded in agreement. One raised his hand and, in broken English, said, "They are always out same times too. At the lunch, there is no one. Not a soul anywhere near lunch, then they are back at the afternoon. After five they are all gone again."

"Exactly!" Rex said. "People know they're fake. How can they tell? An obvious clue is a low follower count. So before you get back at it, I want everyone in this room to 'like' every person on our master Facebook and Twitter lists, from each of your five accounts. In the next twenty minutes, everyone will have a hundred new followers."

He paused for Ruben to translate, then continued. "Think of yourselves as actors playing five different roles simultaneously. Start treating each account like a real person. Use interesting profile pics. Make sure one of your accounts supports Martinez and that another supports Diego. Tonight, your pro-Vasquez accounts should be merciless, but your pro-Martinez accounts could say something a little softer, like, 'I support Martinez and he has done well in so many areas, but I don't support these ads. It's just not right to spend tax money on politics.' Everyone understand?"

The phone bankers nodded. "*Claro*, Mr. Rex," one said.

"Later tonight, when we call into *The Juan Carlos Tapia Show*, we'll have far less room for creativity. We will only get one or two shots to be on-air, so if you make it onto the show, I want you to stick word for word to what's on the talking points and call-in script. Before that, I want everyone to head over to the Electoral Tribunal at seven o'clock for our press conference. We need as many people in the background behind the candidate as possible. Wear regular clothes too. It should look like we're all just concerned citizens, not a bunch of campaign staffers. No Vasquez hats or T-shirts. It's a critical moment for the campaign, and we're going to have to fight hard tonight to turn the tide."

Sergio tapped him on the shoulder. "Hey, Rex, the spokespeople are waiting for you in the next room."

#

As the afternoon grew late at the Palacio de las Garzas, Juan Gonzalas hurried toward the back office in search of the president. He looked down at his phone and cringed. How had the time slipped away? The president would be furious to know how long it took to tell him.

Juan had delayed informing the president about the counteroffensive from the Vasquez campaign because he'd wanted to get a handle on things first and demonstrate that he was on top of them. What had started as a little smoke—he'd waved his communications director away the first time it was brought up—had turned into a four-alarm fire in a matter of hours.

By now the flames had spread to every major social media platform. He had drafted up lines of communication and delivered them throughout his network. He'd also rounded up the phone bankers who had already left for the day, and gotten them back to work.

Finally he entered the president's office but he was bewildered to find only the president's portrait there to greet him. He nervously eyed the empty chair. Where had President Martinez gone? He had to be told, and certainly before he found out on his own.

Juan noticed an empty tumbler resting on the president's desk. The glass was still sweating with moisture around the sides.

Real Madrid.

Earlier in the week, Martinez had mentioned something about leaving early on the day of the Real Madrid game, his second-favorite team.

Juan felt his phone rattle in his hand, and an even greater sense of dread came over him.

#

Rex had sworn to himself over and over again that he would stop drinking coffee after four in the afternoon. His body was slow to digest caffeine, and just a few sips late in the day wreaked havoc on his ability to sleep. It was almost five right now, but in this moment all memory of his vow of abstention faded away. He poured another cup: black, with three packets of sugar. He felt the steam dampen his fingers as he stirred, and his mind began to race.

He mentally reviewed his checklist. He had already rallied the campaign's spokespersons and they were more than enthusiastic about taking on Martinez over his use of public money on negative ads. The prominent group of politicians and industry leaders designated to speak publicly for the campaign were usually pretty slow to embrace new ideas, so he was comforted knowing they were fully on board.

Did he have all the news outlets covered? He couldn't think of one he'd missed. He worried over his teams of internet warriors and phone bankers but he knew he'd set them on the right path and trusted Ruben to push them forward. So he'd covered all the bases. But something was nagging at him—something he'd missed.

Rex sat back down at his desk and sipped his coffee. Taking a deep breath, he relaxed his muscles, then exhaled and picked up his phone.

#

Charles Lee was replacing a freshly cleaned rifle on the gun rack behind his desk at the moment his phone rang. He hated unannounced company, phone calls included, which was one of many reasons that Vasquez was the only client in years he'd officially agreed to help in the role of a general consultant.

Because of his experience, he was often pulled into general consultant territory and tasked with headhunting or other chores anyway, despite trying his best to avoid it. His tenacity for sticking every item and minute of extra services in his bill, thoroughly itemized, at least helped him to minimize the annoyance.

The gun in place, Charles reluctantly stepped down from the chair. In moments of conflict, turmoil, and the unexpected, a general consultant did have to be available to pick up the phone.

He listened as Rex gave him a rundown on the day's events.

"I think you're taking the right steps, but the situation is a bit worrisome," Charles said. "I'm not sure how we drive a message if we're being drowned in an onslaught of two thousand gross rating points of government-paid negative ads every week. It's over if they don't back off."

"Sure, we've been dealt a bad hand at the flop here, but I've pulled out a win before with a lesser hand at the turn," Rex said. "We could try for a long-shot Hail Mary. Run under the radar using radio and grassroots."

"Maybe in times past," Charles said.

"With cell phones, the internet, and social media, it should be easier," Rex said.

"But people are far more isolated these days—that's a new reality across the board whether it's the U.S. or Panama," Charles said. "Peer-to-peer marketing doesn't work if people can't effectively advocate their political views to one another."

"Isolated how?" Rex asked.

"Our polling data has been showing it getting worse for years," Charles said. "Attendance has been rapidly falling in everything from churches to bowling leagues. Only the tip of the iceberg. The data showed it happening even in family units. They no longer eat together or even vacation together. And that's two-parent households."

"Hold on. Technology gives people access to so much more data about everything, extremely quickly," Rex said. "It expands our ability to reach more people, and for cheap!"

"Maybe in the broader sense, but it also cuts people off from having face-to-face interactions," Charles said.

"Then speak to people where they are. Put more effort into winning the battle online," Rex said.

"Not that simple," Charles said. "There are no direct interactions on the internet; there's always an intermediary."

"So?"

"So this is Panama, Rex. People know better. They're too afraid to talk politics online."

"Yeah, you're probably right," Rex said.

"And then, as you know, there's the echo chamber problem," Charles said. "Social media platforms all use algorithmic grouping. It makes the user see mostly things they already agree with. It's a great tool to reinforce previously held beliefs, but less of a one when it comes to changing how people vote."

"Good turnout tool, at least," Rex said.

"This isn't the United States," Charles cautioned. "Panamanians take voting a lot more seriously. The turnout is always over ninety percent here anyway, in every election. The good old tried-and-true U.S. tactic of juicing the margins with higher turnout is a futile endeavor in Panama. They are going to show up to vote regardless of what we do."

"So what else is left?" Rex asked.

"I'm not sure, but if you want to keep the campaign alive, you'd better win this fight tonight," Charles said.

Rex sighed. "What are we missing?"

"You made the right move pressing earned media," Charles said. "The message might be too high-minded, though. A good media story needs a great visual."

"I think you're right," Rex said. "It's a tall order to conjure up an exciting image for the ills of spending public money on advertising, though."

"That's why we need to sex things up a bit," Charles said.

"Martinez is a super-rich guy, right?" Rex asked.

"Yes, but so is Vasquez," Charles replied.

"True, but *our* rich guy isn't the center of attention tonight," Rex said. "Their rich guy is the one taking money out of the hands of starving Panamanians to fund his own campaign."

"Yes, I like it—make him into the Monopoly Man: top hat, monocle, the whole nine yards. Please tell me you have something good in the opposition research file."

"I just pulled up a nice little photo on my screen of Martinez standing on a yacht, holding a glass of champagne. Ohhh, here's one of his mansions at the beach."

"Bingo!" Charles said.

#

As the crowd erupted around him, Martinez lifted his head to see what was happening. He looked to the projector screen on the pub's far wall. Before he could decipher the images dancing across it, he already sensed what had happened. Real Madrid had scored in the final moment, winning the game, 3-2.

He had missed all the goals that night, always just a half-second late looking up from his phone. Someone handed Martinez another shot of vodka. This one hit him a little harder than the last, and he shivered. Then, for a moment, he was alive and awake, hugging and cheering with the crowd.

A banner ad ran along the bottom of the screen: "Tell President Martinez to stop stealing the people's money to fund his dirty campaign."

Martinez tried to ignore it, but a deep sense of disappointment crept back into his mind. Hoping to silence it with another gin and tonic, he headed to the back bar and ordered the bartender to put the local Telemetro network on one of the wall-mounted TVs. After grabbing his drink, he plucked a lime out of the garnish tray behind the bar and mashed it with his palm, spraying lime juice both inside and outside his drink. He tossed the rind onto the floor and swallowed half of his drink in a single gulp.

Out of the corner of his eye, he noticed something familiar on Telemetro's evening news: an image of himself standing on a yacht, holding a glass of champagne.

"Change it. Fuck Telemetro."

The bartender pressed NEXT CHANNEL on the remote. TVN News was showing the president's beach home with dollar-sign graphics running across the bottom.

Martinez knew what people said of him. They called him a madman and a drunk, not solely on alcohol, but also in terms of power and greed. He knew these things were said, but he truly didn't care. From fast food to prostitutes, he occupied his mind with every form of instant gratification. Friends and family members often urged him to dial it back, but he had no intention of falling victim to any sobriety-induced reckoning with his own conscience.

Some of his actions might have mirrored those of an addict, yes. But addicts couldn't operate at his level and they certainly couldn't accomplish the great things he had done. An addict? He was no such thing. An addict knew nothing of proportion, and while Martinez partook in many things, they always ended up balancing each other out: pain pills and smartphones, social media and gossip, cigarettes and gin, polling results and day trading, women and blackjack, and more. He gave his entire self to none of them. He used them freely, but did not live for them. He was no slave.

The only thing he really lived for was power. Politics fed all of his lesser passions like gasoline fed a fire. He sought always to win the day. Men who spoke of "bigger battles"—whether they called it the "greater good" proposed by some political ideology, or were referring to a victory on Election Day—did not understand true victory, the gratification of ending each day having prevailed.

By the time his drink was empty, Martinez could feel that his face had grown bright red. He couldn't bear to stare another moment at that TV. The glass soon left the grip of his fingers and sailed through the air. How dare they!

The sudden explosive pop followed by shards of glass spraying across the floor brought the activity of the room to a halt. The cheering and laughter cut to silence. The bartender cowered and patrons stared.

On his way toward the exit, he grabbed his scheduling assistant by the collar.

"*Pendejo estúpido!*" he yelled as he shook the man like a rag doll.

The assistant tried to wiggle free of the president's grip. "*Tranquilo!*"

Martinez paused for a split second and gave the assistant an affirming nod. Then he tossed the man into a wall. *"El Marica!"*

He turned toward the other patrons and scowled before walking outside and tracking down his driver just outside the door. *"Tele Metro. Vamos, rápido!"*

The driver waved his hands back and forth, pleading with him to reconsider and reminding him how many drinks he'd had. "No, no, *Presidente. Demasiadas cervezas.*"

Martinez pointed back at the assistant he'd thrown against the wall. The driver nodded and quickly went about the business of getting President Martinez to the Telemetro News headquarters.

#

Alfanzo stretched his legs out in the back seat of Vargas's Jeep Cherokee, a relief after having spent the past twenty minutes sandwiched between two fat phone bankers. They'd needed to get those guys to the electoral tribunal, but it had been one hell of a long ride, and he'd worried that he wouldn't get to the El Panama on time.

"Vargas!" Alfanzo said. "Why are you turning left? We need to go straight here." The last thing he needed was for Vargas to get sidetracked again.

Vargas pulled the car off the main road and onto a dark street. "Hang on," he said. "I have to pick something up. It will only take a second."

He drove a bit further and then parked along the curb. Alfanzo watched impatiently as Vargas walked up to a small house and spoke to a man standing outside the front door. The man was wearing khakis, expensive brown leather shoes, and a flashy watch, but Alfanzo couldn't see his face or hear the conversation.

Vargas returned to the car. "We need to put something in the back," he said. "Reach over the seat and move some of that crap around to make space for Marco."

Hijo de puta, Alfanzo thought. He was going to pull a muscle doing this. But he reached into the back anyway and slid a backpack and a case of bottled water to the side as the door of the hatch opened. He looked up and saw the unforgettable face of the man who'd pushed that young woman off the roof of that building. Those same evil, deep black eyes, much like those of a shark, were once again locked onto his own.

REX NASH

February 21
Panama City, Panama
(73 days left)

At eleven thirty, the table for six on the outdoor front patio of the Jaleo restaurant in the Casco Viejo district was littered with wineglasses. Rex, Vasquez, and several others sat and drank and talked. Half-eaten plates covered the table: *carimañolas, ceviche,* tuna tartare, and sautéed octopus. Some dignitaries had joined them, including Freddy Ramos.

Freddy had been an idealist in his youth, but then he became a lawyer. Now, at fifty-six, he was far more tempered and cynical, but he still loved the thrill of politics. He'd always kept a toe in the water, but during Vasquez's campaign, he'd decided to really get involved, taking on his first official political position when Vasquez backed him to become the chairman of the Molirena party.

"Tonight was amazing, Nash," Freddy said. "The media was—how do you say in English?—jumping on Martinez."

"Yes, they piled on, didn't they?" Rex said.

"Could not have gone better," Vasquez agreed.

"It was crazy," Rex said. "I think almost every one of our guys got airtime, and each of them slammed him. And talk about an overreaction from Martinez. Wow!"

"Unbelievable," Freddy agreed.

"A disaster!" Vasquez said. "Martinez went berserk. He panicked. Our poll numbers must be flying right now. Bet that's why they ran that ad today. They are getting desperate. After tonight, it's panic on the *Titanic*, for sure."

"I called my old friend Fernandez who works over at the Partido Popular, to laugh at him," Freddy said. "He said that after slamming drinks all afternoon, President Martinez went straight to the TV station, pissed and drunk as shit. *Chucha!*"

Vasquez laughed. "Did you see when he tried to stand up and wag his finger at the camera? That poor anchorwoman had to catch him. And then he kept slobbering and wiping his mouth!"

"Never seen anything quite like it," Rex replied.

"Welcome to Panama, Nash," Vasquez said.

"Even Diego Dopazo and the PRD jumped in to throw some shit at Martinez," Freddy said.

Rex cautiously nodded and rubbed his thumb under his chin. Even though Diego Dopazo was behind in the polls, he could become a concern. Rex worried that Diego's weak showing could be a temporary illusion given that Diego was the last of the three major presidential candidates to jump into the race. It would take time to gauge how well his candidacy would resonate. He was the sitting chairman of the Partido Revolucionario Democrático, and that party could never be counted out. Panama had an endless list of political parties. They rose and fell in prominence every five years on the single day when all elected positions in the government were held. The PRD was the only political party with a deep enough base and the financial ties to be a contender in every election.

"Oh, that was another disaster," Vasquez said. "They interviewed Dopazo just as he walked out of the PRD party headquarters."

Rex's heart started pumping extra blood out into his muscles and he began to anxiously bounce the front of his foot up and down on the floor under the table. He had done his research in the lead-up to Panama and knew the PRD was a viper's nest beyond anything he had dealt with before. It had been the party of General Omar Torrijos, the party of the dictatorship. Torrijos took power following a 1968 coup and remained the country's dictator through 1981. While most Panamanians fundamentally disliked the dictatorship, much was forgiven after Torrijos had convinced Jimmy Carter to give the canal to the Panamanians. Torrijos died soon after in a mysterious plane crash in 1981. He was succeeded by the CIA-backed *de facto* PRD leader Manuel Noriega, who consolidated full control of Panama in 1983.

Corruption was widespread during Noriega's rule, and he was able to use his power to imprison and kill those who opposed him. Noriega's penchant for waving a machete around in political ads, intended as a symbol of agricultural communities living off the land, did little to soften his image. After Hugo Spadafora, a political enemy of Noriega's, was found beheaded, the dictator's bad behavior became a source of public embarrassment to the CIA.

"The worst part was, he was standing with two of Noriega's most hated former lieutenants in the background," said Freddy.

"Trying to talk about human rights with those assholes right there," Vasquez said, "made him look ridiculous."

"The people, they *knows* who those guys are," Freddy said. "Believe me, Nash. It's no good."

"The PRD are a bunch of clowns," Vasquez declared. "Nash, if I lose this race to Martinez, I get it. He's the government, so that's one thing. But if I lose to Diego Dopazo and a bunch of PRD, Noriega-loving clowns? I refuse to lose to those guys. That happens, Nash, and I will have to take you on a special ride in my boat. We can talk all about what went wrong on a nice day out in the deep water. Then I'm going to throw you to the fucking sharks."

Two waitresses arrived, delivering bowls of *sancocho* to everyone at the table.

"This is for you, Nash," Vasquez said. "You know what is *sancocho?*"

"Shark soup?"

Vasquez grinned. "Shark soup, he says."

"He really thinks we'd throw him out in the ocean," Freddy said.

"Come on Nash, we'd never do that," Vasquez said. "I mean, there is no chance we'd lose to Dopazo."

"Of course not," Rex replied.

"Go ahead and take a bite," Vasquez said. "It's only chicken and yuca."

"Yes and heavy on the cilantro. I've had it. It's good."

"It's Panama's national dish," Vasquez explained. "Everybody makes it a little different, adding their own touch. The people prepare it with a lot of pride, so it's almost always good. In every one of the hundreds of homes I visit on the campaign trail, I eat *sancocho*. That's hundreds of different recipes all across Panama. This place here? They have one of the best."

"I don't know that anyone has ever taken a swing at Martinez like that before. This could be dangerous," said Freddy, changing the subject back.

"He's a bully," said Vasquez. "That's what you have to do with bullies. You just punch them in the nose."

"That's exactly what he is, but a bully can also be dangerous," Freddy said. "Nash, listen to me when I say this. I know this man. He is not above murdering someone. I know this man's thinking."

"You know this man?" Rex asked.

"Looking up at the skyscrapers, Panama seems vast and large," Freddy said. "The barrios on the outskirts are packed with millions of people, stacked one on top of the other. But I tell you that we are still a very small country. This is because, in the world of business and politics in Panama, Nash, everybody knows everybody."

"He is right about that," Vasquez said. "We will probably see some of the administration people here tonight, maybe even have a drink with them. It's strange, but unavoidable."

"Half of us grew up with Martinez," Freddy said. "I have known him since childhood. I went to the same school. He was in my class. I know this man. He has always been this way. He will stop at nothing to hold on to power."

#

Rex stayed long after Vasquez had left, meeting with dozens of politicians and money people, all eager to give advice.

Eventually, only he and Freddy remained. Fresh drinks had just arrived when Rex noticed someone familiar walking toward their table.

"Roberto Marcelli!" Rex said. "Where have you been? You just missed everybody."

"I was at the assembly all night," Roberto said.

"No one works over there during the day, let alone at one in the morning," Rex said. "What's going on?"

"Something important is happening with this judicial reform bill."

"Judicial reform? Really? That's what finally got you to show up?"

Roberto chuckled. "Okay, I agree. There's zero chance I would be up there just to vote on that. My wife got pissed after Martinez posted that YouTube video of me going to the house of my mistress. I still see her every Wednesday like usual, only now I fuck her right in my assembly office."

Rex heaved a sigh. "Figures."

"I know you don't approve," Roberto said. "Nash, you're always too uptight. It's because of her, though, that I was tipped off about the judicial reform bill. She found out something big. She's friends with the mistress of the president of the National Assembly."

"Ah," Rex said. "Of course." Rex shook his head, stirred his drink.

"I tried to rally some guys against the bill late tonight, but it passed anyway," Roberto said. "It will be voted on in a second debate tomorrow. Then, if it passes through a third debate, it becomes law. We have to stop it."

"Stop judicial reform? Why?" Rex asked.

"*Sala Quinta.*"

Rex just stared at him.

"The fifth chamber, Nash," Roberto said. "They are going to add a fifth chamber to the Supreme Court."

"And?"

"Right now, the court is evenly split between Martinez-appointed judges and opposition judges," Roberto explained. "If they add another chamber to the court, Martinez will be able to appoint two new judges. That would give him full control of the Supreme Court."

"Bold move," Rex said. "Why the risk? What is he trying to achieve?"

"The Supreme Court ultimately decides on matters of the election," Roberto said. "Martinez is hurting in the polls right now. He wants to postpone the election another year until his numbers are back up. He plans to create some temporary crisis, then say that the election must be delayed. Without *Sala Quinta*, the court would never back it."

Rex felt his world drop out from under him. "How much time do we have before this reaches third debate?"

"Two or three days, max."

"Shit," Rex said. "I'll wake up Vasquez."

RUBEN

February 22
Panama City, Panama
(72 days left)

Ruben stood when Yolma gave him the news.

"Sí, voy allí ahora."

He grabbed the car keys off his desk and quietly dashed out of the office. He sped along that familiar route to Currundú that he'd driven so many times to get Alfanzo. The kid didn't know how to drive, and in any case it wasn't as though there was anyone in his neighborhood that owned a car. He'd known better than to suggest Alfanzo ride the bus, as the city system was famously unreliable, and while a notoriously large number of independent buses filled the void, they usually stayed away from high-crime zones.

In the back of Ruben's mind, he still expected to see Alfanzo waiting to be picked up there at the apartment complex. He knocked on Alfanzo's door. When it swung open, only Yolma was there to greet him, standing inside the doorway with little Pablo tugging on her shirt behind her. He gave them both hugs and tried to offer words of comfort and condolence, but he didn't have time to linger.

"I need to get down to where they found him."

Yolma nodded. "Pablo, put your shoes on."

She walked Ruben out behind the apartment complex and pointed to a group of police cars that were parked off in the distance along the tree line at the edge of the soccer field.

Alfanzo's arms had been severed, and just a thin rag of skin still connected the head to the torso. The corpse had been found within a block of an apartment complex, which suggested the killer was sending a message. In Currundú, rival gangs clashed constantly, with each member doing whatever it took to survive. While they looked, in many ways, like American inner-city gangs, when it came to sending a message, they had a style all their own.

Alfanzo had been one of his best guys, and Ruben had spent almost every other day with him over the past year. He was just a kid.

The police held Ruben back. He argued and threatened, even as the smell overwhelmed him. Given the temperature—in Panama City, it was always around eighty-five degrees Fahrenheit—and the stifling humidity, it didn't take long for a dead body to start reeking.

The cops tried to be polite—Martinez was their boss today, but it might be Vasquez tomorrow.

Ruben searched around the neighborhood for the local gang leaders. He emptied his pockets, handing out hundred-dollar bills, asking for their help in finding those responsible. But as the morning dragged on, he didn't learn a thing.

He sat on the curb and lit a cigarette. When he'd smoked it down to the filter, he called Rex.

REX NASH

February 22 (night)
Panama City, Panama
(72 days left)

Rex stood in the audience of the convention hall attached to the El Panama hotel, which political parties of all stripes used for countless large rallies every election. Tonight, it was packed with Vasquez supporters, the crowd swallowing every word as his candidate pounded into Martinez from the podium.

"Mr. President, the people do not want the fifth chamber in Panama!" Vasquez shouted.

The crowd erupted.

"The people want democracy in Panama!" Vasquez added forcefully, to thunderous applause.

He peered over at some movement near a pillar in the middle of the crowd. Something flickered. The flickering turned into a blazing spotlight. Vasquez winced and squinted at the teleprompter.

Something was wrong. Rex tapped Sergio and Ruben who were standing in front of him. "What's going on? Did he change the speech at the last minute?"

"No, no," Sergio said. "On the prompter, this speech... you approve."

"*Gracias, gracias,*" Vasquez said, waving to the crowd. He bent at the edge of the stage and shook hands with his supporters as he walked off.

Once offstage, he pointed at Rex, Ruben, and Sergio, and they huddled up as bodyguards surrounded them.

"What happened at the end?" Rex asked. "Did you go off script?"

"You guys screwed up the teleprompter. That's what happened," Vasquez said. "I couldn't see a thing. I had to read off my paper notes. This was a total disaster."

"Don't worry about it," said Rex. "The crowd thought you were great."

"No thanks to my staff," Vasquez replied. "This is supposed to be a professional presidential campaign. What is this? I should fire all of you right now."

"What exactly happened?" Rex asked.

"A spotlight in my face," said Vasquez. "It came at me from near that pillar. Then the teleprompter went blank."

"Was it one of our lighting guys, or maybe a news team?" Rex asked.

"What am I paying you for?" Vasquez said. "Find out!"

News crews flooded in, shoving past the bodyguards and supporters to surround the candidate. Rex wove through the crowd to the pillar, but found nothing amiss. There were only a few slow-moving elderly supporters dallying nearby.

"Did you happen to see who was standing here during the speech? The person with a large light in their hand?"

They responded with confused looks.

"Was it a reporter from Telemetro? Maybe someone from the hotel?"

A woman in her late eighties shook her head. "We wouldn't know. We were over there by the stage."

"Front row," her husband added proudly.

The old woman grabbed Rex by the hand. "Great speech tonight. You keep up the good work. Tell Vasquez we're voting for him."

Rex smiled and gave her a hug. "I promise. Thank you for everything you do to support us. It's going to be a long battle, but we're going to win."

Rex lingered around the event hall, investigating. He talked to the remaining supporters from the crowd as they straggled out the door, questioned camera crews as they packed up their gear, and interrogated members of the hotel staff. He learned nothing meaningful. *Whoever it was, they brought their A-game. Vasquez will be searching for saboteurs every time he steps in front of a crowd now. The guy was already paranoid enough as it was.*

Empty-handed, dispirited, and alone, Rex left the El Panama and walked along the dark side streets leading back to his apartment. He cursed as he stumbled over a large hump in the sidewalk left by the roots of an overgrown rain-forest tree in an adjacent yard. He paused and looked over the obstacle course ahead—missing manhole covers, spilled garbage, stray cats, and several street hookers scurrying about. No thanks. Reversing course, he headed back toward the El Panama Hotel and into the nearby Istmo Brew Pub.

He ordered a glass of the local cane liquor at the bar and pulled up the latest news coverage on his phone as he waited. He couldn't find anything about Vasquez and his fight to stop Sala Quinta. The big news of the night was "American advisor for Vasquez is getting the boot." Clips of Vasquez yelling at Rex and the rest of the team had been wrenched from their context: "I should fire all you guys... What am I paying you for?" Rex slammed his drink in a single gulp.

Next to him, a black man of about thirty sporting a suit ordered a Grey Goose and soda, his accent American. The guy watched as Rex winced from the booze, then gave a nod. Rex turned away, started scrolling through pictures on his phone until he found an old one of him and Jessica together at the beach.

He remembered how beautiful her smile had been that day. How her hair had dangled and grazed his cheek as he'd stared back at her. He closed his eyes as he allowed the entire memory to return.

"Get up, lazy," Jessica had said. "The ocean is waiting."

He lifted his hand and brushed her hair aside, pulling the strands over her forehead with his fingers, revealing more of her face. He turned his body and pulled her close to kiss her. She smiled and snuggled her head into his shoulder.

"Rex, I missed you so much," Jessica said.

"I know, and I missed you more," Rex said. "I don't know what drives it, but there's something about you that captures my interest more than anyone I have ever known."

"Hmm, tell me more," Jessica said.

"No, seriously," Rex said. "Even when we were younger, I would watch you do some silly, odd thing and then smile and think, 'Why am I not horrified?'"

"Horrified?" she questioned. "I liked where this started much more than where it's going."

Rex laughed and sat up on the bed, grabbing her hand.

"What I mean is, no matter what you did, even if it was goofy, it always made you even more perfect to me."

"Now, *that* I like to hear," she said.

"Don't ask why," Rex said with a grin. "Maybe on some genetic level we're just a rare perfect match—because all I know is I can't escape it."

"Is that what you tell every girl you wake up next to?"

"No, I mean it."

"Well, you'd better not slip away from me again," Jessica said. "I need you."

Rex had stood up and stretched, feeling the blood drum through his veins. "Are you ready?"

"Let me get my stuff," Jessica said as she hopped off the bed and reached for her beach bag.

Light poured in as Rex opened the door. The cloudless blue sky hung over the ocean, and the breeze danced over the waves and sand.

"Jessica called out behind him. "Wait! Let me get a picture."

Rex closed the picture on his phone and his thoughts returned to the present. There wasn't a moment more left to waste. He scrolled through his contacts until he found Jessica. Pressing his thumb down on her name, he leaned against the bar and placed his phone tightly to his ear. He could barely hear the ringing.

No answer.

He felt an elbow nudging him in the rib. It was the black guy in the suit next to him. The man nodded over to two gorgeous Panamanian women as they strolled past. Rex smiled and turned off his phone. He gave the women an approving smile.

"Not a bad sight," Rex said.

"For sure," the man replied. "I think they may have caught us looking, though."

"Well, it was like seeing a couple of unicorns walk into this dump."

From their table, one of the women gave Rex a little wave and a flirty smile.

"Two of them and two of us," the fellow said. "I like our chances."

"What's your name, man? I'm Rex."

"Eddie. Eddie Avery."

"American?"

"Panamanian, but I grew up in Chicago. What brings you to Panama, Rex?"

"Just moved down here for work about a couple months ago."

"What do you do?"

"I'm a... marketing consultant."

"And how are you liking Panama so far?"

"It's good." Rex shrugged. "I like it."

"Made it outside the city yet?" Eddie asked. "That's where the best places are, man."

"Yeah, I keep hearing that," Rex said. "What's the best beach?"

"Playa Blanca is good," Eddie replied. "It's close. You really have to see Bocas del Toro, though. That's the spot, man. Right on the Caribbean, clear water—you can see right down to the bottom. Totally undeveloped, real nature."

"Any good-looking women there?"

"There are, for sure. Mostly hippie white girls," Eddie said.

"That could work," Rex said.

"Oh no, not for you. Won't work out," Eddie said. "They're the worst. It took me forever to finally develop a rap."

"What was the issue?" Rex asked.

"They only like black dudes," Eddie said.

"Wait, what?" Rex asked. "I guess that would suck for me, but... I don't want to be the one to have to break it to you, but, dude, you *are* black!"

"No, Bocas-del-Toro black is totally different," Eddie said. "I'm a young professional with a job, education, and money."

"Women tend to like that," Rex said.

"Not the ones who come to Bocas del Toro," Eddie said. "It may not look like it, but they already all have a ton of money. It's not cheap to just trip off out to Bocas."

"Oh, trustafarians!" Rex said.

"What's a trustafarian?" Eddie asked.

"White girls who have trust funds and dress like Rastafarians," Rex said. "They choose to live like bums to prove how much they hate Daddy, I guess."

"Never heard it put like that, but it's about right," Eddie said. "Totally not impressed with cash 'cause they already have it. Refuse to talk to anyone professional looking."

"Trustafarians, for sure," Rex said. "How did you finally get your rap going there?"

"Oh, I clean house at Bocas nowadays!" Eddie said. "My secret: I stop washing and combing my hair for, like, a week before heading there. Avoid using any lotion until I have a nice ash going."

"Ah, that's fucked up," Rex said.

"Yep. Then I just throw on, like, the dirtiest, most mustard-stained wifebeater I can find and roll out," Eddie said. "Once I get there, I grab some dirt and rub that shit on my forehead. They swoon over that, for sure. When I start talking game, instead of saying like, 'Hey, baby, come by my apartment over in Panama City,' I just tell them I live in a dumpster, or, like, in the bushes. For them, it's exotic. The jungle gets them wet. What they really want is to have sex with some dude living up in the trees, like fucking Tarzan."

Rex laughed. "That's funny shit."

"I'm serious, man. You've got to give them what they want."

The two women stood up from their table, drawing packs of cigarettes from their purses as they walked past Rex and Eddie toward the patio.

"Looks like our cue," Rex said, pulling a pack from his pocket. "Do you smoke?"

"Not really, but it sure seems like a good time to start," Eddie said.

"Indeed. Here you go," Rex said, handing Eddie a cigarette. They walked out to the patio and lit up right behind the women.

"Hey, I think I've seen you here before," said the cute one with long black hair and a mischievous smile. "What's your name?"

"Rex Nash, and this is Eddie."

"I'm Sara, and this is my friend Christina," Sara said. "We've definitely seen you both before. Not too many *gringos* coming through this bar as repeat customers."

"What?" Rex asked. "I thought I blended in perfectly. Look, I'm even wearing that Colombia fishing shirt that's all the rage."

"You've got the outfit down," Eddie said. "I have to give you that."

"Christina swears you must be in the FBI or DEA, but I told her, 'No way. He's a tourist for sure.' Then here you are again tonight, so which is it?" Sara asked.

"Definitely not the FBI," Rex said, laughing. "I came here for work last month."

"Are you living here in Panama?" Sara asked.

"Yep, full-time. My apartment is right down the street," Rex replied.

"So, what work do you do in Panama, exactly?" Christina asked.

"Just a marketing consultant," Rex said. "Not that exciting."

"You are not married?" Sara asked.

"Nope. It's just me," Rex said.

"Not married and new to Panama," Sara said. "Well, Christina and I will have to introduce you around."

"You, too, Eddie?" Christina asked.

"Not married as of yet, but let's see where the night goes."

"Let's have a drink back at our table, then," Sara said.

"I'd like that," Rex said.

Two hours later, Christina and Eddie had wandered off and Sara and Rex danced together on the patio, having left the carnage of empty shot glasses and half-empty mixed drinks scattered over their table inside. Sara pressed her hips against his as they swayed with the music. She drank him in with her eyes and, just as he closed in for a kiss, giggled and turned away.

"You know what? I need to introduce you to Juan Gonzalas," she said.

"Who is that?" Rex asked.

"Oh, some super-old guy I ran into earlier this evening," Sara said. "He says he's famous here, though."

"How do you know him?" Rex asked.

"He's like my great uncle or something," Sara said. "I didn't even realize it until I was talking with him."

"Randomly your unknown uncle?" Rex asked.

"The web of families runs deep in Panama," Sara said.

"Sure," Rex replied.

"He's over there now, just behind that group of people at the end of the bar."

Rex saw a well-dressed older gentleman with slicked-back hair and Rick Perry eyeglasses.

"Let's go say hi," Sara said.

Juan Gonzalas sat on his barstool, both hands folded over the handle of a black walking cane. He was flanked by two large, rough-looking guys.

"Juan, meet my friend Rex Nash," Sara said. "He is brand new to Panama."

"Welcome, Rex," Juan said. "I see you've met Sara. That's a pretty good start."

"Indeed," Rex replied.

"So what brings you to Panama?" Juan asked.

"I'm a marketing consultant," Rex said. "We make TV and radio ads, mostly."

"Marketing?" one of the men asked. "Hey, let me know if you need any market research. I have the best research company in Panama. We can find out anything about anybody. I'm Rafi."

"I may be interested," Rex said. "Do you have a card?"

Rafi handed it over.

"So you dig dirt for Juan here?" Rex asked.

"No, no. I'm the head of his cybersecurity team, but I still hold on to my side business," Rafi said. "In Panama, we wear many hats. There is also an endless supply of dirt to uncover here."

"I'll bet," Rex said.

"Yep, our people are so good they can get into any computer or laptop," Rafi said. "They can turn on your phone remotely and record any sound or image within reach of the mic or camera lens. Anything to hide, we will find out."

"Good thing I have nothing to hide," Rex said.

"You need another?" the bartender asked Rex.

"Sure, I'll have a Seco and club with lime, plus another round of whatever these guys are having," Rex said.

"Ah, that's the spirit, Rex," Juan said. "You know how to make friends quickly. Hey, if you ever want to go out and get a bunch of whores, well, just ask. I'm telling you, I can get us the best Colombians in all of Panama. Believe in this."

"Ugh, Juan, you are so gross," Sara said.

"Okay, okay," Juan said, as the bartender set the drinks in front of them. "So, Nash, who is it that you do this marketing work for?"

"I would prefer not to say," Rex replied. "A lot of our work is confidential."

"Why is that?"

"Leave him alone, Juan," Sara said.

"So what do you do, that people say you are famous?" Rex asked.

"What?" Juan waved. "I'm not famous."

"Bartender, Sara claims this guy is famous," Rex said. "Is that true?"

"Oh, him?" the bartender said. "He is definitely famous."

"All right, even the bartender agrees," Rex said. "So does he mean you're, like, a famous drunk or what?"

"No, no, I just work for the government," Juan said. "The problem is, Panama has no good sports or celebrities, so the news focuses nonstop on anyone in politics. It's a soap opera. It's crazy."

He handed Rex a business card with the seal of the government of Panama on it.

"Come on, now. *I just work for the government*," Rafi said. "Pfft. Rex, this man is the right hand of the king."

Rex tried to mask his panic. "Now that is impressive," he said. "Bartender, let's get a round of Grey Goose and lime shots for all the king's men."

"I do like Grey Goose," Juan said.

"Sara, here. Take my phone," Rafi said. "We need to get a picture of this. Get in here, Rex."

Juan, Rafi, and Rex raised their shots and threw their arms around each other to pose.

Juan drank and wiped his mouth. "Thanks for the shot, Rex. But I really do have to ask—what the fuck is it you do here in Panama?"

"I said to leave him alone," Sara complained. "You're ruining my chances. What's wrong with you?"

"Okay, okay," Juan said.

Sara put her hand on Rex's shoulder and whispered into his ear, "Do you want to spend all night talking to Juan and Rafi, or do you want to spend the night with me?"

"Not even a question," Rex said. He signaled the bartender for the check.

"Here's your tab," the bartender said.

"Great. Let me pay for Sara and her friend's tab too. Is it still open?"

"Don't worry," the bartender said. "Juan usually pays for everyone at the ministry when he is here."

"*Gracias*," Rex replied.

As he turned, he caught a glimpse of Sara abruptly pulling away from Juan. Whatever it was those two were talking about, Sara had seemed intent on keeping it a secret. She looked back at Rex and smiled, as if he hadn't noticed.

"Ready?"

Rex pulled her close and kissed her. She pressed herself against him even more tightly. When he pulled back, she opened her mouth as if she was about to say something.

"Hold that thought," Rex said. "I need to hit the bathroom first, okay?"

"I'll be here," Sara said.

Rex walked toward the restroom and the sign beyond it that read EXIT. He glanced back over his shoulder at Sara, who stood alone, beautiful in the dim light, and then at Juan, who peered back at him from his barstool with both hands resting on top of his cane. *A sinister grin if I've ever seen one*, Rex thought.

He passed the bathroom, walked through the back door, and hailed a cab.

REX NASH

February 23
Panama City, Panama
(71 days left)

On the outskirts of Panama City in the hilly slums of San Migueli-to, three black SUVs wound through the streets. Ramirez, Vasquez's driver, reached out the window and signaled to the car at the front of their motorcade. Rex pondered what that meant, while Vasquez stared at his phone, oblivious.

Finally, Vasquez gave him a grave look. "We need to talk about last night."

"Sure, what's on your mind?"

"I'm sure you heard the news reports, but I wanted to let you know in person," Vasquez said. "The reports are true. We are going to have to let you go."

"What?" Rex was stunned. "Because of this teleprompter bull-shit?"

Vasquez laughed. "*Ah! Chuchu!* Ramirez, you see the look on his face? Wow. You are gullible, Nash."

"Man, that was not funny," Rex said.

"Yes, it was." Vasquez laughed harder. "Look, Ramirez is still laughing."

Ramirez looked back at Rex in the rearview mirror and grinned. "*Graciosísimo.*"

"Nash, don't pay attention to that bullshit," Vasquez said. "The media here love to make everything in politics like it's a big soap opera."

"Yeah, so I have heard." Rex was still annoyed.

"Don't worry about that stuff," Vasquez said. "You are not going anywhere. I brought you here for a reason. We are going to do this thing together. There are storm clouds gathering against us, and we both will be put to the test. I can't have you saddled with any doubts on where you stand."

"Thanks. That means a lot," said Rex. "I'm all in on this campaign. Regardless of what we face, I have your back."

"Trust first in logic, faith, and your own mind," Vasquez said.

"Say what?" Rex replied.

"Something a priest told me once. He knew my mother really well. I started to talk to him a lot after she passed."

"That's a difficult loss to go through," Rex replied.

"It was," Vasquez said. "It changed my thinking, though. You met him, the priest. Father Abasolo."

"Yes, you introduced us a few weeks ago," Rex said. "He's the one that talks about golf all the time, right?"

"That's him," Vasquez said. "Silly game, golf, but he loves it."

"Seems like a good guy," Rex said.

Vasquez jerked his thumb toward the window. "This neighborhood we are entering now is San Miguelito, one of the most dangerous, poorest areas in all of Panama."

"Great," Rex said.

"No, no. This is important," Vasquez said. "I want to show you why it is I'm running. The people I'm doing this for. I want you to understand, see who they are, know what it is they are going through. Sure, you have rich and poor back in *gringo*-land, but it's on a whole different level here. Panama City is basically Manhattan surrounded by Haiti." He pointed ahead through the windshield as the car reached an overlook. The immense skyline of Panama City was indeed an island in a sea of tin shacks, tents, and other makeshift dwellings.

"Striking view," Rex said. "Tin roofs just blocks from the Trump Ocean Club."

The SUV turned onto a street lined with people wearing Vasquez T-shirts and waving Molirena party flags. The crowd grew bigger as the car advanced. A junker with speakers in its open trunk joined the motorcade. Salsa and rap music blasted, peppered with shout-outs to Vasquez.

"I think someone was playing games with us the other night," Vasquez said.

"How so?"

"The prompter thing. It didn't seem right. Either the media screwed us, or maybe someone inside our own campaign."

"My sense, too, is that it was intentional," Rex responded. "Probably the media. I don't see how it could have been an inside job."

Vasquez shrugged. "Here, everybody is playing all sides, always. I don't even trust myself half the time."

"You might have just a slight touch of paranoia," Rex said.

"Yeah, but we Panamanians love intrigue and all that shit," Vasquez said. "The city is a bunch of spies, drug dealers, billionaires, fugitives, con artists, terrorists, and mobsters, all just floating around together in this crazy place."

The motorcade slowed to a crawl as a marching band appeared in front of them from a side street.

"This election is too important not to be paranoid," Vasquez said. "We have pissed off some powerful people, and the closer we get to winning, the tougher they are going to make it for us."

"Exactly why I've been begging you to dial back the rhetoric," Rex said. "You may be in the right, but it's a little early to be calling out billionaires by name."

"There is too much at stake to be quiet," Vasquez said.

"I know how you feel, but let's pretend for a moment that Armando Delgado, your favorite billionaire to agitate, really is the primary source of all evil. Let's accept that he is the mystery man lurking behind every one of the wild conspiracy theories and paranoid pieces of folklore the wonderful ladies of our volunteer force, God bless them, conjure up and continue to ask me to investigate." Everyone from the biggest donors and political leaders to the phone bankers and envelope stuffers all had their own ideas about which hidden issue or silver bullet would be the one that could win it all. The fight to maintain message discipline was an unceasing daily battle. In order to win, he needed to keep every part of the organization focused on the core poll-tested issues of clean drinking water, reliable trash collection, fighting corruption, and putting more money into people's pockets.

It was also a campaign manager's job to build the esprit de corps within a campaign. At the end of the day, campaigns were fundamentally about people. Regardless of which burning priorities topped the list at any given moment, a good campaign manager knows to listen to the supporters and treat their concerns with respect, no matter how wild those concerns might be. It was his job to infuse the campaign with a contagious enthusiasm and spark a creative energy in people that would inspire them to keep working, regardless of the prospects for a victory.

The esteemed ladies who headed up the party's regional volunteer and fundraising committees were no exception. They were of significant importance in this regard, and woe to the campaign manager who failed to recognize it.

"You never know, Rex. Those gossipy old women might be smarter than you think. They hear everything. They have the wisdom of the streets."

"I don't doubt it. For argument's sake, let's accept that some of their theories are true: the Zika virus was released in Panama as part of a top-secret eugenics program, and the remote wealthy communities being built near the Chiriquí Province and the Pearl Islands are really John Galt doomsday hideouts. And, of course, the one about Nazi drug lords living out in the jungle. That's my favorite."

"Those senoritas might actually be onto something with that last one," Vasquez said. "Ever hear about Carlos Lehder?"

"Sure. I watched *Narcos*." It never seemed wise to put much stock into dramatized or fictional retellings of historical events via Netflix, but then again some of the characters on the show were somewhat based on actual people. One featured character was Carlos Lehder, a real-life German-Colombian who had helped Pablo Escobar and the Medellin Cartel make billions. Lehder used aircraft flying at low altitudes to smuggle legendary amounts of cocaine during much of the seventies and early eighties. A vocal anti-Semite and Holocaust denier, Lehder founded a neo-Nazi Party called the National Latin Movement, which had sought to install a neo-Nazi government in Colombia.

Vasquez shook his head. "*Narcos*? Oh no. Watch *El Patrón del Mal*. It's much better."

"I'll put it on my list."

"Rex, you can't blame the Panamanian people for having so much creativity after everything we have seen and been through."

"No. But as I was saying, even if we assumed that all of these terrible things were true and provable, the fact would still remain that you are not running in an election against Armando Delgado. The only names on that ballot are President Martinez, Diego Depazo, and you."

"You must understand. This guy... he has his hands in everything."

"Why would I spend time personally keeping tabs on Armando Delgado's mysterious dealings around the world? The only thing I know about the man for sure is the degree to which he can crush a campaign, a reality I personally experienced when he decided to set his thumb on the scale against the campaign I managed for Senator Sheehan."

"How did you know he was involved?"

"We heard rumors, and not long afterwards millions of dollars in third-party advertising dropped out of the sky against us. Scores of weird advocacy groups began attacking us from out of the woodwork. Every local television station suddenly turned on us. It was a nightmare."

"I thought you won? The Sheehan woman, she did become a senator, right?"

"Yes, but only because of a degree of trickery."

"Trickery?"

"Yes, we lured their polling outfits into falsely believing they were ahead by far. That convinced them to delay adding more resources before it became too late."

"How did you do that?"

"First we identified the underrepresented areas in our opponent's survey sampling models, and then we targeted our early resources in those underrepresented areas. We poured massive amounts of advertising via radio, phone, cable television, and mail specifically into those off-the-radar regions. Money has an interesting property because it's equivalent to time. For each day that passes during an election period, money becomes less and less valuable in terms of time, and time becomes more valuable in terms of money. In the final weeks, money loses all of its value. At that point, you simply can't buy any more TV, radio, or mail—or anything of material advantage. Even if you could, most voters would have already solidified their choices. Charles once told me it seemed as if we'd flipped a light switch when we suddenly surged ahead and beat him. I never told him how we did it."

"Charles worked with Armando Delgado?"

"No, no. In the United States all of the big money, especially from interests such as Armando Delgado, is funneled through third-party organizations. By law, they're not allowed to coordinate directly with a candidate's campaign."

"That's *loco*."

"Yes, it is."

"Rex, my country has been passed around between the same four families for generations. I'm not just looking to change the management—I'm talking about changing the ownership. I don't care, Nash. I'm willing to put my life on the line for this. This is a dangerous endeavor, but somebody has to stand up to these *currup-tos*."

"Let's not go there," Rex said. "It's unproductive. Just because Martinez is capable of coming after you does not mean he is stupid enough to pull that shit with the U.S. watching."

"Noriega was," Vasquez said.

"Well, that guy was straight-up crazy."

"True." Vasquez rolled down his window and waved to the crowd.

Supporters, local politicians, and security personnel were walking alongside their vehicle now. There were construction workers and elderly men and working mothers and local drunks and gang members—all waving and grinning, hoping to get a glimpse of Vasquez.

"Welcome to San Miguelito, Mr. Nash," Ramirez said.

Rex and Vasquez stepped out of the car and were immediately mobbed by the cheering crowd. Vasquez was a natural. He didn't flinch, just smiled and shook hands and doled out hugs.

When he ambled ahead, the crowd moved with him. Rex hung back by the car, lit a cigarette, and took in the spectacle. Hearing a whistle, he saw Ruben waving for him to follow Vasquez up a side alley. Rex caught up to the candidate just as he was greeting an elderly woman at her front door. Vasquez kissed her hand and patted her shoulder. She invited him inside, and Rex followed.

On the way in, Vasquez whispered, "I want to show you the poverty of this place. The rich come into the government and make themselves richer, while these people always have nothing. Dirt floors. Hardly any of them have basic plumbing or running water. They use latrines. Some don't even have a latrine. They have to shit into plastic bags. It's a humanitarian disgrace. Assholes like President Martinez steal hundreds of millions from bullshit government contracts but somehow never find money in the budget to fix this."

The old woman motioned for Vasquez to sit down at her table for coffee, and he turned his full attention to her. Rex walked back to the doorway, where Ruben was waiting.

"What's our next stop?" Rex asked.

"Veraguas Province," Ruben said. "Catholic procession in a small town, way out in the interior."

"That's two hours away," Rex said. "Why waste time in the middle of nowhere?"

"Oh, this is a big procession," Ruben said.

"Really?" Rex asked. "There are zero voters in all of Veraguas, let alone one town."

"The people, they come from all over for this," Ruben said. "It's actually five different towns that come together once a year. People will walk, like, five to ten miles on foot just so they can walk another three when they get there."

"We are going to walk three miles?" Rex said. "Ugh. Give me a cigarette?"

\#

Sweating in the heat of the sun, Rex, Vasquez, and Ruben made frequent use of their water bottles as they walked, flanked by leaders from the five villages.

They were an hour's walk above a town at the center of a large valley. The procession had started at a church in the middle of the town. Rex and Vasquez had accompanied the hundreds of people as they walked up a dirt road, through the neighborhoods, and up into the hills.

As they marched through yet another neighborhood, a man to Rex's right elbowed him and pointed at a peculiar bush in one of the house's yards. "*Gringo*, look."

He grabbed a handful of leaves from the bush.

"What is it?" Rex asked.

"*Esta coca*," the man said. He shoved half the leaves in his mouth and started chewing, then extended his hand to share the rest. Rex lifted his shades over his forehead to take a closer look. Sure enough, it was a coca plant, the plant from which the highly valued psychoactive alkaloid known as cocaine is extracted. Rex smiled in amusement, but shook his head. His new friend offered it to another man nearby, who stuffed the leaves into his mouth. Several others plucked the bush behind Rex.

"Nash, put your shades on," Vasquez said. "If people see I have this *gringo* by my side wearing dark shades, they'll think you must be CIA and that the U.S. is backing me."

"Are you sure being backed by white foreigners is a plus?" Rex said.

Vasquez shrugged. "My people, they are gamblers. More than anything else, Panamanians love winners!"

"Good thing winning is exactly what we are going to do," Rex said.

"If not, it will be a total disaster," Vasquez replied. "What Martinez is doing with *Sala Quinta* could destroy our democracy. He just doesn't give a fuck. And the U.S. is silent."

"Their priorities are elsewhere, and life's not a TV show," Rex said. "A lesson I learned back in the war when I had to wipe a great friend's brains off my arm."

Vasquez's eyes widened. "Sorry that happened. That's horrible."

"It's why I got into politics. I wanted to take the battle forward and fight each day to help all the congressmen and officials pull their heads out of their asses. But it's a much more difficult task than you would think. Most of them seem to enjoy having their heads up there."

"In their asses?"

"Yes," Rex replied. "Who knows why. Maybe they start getting used to the smell after spending so much time in there."

Vasquez shoved him in the shoulder and laughed. "You're too much."

Rex stumbled back a step, juggling his water bottle to keep it from spilling. "Just pointing out it's what we do ourselves that's really going to count. As long as Martinez toes the line on drugs and security, the U.S. doesn't really give a shit. Latin America is not on the radar right now. The focus is on the Middle East."

"Martinez, he is a lot of things, but I don't see him fucking up on drugs," Vasquez said. "He makes too much money elsewhere."

"What about Diego Dopazo?" Rex said.

"You have no idea, Nash," Vasquez said. "His whole operation is funded by that shit. After Noriega, things got cleaned up in Panama, and we have been very lucky for it. If Diego wins, it would be the worst possible outcome."

"Well, anyway, the first step to winning is this protest tomorrow," Rex said. "It's going to be a historic deal, with every opposition party in the country involved."

"Yeah, and also the hard left," Vasquez said.

"The SUNTRACS union signed onto the protest?" Rex asked.

"Yes. I sealed the deal during the car ride over from San Miguelito."

"That could be a disaster," Rex replied. The National Union of Workers of Construction and Similar Industries, as it was otherwise known, was by far the most radical and militant union or large political group in Panama.

Vasquez gave a dismissive wave. "We have to make it at least a little exciting. Otherwise, holding a protest won't accomplish much. How are we supposed to get anywhere by just gathering a bunch of people together to stand around and look at each other?"

Rex shrugged. "Like I said when we talked about this the other night, we need to be very cautious in dealing with these people. After all, they are totally nuts."

"Doesn't matter," Vasquez said. "Even after everything the PRD has done to our party, this one day we will put aside our differences to stand against Martinez. That is something I never thought I would see. I'm sure we can handle whatever stupid shit SUNTRACS pulls."

"I hope you're right," Rex said.

#

Rex paid for his coffee at the convenience store near his apartment the next day and looked through the morning papers in the newsstand. He noticed a familiar paper with an unfamiliar headline. The bottom corner of that morning's *New York Times* read: "Martinez Power Grab a Threat to Democracy in Panama."

Rex smiled and bought the paper. He chuckled as he read the article in a cab. The *Times* was lifting directly from his press releases.

Breaking news came over the cab's radio: a workers' strike was in effect across the nation.

The cab slowed and Rex looked up. A motley group of protesters in SUNTRACS shirts packed the corner. As they chucked trash cans and debris into the intersection, they chanted, "*Justicia por democracia!*"

"*Bajo Martinez!*" others chanted, followed by, "*No más Sala Quinta!*"

Rex's driver honked at two protesters, who had their shirts wrapped around their faces, and they started heading toward the cab. One of them grabbed a trash can and threw it at the windshield.

"Fuck!" Rex yelled. He threw his fare money at the driver and reached for the door as an irate protester ran up behind him with a club in hand. The driver stepped out of the cab and began waving his fists in the air, which bought Rex enough time to jump out, cut down a side street, and make it to the campaign headquarters.

The television in Rex's office showed more protesters in front of the National Assembly Building, rocking a chain-link fence on its feeble foundation. A wall of cops in riot gear, equipped with gas masks and billy clubs, pushed against the other side of the fence.

Rex paced around his desk as he talked into his phone. "Charles, I'm telling you, these SUNTRACS idiots are going to turn this thing into a nightmare."

"Well, at the end of the day, we have no control over those people."

"They threw a fucking roadblock up in front of my cab."

"Panamanians always throw up roadblocks when they protest," Charles said. "Protesting is their national pastime. Par for the course. Don't get too worried."

The images on the TV turned ugly: tear gas, broken shop windows, burning tires, and bloody noses.

"I'm telling you, the place is in meltdown mode."

The protesters overtook the security guards at the entrance of the National Assembly and broke through, flooding into the public seating in the back.

"Holy shit!" Rex said. "They just bum-rushed the assembly."

The office door burst open, and Ruben ran in with a gun holster strapped to his chest. A worried-looking Ramirez was right behind him.

"*Casa de jefe!*" Ruben yelled. "*Nash, vamos!*"

"Where?" Rex asked.

"No time, *rapido. Casa de jefe,*" Ruben said. "*Vamos!*" He put his hand on Rex's shoulder.

Rex hung up on Charles and let Ruben guide him out. They hurried down the stairs and outside into a black SUV. Ruben grabbed another gun and holster from beneath his driver's seat and tossed it onto Ramirez's lap.

"What's happening?" Rex asked from the back seat.

Ruben spoke into a walkie-talkie, ignoring him. "I've got him."

A voice, scratchy and distorted, replied, "*Claro.*"

Ruben slammed the gas pedal and the SUV flew through smoke and crushed glass and nails, screeching as it dodged the burning tires and broken furniture littering the streets.

There was a car in the middle of the road ahead, its windows shattered, tires punctured, hubcaps gone, and interior ablaze. Ruben tried to swerve, but the SUV's left headlight smacked the vehicle hard and sent them skidding through the street.

The SUV finally came to a stop. Rex coughed as Ramirez sighed and bit his knuckle.

A man with dirty dreadlocks, a ripped shirt, and wild, unblinking eyes was headed their way. He was shouting and holding a Molotov cocktail.

"Shit!" Ruben slammed the gas again, just as the Molotov cocktail hit the right rear door. Flames lapped at the window for a second, then died. Rex looked back and saw the man dancing and screaming profanities.

Moments later, Ruben pulled the damaged SUV up to a modern skyscraper apartment building. Rex and Ruben hopped out of the car and ran inside to an elevator. At the top floor, the doors opened onto a long, ornate hallway. At the far end, two bodyguards stood on either side of a set of tall mahogany doors.

Rex proceeded down the hall, through the doors, and into a large living room with tile floors and modern décor. The room, empty of people, was chilled by excessive air-conditioning. One wall was constructed entirely of glass, offering a panoramic view of the ocean. Notepads were scattered over the couch cushions, and half-empty cups of coffee littered the table. A flip chart was posted on an easel in the middle of the room.

He noticed a light on in the library and walked toward it, wiping sweat from his forehead.

Vasquez was trying on ties. Behind him were Sergio, Freddy Ramos, and a man Rex didn't know. All eyes were glued to the room's television.

Behind Rex, Ruben said, *"Señor Nash, Jefe!"*

Vasquez turned. "Sorry about the rush, Nash, but we needed you here right away. This is critical. I need your counsel."

"I'm here," Rex replied.

"Red or blue?" Vasquez held up two neckties.

"That's what all this was about?" Rex said.

"Neither," Freddy suggested. "Don't wear a suit. You must look like a man of the people out there."

"So Freddy thinks no suit at all," Vasquez said. "What should I do, Nash?"

"You're kidding me, right?" Rex said. "I thought I was going to die on the way over here."

"We need a decision," Vasquez said.

"Okay," Rex said. "Wear a suit, no tie. You would look too stuck-up with a tie, but it's also way too crazy of a scene to try and play 'Mr. Man of the People.' The last thing you want is to look like another one of the lunatic rabble out there. Your image should be one of authority, a voice of reason. Show your support for the protest, but not as a common protester—as a leader, a force of stability that stands apart from the madness."

Vasquez smiled. "I knew I hired this guy for a reason."

Rex felt a tap on his shoulder. It was one of the drivers from the security detail.

"Señor Nash, computadoro?" the driver asked.

"Ah, thanks," Rex said, taking the laptop in its case. "Vargas, right?"

"Yes, señor," Vargas replied. "We met that night... I think it was before the big speech."

Rex shook his hand. *"Gracias."*

"Nash, put that with everybody else's stuff in the living room," Vasquez said.

"Got it," Rex said, and did as he was instructed.

"Oh, Nash, come back quick," Vasquez called. "You have to see this!"

Rex entered the library again and saw all the men gathered around the TV.

"Hey, isn't that Roberto Marcelli?" Rex asked.

Assemblyman Marcelli was going nuts, pinching at a fence with a pair of bolt cutters and screaming with the rest of the protesters.

"That's him, all right," Freddy said.

"That crazy guy." Vasquez shook his head.

The words were still echoing in Rex's mind when something slammed into him hard, followed by a terrible, deathly stillness. Everything seemed to be happening in slow motion, as if he were suspended in ether, and then it hit him.

I'm on the ground.

There was smoke. And blood.

Dust was everywhere; his head throbbed. Rex pushed himself up as a wad of mealy gore dribbled from his lips. Five feet away, a mangled body burned. Freddy was screaming and grabbing his leg, gripping an open wound leaking blood with every heartbeat.

Rex felt an immediate drowsiness overtake him. *Like a blanket,* he thought. A scary blanket.

Some part of his brain told him to get up. If he didn't stay awake, he'd fall into a coma.

Wake up. Get up. Eyes open.

But it was no use.

#

Rex found himself on a beach, barefoot. The breeze felt cool on his skin. The sound of the waves crashing against the shore repeated in his ears like a drumbeat.

A cigarette dangled from his fingers, and no matter how much he smoked, it didn't get any shorter. But the smoke tasted like chemicals. Like a plastic bottle in a fire.

The sand burned his feet.

The sun was pastel orange, as though it had been painted on the firmament. It emitted no heat, and the sky, though cloudless, was an ashen gray.

Am I on Earth? Am I dead? I must be dead. He turned his eyes from water to land and searched for another living soul, but there was no one.

A soft hand touched his shoulder.

"There you are," Rex said.

Jessica stood next to him, holding two sweaty sodas. "I hope you like Pepsi. It's all they had that was cold."

Rex smiled. "Thanks. This is perfect."

She placed her soda upright in the sand and took off her shirt, revealing a bikini top beneath. She pulled the scrunchie from her ponytail and let her long hair fall loose over her shoulders.

"Time to go in the water," Jessica said. "Come with me."

Rex looked down and saw that he was sitting in a beach chair, holding an open notebook in one hand and a phone in the other.

"Just let me finish this, and I'll be right there," he said.

"Let it go."

"Two seconds," Rex said.

"He's hiding, just like you."

"It's my job; I have to respond."

"The fate of kings is to be eaten by worms," she replied.

"Just go ahead. I'll join you in a minute," Rex said.

Jessica dropped her shirt and scrunchie in the sand next to Rex. "Well, *I'm* going in," she said.

She ran into the water, graceful as usual. He looked down again at his lap, but the notebook and the phone were gone. He shaded his eyes and gazed at the water. Jessica was far out there, and deep.

"Come on in!" Jessica shouted.

Rex ran across the sand, stopping at the edge of the water. Spotting her was difficult now, as a mist, thin as gossamer, covered the water. Her head bobbed in and out of view as the waves rolled by.

"Rex!" Jessica called from somewhere far away.

He jumped in the water and began to swim out toward the voice. The sound was so faint, almost a whisper, and it kept getting softer. The noise of his splashes drowned it out, and he was left treading water, listening. He swam for maybe ten minutes, maybe a decade—time didn't seem to work the same way anymore—until he realized, with horror, that he had lost track of both Jessica and the shore in the growing mist.

"Jessica!" he yelled, but all that came out was a hoarse bark. He was tired, but he didn't care. Ignoring his fear, he started swimming again. He couldn't die twice.

"Rex! Help!"

Suddenly, he no longer felt any exhaustion or pain. He just swam out faster and faster until he came to an open space where the mist had begun to dissipate.

"Jessica?" he called, with all the force his voice would allow.

He waited, listening, but there was no reply. He looked around him through the mist as it began to thin out and change texture. Now he could see farther, but it burned his eyes to look. He kept them open anyway, searching.

A deep sorrow consumed him. Jessica was gone. The mist turned into a bitter, acid-tasting smoke, like a big cigarette. Then he felt pain, savage and immense.

Rex sat up on the tile floor. He looked at his hands and felt his shirt, relieved to find them dry. From somewhere, people screamed, and his ears rang. Dust and debris, much of it on fire, littered the room. He pinched his cheeks and pulled on his hair. *This is real. I'm alive. I'm okay.*

He stumbled out of the library and into what was left of the living room. The windows had been blown out, and the hardwood was charred. Bodyguards rushed past him and into the library to collect Vasquez, hurt but alive. Rex tried to see what was wrong with the candidate, but he had to grip his own head to stop the ringing. He hobbled his way through the mahogany doors, the shining lacquer still visible beneath the soot, and found the staircase.

I'm in shock, he told himself. He took the stairs slowly, gripping the cool handrail and letting his head glide along the slick white tiles of the wall.

By the time he made it into the lobby, Vasquez was gone. The hospital, for sure.

Still dazed, he left the apartment building and walked right into the roadway. Cars honked, but likely not at him. Dozens of protesters were shouting and throwing bottles at an overturned police car down the block. Rex spotted a restaurant across the street and headed that way. A plume of black smoke emerged in the sky after the overturned police car became engulfed in flames. Frantic protesters started to scatter and flee in every direction. Several ran right past him as he walked to the restaurant. As Rex opened the door, cops fired tear gas canisters into the streets behind him.

No one in the restaurant cared. They drank and laughed and dined, and few eyes even turned toward the windows. Rex sat at the bar and used a cocktail napkin to dab up the blood that was still leaking from the corner of his mouth. He easily ordered a beer and was perplexed by the atmosphere around him, where life moved on with indifference to the surrounding insanity.

His eyes drifted to the television, where he was startled to see his own image. Breaking news: Vasquez had been hospitalized, and Rex was the chief suspect. Under his photo—one that made him look like a particularly nasty character—scrolled a caption: *"Gringo loco, Problemas con el jefe."* Then came the clip of Vasquez yelling at him about the teleprompter incident.

Gravity suddenly increased on his internal organs.

He lowered his beer, trying to avoid drawing any attention to himself. The campaign train had gone off the rails, and the only thing at the end of this line was death.

Time to get off the ride. He threw some cash on the bar and headed for the door.

"Señor Rex!" The bartender's voice boomed across the room.

Rex paused, inches from the door, contemplating his next move. Should he make a run for it? How far could he get?

Slowly, he took his hand from the door. He turned and looked the bartender dead in the eye, searching for any facial clues of the man's intentions.

"Cambio?"

Rex gave him a smile and a wave. *"Gracias, amigo.* Keep the change."

The bartender smiled back.

#

Rex gulped in air as he rounded the last flight of stairs to his apartment. He rushed through the door, ran to change his shirt, and grabbed some cash from under his mattress. After throwing a pile of clothes into a suitcase, he headed back out the door.

He saw two men in white fishing shirts making their way up the stairs and froze in place on the landing. *This looks bad.* Who were these guys?

The far one drew a gun.

Rex sidestepped to his left, and launched his suitcase their way. *Act or die. Get the gun.*

As the suitcase hit the men, he leaped forward and tackled the closest guy. The two of them hit the hard steps and rolled to the edge of the next flight. Rex grabbed the gunman's shirt and fell backward, pulling the man down the steps with him. Rex kicked off the wall as they fell, pushing the man's head toward the railing.

They came to a stop when the gunman's neck slipped through the bars, got caught between them, and broke with a wet snap. The man's legs twitched and he gurgled, then stilled.

Rex reached for the gun at the bottom of the steps as the other guy crashed into his back. The impact jolted Rex's arm forward, bumping the weapon across the floor. As Rex lurched after it, the man swung wildly at Rex's head. Finally, Rex grasped the gun and tucked it in under his chest like a football player protecting against a fumble. He squirmed and swung his elbows as the man tried to hold him down and pry the gun away. Rex strove to angle it under his armpit for a clear shot at the man on top of his back. He fired, landing two rounds in the man's gut. His attacker yelped and fell in front of the exit door just a few feet away, kicking and squirming. Rex stuffed the gun in the back of his pants and pulled his shirt over it as he stepped over the man.

Out on the street, police cars whizzed past as he walked to the edge of the parking lot. Trying to keep a cool pace, he set course for the side entrance of the Venito Casino, the largest in Panama.

As he headed down the hallway to the casino floor, Rex saw a souvenir shop operated by an indigenous woman who, by the look of the brightly colored mola patterns she wore, appeared to be from the Guna Yalla. Her wares included an assortment of handmade trinkets and traditional Panamanian hats. Rex pointed at one that was big and handwoven and white, handed her a U.S. hundred-dollar bill for a ninety-dollar hat, and shoved it onto his head.

The cacophony of slot machines and salsa music rang in his ears as he walked onto the floor. He headed straight to a crowded craps table to blend in and noticed two prostitutes sizing him up from a nearby row of machines. He approached them and whispered in their ears, then walked out the casino's main entrance, one woman on each arm. They hopped into a cab, and Rex told the driver to drop them off a short distance around the block at the Hotel El Panama. Rex knew well the layout of the place, with its old labyrinthine hallways and discreet unmonitored side exits and entrances. He gave one of the ladies some cash and sent her into the lobby to purchase a room while he waited outside in the cab.

FRANK BAKER

February 24 (Afternoon)
Langley, Virginia

Frank Baker leaned back in his chair, phone to his ear. The sign on his door read, "Regional Director for Central America."

Frank had grown weary of having to repeat himself over and over again to Vasquez. Each time he made his case, Vasquez would immediately dismiss it outright. Then, before Frank could get a word in edgewise, he would have to endure another one of Vasquez's angry tirades—mostly filled with accusations thrown in every direction but the one Frank had so laboriously spelled out for him.

He gazed across the room at a picture of his father, wishing his father could hear him. Maybe Dad could tell him why he had to suffer this call.

Throughout his youth, the man had been a giant in Frank's eyes. A basketball star in high school, he'd had perfect SAT scores and earned a full scholarship to Yale. Like his fellow students, he'd known the history of World War I and that there was no support for entering another world war in Europe, but he'd felt it rolling in like the change of seasons. Like an old man with a bum leg that could predict rain, Frank's father had sensed the political pressure in the air.

He couldn't stomach the idea of history passing him by while he hid out in some library. So, in 1941, at the end of his sophomore year, he tried to enlist.

Frank's father had a problem with his knee, though—an old basketball injury that made him ineligible for the infantry. But then he received a call about a new department opening that summer, the Office of the Coordinator of Information, which was being established to monitor and shape public opinion at home and abroad. He joined, and within a year the department had evolved to become the Office of Strategic Services (OSS).

Frank had always tried to live up to his father's example. He studied hard and kept his grades up so he could follow in his footsteps to Yale. After graduation, he applied for a job at his father's office, which was by that time operating under the name Central Intelligence Agency.

"Vasquez, regardless of what it is you think you know about this guy, I'm telling you, it's wrong," Frank said. "He did it."

"I disagree," Vasquez fired back. "Nash is solid. How could he be getting revenge for being fired when I never fired him? *Las mentiras.* How is it you have Edward Snowden over there spying on everyone's telephone calls across the planet, and all you can come up with is this retarded shit?"

"We have hard evidence," Frank said. "It's almost never this clear. The fact is, your good friend is an unstable character. He posed a danger to you from the start."

"That's crazy," Vasquez responded. "I promise you, Martinez is behind this. So don't give me this 'disgruntled employee' bullshit!"

"Okay, but let me ask you this," Frank said. "Were you aware that Nash was charged with assault just a few months ago?"

"So?"

"Not much on its own, I agree. But add a history of threatening former employers to that. He was fired a couple weeks before heading your way. He threatened to physically injure the candidate. Haskins was the name. Were you aware of that?"

"I never heard of it, but even so, I still don't see it."

"We also have evidence of him meeting with Martinez's people two nights before the bombing. Check your email."

"I'm opening it now, but I will need to call you back. There is someone that I must speak to on the other line."

Frank heard the candidate curse as he hung up the phone. He must have read the email.

REX NASH

February 24 (Afternoon)
Panama City, Panama,

"Vasquez, you know I have nothing to do with this!" Rex said into the phone as he followed the two women down a long hallway toward the ground-level pool at the center of the El Panama.

"I certainly hope the fuck not," Vasquez said.

"Look, it's too dangerous to use the phone. We need to meet in person."

"All right," Vasquez said. "Ancon Hill, eight o'clock. We will pick you up."

"See you there."

Just before the pool entrance, Rex turned his phone off and keyed open his room. He placed the phone on top of a minibar near the door, walked past the first of the twin double beds, and sat down on the edge of the one farthest from the door. He glanced at the pool through the window, then stood up to close the blinds. When he sat back down, he closed his eyes and rubbed his temples with his fingers.

The hookers climbed up at either side of him on the bed. One slung her arm around him and ran the fingertips of her other hand along his thigh. The second woman crawled behind him, took off her shirt, and rested her arms around his neck.

"*Uno momento, eh?*" Rex whispered. "Hold off a second, *por favor.*"

He opened his eyes, rubbing the bridge of his nose. *"Señorita, que hora es?"*

"Por qué?" the woman behind him asked.

"Muy importante—rapido!" Rex said.

He nodded at his phone, and the woman tickling his thigh jumped up and grabbed it from the top of the minibar. *"Son las seis y media,"* she said, tossing the phone across the room to Rex.

He caught the phone in his palm just as someone knocked on the door.

"Tareas domesticas," a muffled voice announced from the other side.

"Come back later," Rex shouted.

The first woman walked over to the door.

"No, don't do that," Rex said.

She glanced back at him with a confused look and unlocked it.

Rex rolled behind the bed and pulled the gun from his waistband.

The woman was pulled by her arm and tossed into the hallway by two men as they barged into the room, one with a pistol and the other with a shotgun. Rex started firing. The guy in front went down, but the guy with the shotgun raised it and fired just as the other girl jumped from the bed. The blast ripped her face right off, her body whirling before crashing to the floor.

Rex fired in the direction of the blast, and the man with the shotgun ducked into the bathroom. Rex leaped up from behind the bed and threw his shoulder hard into the window, shattering it. He tumbled onto a crowded pool deck, where he rolled and stood to his feet. Patrons gasped and backed away.

Rex fired back at the broken window, and people scattered in panic. Out of ammo, he dropped the gun and ran.

#

Not long after sunset, Rex sat atop Ancon Hill, staring out at the city. All those blinking lights and cars. How many were looking for him? He heard the SUVs rumbling his way just before the headlights cast his long shadow before him.

He turned to see Ruben and Vasquez's driver, Ramirez, step from one SUV. He was joined by Oscar, Vasquez's head of security. Maybe it was the dusk, but Oscar's eyes looked black.

The men nodded to Rex as they walked his way.

"Where is Vasquez?" Rex asked.

"Ruben, talk to Mr. Nash," Ramirez called over his shoulder.

Ruben drew a shotgun from the SUV and pointed it at Rex's face.

Rex raised his hands, palms open.

"You will see him soon enough." He broke Rex's nose with a sucker punch that sent him to his knees. Blood streamed through Rex's fingers, and his head spun. Ruben hovered above him, tickling his temple with the gun barrel before resting it on his shoulder.

Then the butt of the gun slammed into Rex's head and everything went black.

#

Rex came to in the back seat, sandwiched between Oscar and Ruben. Ramirez was driving. The SUV was cruising through the city, and his head throbbed with every movement.

"Welcome back to the land of the living," Ruben said. "For now."

Oscar gripped Rex by the collar and stared him down. Those eyes were definitely black. He needed to find a way out of this car, fast. A drop of blood dripped off the tip of his nose and onto his pants leg. He touched the wet red spot with his finger and stared over at Ruben's clean, bright white shirt.

Rex closed his eyes and let his body fall limp. As the SUV made the next left-hand turn, he leaned his body into the turn and pressed his face against Ruben.

"Get off of my shirt!"

Ruben shoved him hard the other way. Rex, now draped over Oscar's lap, grabbed the door handle and kicked off Ruben's side. It almost worked: Oscar fell halfway out the door.

"*Carajo!*" Oscar cursed as he grasped the ceiling handle and slowly pulled himself back inside. Before Oscar could make it all the way back in, Rex grabbed Ramirez's seat belt and tightened it around his neck. Ramirez choked and swerved. With his back pressed against the driver's seat, Rex kicked at Oscar until he finally sank a blow squarely into the center of the man's chest. Oscar lost his grip and fell back, headfirst, out of the vehicle and onto the street.

Ruben swung blindly at Rex, but he was too close and at too much of an awkward angle to deliver any power punches. Rex ducked his head beneath his arms to deflect the blows.

Rex suddenly heard the sound of squealing tires, and the front seat jerked back with a sudden pop. The SUV had crashed into a parked car. He patted his arms and legs to make sure everything was still attached. Fortunately, the back of the front seat had absorbed Rex's forward momentum and spared him from injury. He quickly checked the front of the car. The driver's-side door was caved in. Ruben had been thrown into the front seat.

"*Mi brazo!*" Ruben screamed.

Rex looked over at Ramirez, whose head rested on the steering wheel. He was unconscious but breathing.

Ruben was holding his arm and freaking out. It was bent in the wrong direction at the elbow. He stared back at Rex and pointed at his arm in a plea for help.

"*Mi brazo*, Rex."

"Sorry, Ruben, I have to go." Rex crawled from the car and sprinted across Urracá Park Square and down a side street. He hit the corner of Calle 50 and España and jogged up the sidewalk along España. He heard loud music in the distance and the rumble of a large vehicle heading toward him. Was that bus covered in Christmas lights?

Yes.

It was a Diablo Rojo, one of Panama's famous commuter buses. Underneath the vehicle's exotic exterior, it was probably nothing more than an old school bus, but only the frame bore any visual clues to the mechanical monster's past life. It looked like it had been pimped out by hell's interior decorator, all brightly colored graffiti and blinking lights. Along its sides were murals of explosions and half-naked women, and the speakers blasted music that shook windows for blocks.

A man with a bullhorn hung out of the bus, calling pedestrians to come aboard. He gestured to Rex, who pulled out some cash and waved it over his head. The Diablo Rojo stopped, and he hustled to catch up.

Rex paid his fare and walked down the aisle. He was taking a gamble by getting on the bus, but if he could just make it to a seat without being recognized, he might win a chance to stay alive. As he neared the back, he was surprised to see that the seats weren't occupied by gangsters or partygoers but by working-class folks, all too tired to care about the *gringo* with the busted nose who had just stumbled aboard.

Double shifts and second jobs, he thought, feeling a pang of pity. Even given the blood covering his face and shirt, they barely seemed to notice him.

As he sat, he detected a mound of litter at his feet. Among the plastic bottles and empty cigarette boxes and old wrappers was a battered Panamanian hat. He picked it up and poked it. Clean enough. He leaned back in his seat and laid it over his face.

REX NASH

February 25
Santa Rosa, Panama
(69 days left)

When Rex woke up, his face covered in sweat and dried blood, he saw that the bus had stopped far outside the city. Two scrawny young thugs wearing designer jeans and expensive new sneakers boarded. One had a gun in his waistband. They showed two flyers to the driver as they talked animatedly. Rex ducked down. *Cornered.* Nowhere to go. His foot crunched down on a plastic bottle as he crouched. Maybe a distraction could work. He needed to do something to divert the aim of the gun long enough to make a move. Rex picked the bottle off the floor. He jammed it in between the edge of his seat and the window and then used it to prop his hat up.

The driver stood and pointed in Rex's direction.

"El gringo está por allá."

The thug with the gun started walking to the back as his friend held the bus driver in place.

Rex slid his fingers inside a gash in the green fake leather upholstery that covered the back of the seat in front of him. He ripped it down and leaned into the hole to gain a small amount of cover.

The thug's footsteps grew closer. *Hold still*, Rex told himself. *Wait until you see a hand.* The tip of a gun slowly edged around the corner of the seat. It was pointed at the hat.

Rex reached up and pulled the thug into the seat. He bent the guy's wrist inward as they wrestled, and the gun went off.

The other thug let go of the driver and started toward them.

Rex pushed the body of the first guy, with a fresh hole in the center of his chest, out into the aisle. The other thug turned and ran back to the front of the bus.

Rex bolted for the emergency exit in the back. He jiggled the handle with one hand while aiming the gun toward the front with the other. Finally, he shouldered the door open and jumped out.

Crouching behind a taillight, he watched as his pursuer came bounding around the bus's back corner. He flattened the guy's nose with the butt of the pistol, and the man crumpled as the bus sped off.

Rex frisked the cursing thug and discovered the keys to a Dodge Challenger. Scanning the landscape, he spotted the vehicle soon enough. He rested his knee on the man's chest and pressed the gun barrel to his head.

"Who gave you those flyers?"

"Fuck you, *gringo*." The thug spat in his face.

Rex stood up and wiped off the spit. He kicked the thug in the ribs and lowered the gun over the man's knee. Then he pulled the trigger. The man howled and coughed, until he bit his tongue and blood welled between his lips.

"If you don't speak up, the next one goes in your head," Rex said.

"I don't know nothing," the thug said, from a fetal position. "All I know is, you are dead either way."

Rex kicked the thug's freshly capped knee. The guy screamed and spat blood and sniffled.

"Word is out all over the street," the guy said, between gasps for breath. "A hundred thousand dollars to kill the *gringo*. You pissed off a fucking cartel. You're already dead, *gringo*."

"Well, at least I'm among the walking dead."

Rex dangled the Challenger keys over him. "You know, you really shouldn't be driving with your knee all fucked up like that." He hit the unlock button, heard the doors opened with a satisfying click. A lime green car with black racing stripes glimmered in the direction of the sound.

"I will fucking kill you if you touch that car."

"I'm already dead, remember?" Rex shrugged. "You, on the other hand, could really hurt yourself. Better for you if I hold on to it for a while."

He jumped behind the wheel, slipped the key into the ignition, and felt the car growl and shake. He rolled the window down and drove slowly by its former owner.

"Thanks for the ride," he said and roared off.

DIEGO DOPAZO

February 26
Panama City, Panama
(68 days left)

In a musty dressing room with faded, lime-green peeling paint, Diego Dopazo, the leader and candidate of the PRD, looked back and forth between an old TV and his own reflection. In the mirror was a man with dark, slicked-back hair, a white fishing shirt, and a pair of pressed khakis. He had the face and build of a politician, but there was something dangerous in his eyes.

On the TV, President Martinez walked through a crowd of reporters. "What do you say about those who are making accusations?" one yelled. "Did your administration have a role in the attack on Vasquez?"

Martinez, plump and exhausted, pushed past them, saying nothing.

"True or not, the suggestion that President Martinez's party was in any way involved has the opposition calling for his resignation," the anchor said.

The broadcast switched to a clip of Roberto Marcelli standing just outside the assembly building. He shook his fist and pointed his finger. "There is no way President Martinez can maintain control," he said. "This is the last straw. He must resign."

The broadcast moved on to Freddy Ramos, who spoke from his hospital bed. "President Martinez is behind this, I'm sure of it. Let me tell you something, Dictator Martinez. The people of Panama, we remember the days of Noriega, and we are never going back, no matter what you try to do."

The newscast cut back to the female anchor behind the news desk. "Martinez's silence is fueling speculation. Even after hearing the accusations of the opposition, the president refuses to speak."

A press secretary stuck her head in through the doorway of the dressing room. "It's time."

Diego nodded. He adjusted his coat and straightened his tie.

"The chairman of the PRD and next president of the Republic of Panama, Diego Dopazo!" the announcer told the crowd gathered in the auditorium at Latin University of Panama.

He walked out onstage, waving to over a thousand people packed into the event hall. The crowd roared. He looked directly into the Telemetro and TVN cameras as he approached the mic.

"There comes a moment in a country's history when it meets a crossroads. This is one of those moments," he began. "We must resist the old ways; the politics of violence and chaos have no place in the future of our republic. But we must stand up in the face of violence. We must stand up to President Martinez, and we must say, 'No more!' President Martinez, we will not let you drag our country backward. We will win this election. We will win, and we will move this country forward."

PRESIDENT MARTINEZ

March 5
Panama City, Panama
(61 days left)

President Martinez peered out a window at the end of a long hallway on the second floor of the Palacio de las Garzas. A traffic jam was building outside in Casco Viejo's narrow colonial streets. TV vans were parked on the sidewalk in front of the presidential palace while reporters jockeyed for position before the palace doors.

Unshaken, the president closed the curtains and strode down the hall. He had seen every form of media circus in the past, and he'd made it through all of them unscathed. From the moment of his first entrance into politics, they'd called him crazy, claiming he'd never have a shot. Every time he was up for reelection, they were sure of a victory for his challenger. But he'd proven them wrong every time. On the eve of his latest landslide victory, the opening words of his address had been, "Never mistake someone who seems too crazy to get elected for someone just crazy enough to win."

His steps echoed down the long hallway until he stopped in front of a pair of large wooden doors. Taking a breath, he lifted his head and opened them.

His eyes took in the Persian carpet and then the Moorish carved-wood ceiling. The sound of camera shutters clicking and the lights of their flashes filled the room.

His chief of police and attorney general stood waiting for him. The police chief lined up beside him as they gathered behind the attorney general, who took the microphone first.

"I apologize for the delay in public information," the attorney general said. "This was a massive investigation, with multiple agencies in Panama and *los Estados Unidos*. We needed to ensure we had all the facts and that we didn't report anything that might hinder our investigation. The explosion at the home of Candidate Vasquez resulted from the actions of one disturbed person acting alone. Rex Nash, an American member of Vasquez's own campaign, was immediately identified as a person of interest. Vasquez had threatened to fire him on TV just days earlier."

The attorney general continued, "With the help of the U.S. State Department, we quickly gained access to background records on Mr. Nash, which revealed a disturbed young man with a history of violence and threats against his employers. He was twice fired in the past year.

What we are about to play for you now is a recording made by U.S. congressman Bob Haskins."

President Martinez covered his mouth, resting his chin in his hand in an attempt to conceal a widening smile. He cocked one eyebrow and pretended to focus on learning the contents of the audio recording:

Rex Nash: What you're really saying is you want me to kick your ass. Because if you don't cut me my check, that's exactly what's going happen.

Bob Haskins: Watch the threats, Rex. I am recording this conversation.

The attorney general returned to the microphone. "We can clearly hear a psychotic Mr. Nash threatening Mr. Haskins with physical violence and harm. When we interviewed Mr. Haskins, he stated that he felt the need to fire Nash out of fear for his own safety.

"Angry and dangerous, Mr. Nash joined the desperate Vasquez campaign. With the campaign already out of money and hurting in the polls, Vasquez passed the blame on to Nash. This pushed the already deranged American over the edge, and he lashed out again, this time much more violently. Finally, further analysis of the crime scene confirmed that the blast generated from a briefcase belonging to Mr. Nash. Contrary to the prayers of the opposition, there was no conspiracy. This was just a simple case of revenge perpetrated by a lone, disturbed, and disgruntled employee."

#

Vasquez and his deputies huddled around a large TV in his office, staring at Martinez with open mouths as he stepped up to the podium.

"Oh, no, here it comes!" Roberto Marcelli cried out over the sighs and gasps muttered around the room.

"Vasquez wants to point fingers at others," President Martinez said. "He likes to spread lies about conspiracies. If he needs someone to blame, he should take a long look in the mirror. Maybe if he treated his employees better, they wouldn't want to blow him up. That's why the employees at his coffee company are on strike right now. He mistreats them too. Now he wants to be president? Why? So he can mistreat the rest of us?"

Vasquez stayed silent as his deputies moaned and yelled. "Bullshit! *Mentiras!* Liars!"

"Vasquez is going nowhere," Martinez went on. "Who would vote for someone whose own campaign wants to kill him?"

"Motherfucker!" Roberto shouted at the screen.

Vasquez soaked up each insult like a sponge, his face burning. There was only one thing he wanted now: revenge.

RAUL VASQUEZ

March 6
Panama City, Panama
(60 days left)

Black smoke from burning tires lingered like fog in front of the old palace. Sounds of movement grew, and dark shapes appeared.

Men emerged from the smoke with rags held against their mouths and a crowd of protesters in tow.

Vasquez raised a bullhorn. "President Martinez, we will not let you terrorize our nation. The people want their palace back!" He stared up at the top floor office window. "Martinez has no understanding of the consequences of his actions. He thinks it is amusing to toy with our country with his constant maneuvering, plotting, and scheming. He treats human beings as if they are wooden figurines scattered over a chess board. Play time is over. This is not a game. This is real life, and you're going to be made to see and feel just how real it is."

T-shirts wrapped around their heads, the protestors cheered, flung bottles, and charged. They ran and shoved and pushed and yelled all the way up to the line of cops in riot gear guarding the presidential palace.

They began hurling bottles at the barricade. Others danced, and yet another group burned more tires in the street. Canisters of tear gas, their tails smoking like shot-down planes, sailed into the mob from the police line.

Two TV crews hustled to follow Vasquez.

"Time to step down before we throw you out!" Vasquez shouted toward the palace.

A flood of protesters rushed past him and shoved against the barricade.

JUAN GONZALAS

March 6
Panama City, Panama
(60 days left)

President Martinez stepped away from the window of his palace office.

"We need to put a stop to this," Juan said. "We cannot allow this mob to go any further."

Martinez grabbed a bottle of painkillers off his desk and popped two in his mouth. He washed them down with a gulp of gin and tonic. "Fuck it. Just do it."

Juan picked up his cell phone and made a call. "Send them in," he said, then walked back over to the window and pulled the curtain again.

From a nearby alley, plainclothes goons with clubs rushed in, swinging hard. Dozens of victims dropped, grabbing cracked skulls or broken noses.

But the protesters outnumbered the goons. Grabbing rocks, broken glass, and still-smoking hubcaps from the burned tires, they fought back.

Juan watched. The president poured another drink. *Vasquez has gone mental dragging this band of terrorists out into the streets. All this bullshit about democracy. The people love me. I am democracy. Why does he have to be such an asshole?*

"How bad is it?" Martinez asked.

"Not good," Juan said.

"Vasquez is totally fucking us," Martinez said. "I was supposed to go to Rio tonight—so I can obtain at least some small amount of enjoyment in my life, you know? But now I have to deal with this nonsense."

"The riot is out of control," Juan said. "It's a crisis. We have to deal with it."

"Noooo! I want to go to Rio!" a woman's voice wailed.

The president turned and stared across the room at the three gorgeous Colombian women, less than fully dressed, who sat on a couch, waiting. The coffee table in front of them was littered with empty champagne bottles and glasses. Strewn among the glasses was an assortment of pills, cocaine, and cigarette butts.

"*Presidente*, you promised..." the middle one whined.

"Please, *Presidente*..." the woman on her left begged.

Martinez ignored them and frowned at Juan. "You are right, this is a serious situation."

"We need a plan," Juan responded.

Martinez shrugged and joined him at the window. Through the glass they could see scores of policemen swinging at goons and protesters alike. "Holy shit."

"*Presidente*, what do you want us to do?" Juan asked.

"Here is the plan," Martinez said. "I'm going to Rio. You can stay here and figure out how to deal with this bullshit by yourself."

The women cheered.

REX NASH

March 6
Bocas del Toro, Panama
(59 days left)

Rex sat at a grass hut bar at the end of a long, narrow, and rickety wooden dock, watching and listening.

At one of the barstools, a dark shirtless man, unshaven and wearing a ragged pair of jean shorts, ran his finger across the palm of a college girl with dreadlocks and a tie-dyed T-shirt and explained the meaning of the love line. She giggled.

The bartender smiled as he held back his own laugh; he had clearly seen this guy's fake palmistry routine before. He placed two melon ball shooters in front of them. "On the house."

The Caribbean beach around them was all white sands and still, blue water. Couples sunbathed on lounge chairs, sipping daiquiris and beers, attended by well-tipped waiters required to wear long slacks and polo shirts.

Next to Rex, a couple and their young son were close to finishing their meal. The bartender pulled up their check and brought it over to them. "I hope you enjoyed your time here in Bocas del Toro."

"Oh yes, it was fantastic. So glad we decided to come," the wife said. "We've been to the Bahamas a few times, but this time was totally different."

"So when does your cruise leave port tomorrow?"

"Not until four, so we're looking for something to do in the morning," the husband said.

Rex tipped up his baseball hat and took off his sunglasses, placing them carefully down on the bar.

"I may be able to help you," he said.

They both gave Rex puzzled looks.

"I'm in kind of a predicament," Rex said. "My wife and I booked a fishing tour charter for tomorrow morning. We paid in advance, but her sister is in labor, so we're cutting our trip short. You should take our place. The boat trip runs eight to one, so you would have plenty of time. I'd hate for those pricey tickets to go to waste." Rex laid it on thick with his best salesmanship smile and tried to mask how desperately he needed them to accept.

"That'd be great. Are you sure?" the husband asked.

"Yep," Rex said. He let deep breath. "More than you know." A nice couple and all but they were going to have to take one for the team. No other way around it.

"No refunds, so please, have them."

The husband turned and put his arm around his son. "Hey, little buddy, what do you think? Ready to go out and catch some big fish tomorrow?"

#

The forty-foot, in-board diesel boat with two deep-sea fishing rigs affixed to the sides of the helm cut through the crystal-clear blue Caribbean water, the rods pointed back over the boat's wake. The captain, an older Bokata Indian native, was firmly in charge of his boat. His skin was hard and leathery, and though it puffed up like goggles around his eyes, his pupils still glimmered. He had spent the morning sailing out into deep waters in search of blue marlin. After several hours of trolling without so much as a nibble, he'd realized that the family with him was bored, so he re-rigged things to let them try instead for smaller fish. It had worked, and soon dozens of newly caught dorado, kingfish, and yellow jacks filled the space beneath the hatch in the deck.

They set course to return to Bocas del Toro, and he turned to see the couple staring out across the water from the back of the boat, no land in sight, as their son lifted the hatch to examine the day's catch. Seeming awed, he poked at the bright scales of the different fish and watched as they changed color in the light.

When the boat abruptly slowed, the boy fell face-first onto the fish pile.

The mother reached for her son. "Get out of there!" she scolded. "Are you okay?"

"Why are we slowing down?" the husband yelled up to the helm.

The captain attempted to restart the engine, but it failed to turn over. He banged his leathery fist on the wheel and cursed, then stepped onto the back deck.

"Hey, what's going on?" the husband asked. "I thought we were headed back—"

"The engine broke down," the captain said. "I'm going to have to get someone out here on the CB. Sorry, but it's going to take a while."

"You have to be kidding," the husband said. "This can't be happening. We need to board our cruise back to Miami."

The wife grabbed her purse and rifled through it in a panic. She yanked out her cell phone. "Oh my God," she said. "We need to tell them. They have to wait!"

"Sorry, ma'am," the captain said. "Cell phones hardly work on land in Bocas, let alone way out here."

#

Rex took his time going through the contents of the couple's suitcases in their hotel room. He'd found their passports and the cards they needed to return to the ship. He also found a nice bottle of bourbon, from which he took a long pull.

Rex lifted the husband's passport toward the window and squinted at the picture. This would work.

PRESIDENT MARTINEZ

March 8
Rio de Janeiro, Brazil
(58 days left)

The pool at the Belmond Copacabana Palace in Rio was big and blue and clean, but nobody went out there just to swim. They went to watch the gorgeous women lounging on the deck chairs, order a drink, or smoke a fine cigar.

Three reporters stood in a semicircle on the deck, interviewing a reclining President Martinez, who wore Hawaiian-flower-print swim trunks, flip-flops, and a white T-shirt. An unfinished gin and tonic sweated on the table beside him.

"*Presidente*, Panama is suffering through a third day of rioting," a female reporter asked. "The country is breaking down in chaos. Why have you not returned home to address the situation?"

"I'm in constant contact with my officials, and I've already spoken to the nation on Twitter. Besides, the security minister has the situation under control."

"But the situation is getting worse, not better," the reporter said.

"If you want to point fingers, look to Vasquez." Martinez shrugged. "He is the one creating all of this. This is a crisis of the opposition. Go ask him why there is chaos in the streets."

"*Señor Presidente*, Diego Dopazo says responsibility for the chaos rests with both you and Vasquez," the reporter pressed. "He says he is the only one who can put an end to the corruption and chaos plaguing the country. He is now leading in the polls, so the people seem to agree."

"Dopazo?" Martinez shouted. "He is the most corrupt man in the entire country. Believe me, whatever false scandals Vasquez accuses me of, they are absolutely nothing compared to what Diego would bring. Enough!"

Martinez waved his hand under his chin, letting them know the interview was over. He reached for his drink and sucked down the soggy remainder. "These questions are bullshit. You want something to report on, report on this."

He slammed his empty tumbler on the table and jumped from his lounge chair.

Then his plump, round body broke into a sprint, and he ran as fast as his legs would allow toward the pool, flanks wriggling.

"Cannonball!" he shouted as he leaped.

The splash was colossal. Sunbathers winced and tried to shield themselves from the drops raining down.

Martinez swam along the bottom like a ray, winding around others' feet. At last he emerged, climbed up the ladder, and grabbed a towel. An aide ran up with a cell phone, which he snatched and immediately dialed.

"Juan!" Martinez said. "There is no way Diego Dopazo is stealing the government from us. Track down the fucking *gringo*."

MARCO

March 9
Washington, D.C.

Marco silenced his ringing phone and put it in his pocket, taking one last sip of overpriced, burnt coffee. He hated Starbucks. He left the shop, walked directly to a black Lexus on the corner, and popped the trunk.

The duffel bag inside was gray with black straps, too unassuming not to be dangerous. He unzipped it. On top of the gym clothes was a Beretta 96A1 handgun. Marco threw his phone into the bag and zipped it back up.

He closed the trunk and lit a cigarette. He walked past the parking meter and under a bare cherry blossom tree toward the field of grass. He glared down the mall at the Capitol and took a long drag. He blew out the smoke, turned back toward the car, and looked upward. The Washington Monument really looked as absurd in real life as it did in pictures.

FRANK

March 11
Prince George's County, Maryland

On a bright Saturday morning, a boy of about ten rode his bike swiftly, weaving among cars because it was fun. He did a bunny hop onto the curb, then onto the street, then back to the curb again in a dance he hoped looked both casual and cool.

He passed an upper-middle-class home where an old man was doing yard work. His nose itched and his eyes started to water from the scent of fresh-cut grass. He pedaled harder, whizzing down the sidewalk.

He could see kids on the corner a couple of blocks away, new ones who had come with their parents to D.C. after the change in administration. His old friends had moved, but he was excited to meet the newcomers, so he sped up even more.

Zeroed in on the corner, he gave little attention to what sounded like gloved fists punching the pavement. But then a black blur whizzed into his field of vision, and the fists smacked him just beneath the ribs.

Not fists, paws. The kid wavered and gasped, but didn't fall. He steadied his bike and sped away from the animal as its leash went taut.

"Hey! Watch out, you little shit!" shouted the woman on the other end of the leash.

He would have flipped her the bird if even one of the kids on the corner had looked his way, but none did. They were all staring at something else.

A crowd of adults had gathered near a house with three large black SUVs and several police cars out front. People wearing blue jackets with yellow letters that read "FBI" marched in and out of the house with boxes. The boy rode over to get a closer look.

An older man climbed out of the back seat of one of the SUVs and stepped onto the lawn. A female FBI officer with a clipboard stood in the driveway, peering at the hood of a new Lexus.

The guy on the lawn inspected his suit for something. Who knew what. Wrinkles? Coffee stains? The man plucked a piece of lint off his lapel and tossed it into the air, observing as it wafted down among the blades of grass.

The boy pedaled up and parked on the edge of the lawn. The old man turned toward him and smiled.

"Did Mrs. Nash rob a bank?"

The man snarled at the boy and made his way across the lawn toward the house. He waved at the woman in the FBI jacket, who ignored him, scribbling something on a pad as he approached. He pulled his badge.

"Excuse me, ma'am," the boy heard him say. "My name is Frank Baker."

#

Dolores Hogan Nash took a deep breath and clasped her hands to steady the shaking. It didn't help, so she lowered them under the kitchen table and out of the view of the two bulky men sitting across from her. One had short, black boy-band hair, and the other was blond. They both reeked of cologne and wore their blue jackets a size too tight.

For over an hour, the agents had drowned her mind with detail after detail of the recent events in Panama. They told her every horrible thing her son Rex had been accused of, from the bombing to the shootouts to the political chicanery. Dolores's heartbeat grew faster as they spoke. Her hands felt cold and clammy as she pressed them together. Then a dizzy sensation gripped her, as if the room were suddenly floating on water, with steady waves rolling underneath. She desperately wanted to stand up and leave the room, but she was too scared and fatigued to escape. She worried that she might throw up or pass out. Or both.

"The best thing you can do right now, Mrs. Nash, is to tell us everything you know about what your son has been doing," the blond agent said. "It could help us bring him safely in."

She dug her fingernails into the table. "I... I..." She stopped and then started again. "I don't believe a single word of this garbage."

"Okay, Mrs. Nash. Have it your way," the blond agent said.

"Where did you get that nice Lexus in the driveway?" the black-haired agent asked. "Gift from Rex?"

"That was his father's car. Just something nice he bought for himself in the final months before he passed." Her breath hitched a little. Could these jerks not give her any consideration?

The black-haired agent slammed his hand on the table and leaned toward her.

"Mrs. Nash, are you aware that lying to the FBI is a crime?" he asked. "A felony."

She rubbed her nostrils as he stayed in her face. He smelled like a cat had drunk cologne and peed on his head. Above his collar, a hipster tribal tattoo crept up his neck. She stared at the ugly skin art and sat back in her chair with her arms folded.

"If you two are what they're sending out to play FBI men these days, then God help us all," she said.

"Very protective of Momma's little angel, aren't we?" the blond quipped.

"Where does he hide his money, Mrs. Nash?" the black-haired agent pressed. "If it's here in the house, you'd better tell us now before we find it. And we *will* find it."

"How long has Rex been involved in the drug trade, Mrs. Nash?" the blond asked. "Running around in Panama just seeing the sights, is he? Yeah, I bet. Everyone knows how those people are down there. Bunch of Third World criminals, every one of them. Do you really expect us to believe you didn't know what your little Tony Montana was up to?"

"Now you listen here," she fired back. "You need to go to a doctor and get yourself checked out. Maybe you have some wires crossed in your brain or something, because those are some pretty stupid ideas."

"Mrs. Nash. Do you know just how much trouble your son has put you in?" the black-haired agent asked. "Aiding and abetting, conspiracy, material support of terrorism? The list goes on."

"You don't know anything about Rex." She wiped a tear from her eye, then pointed at both of them. "I gave birth to him. I raised him. What do you know?"

"Well, unless you want to spend the rest of your time left on this earth in a federal penitentiary, you need to do exactly as we tell you," the black-haired agent said.

"Maybe you think you can bully me around because I'm an old woman, and maybe I am. But I didn't fall off the turnip truck just yesterday, and the hell if I'm going to help you destroy the one person left that I love in this world. What do you know? I was the one they called if he messed up at school. I was the one who had to speak with his teachers or principals. I know when he's telling the truth, and if he's lying to get out of trouble. I know his ways and ideas, his hopes and fears. I know what drives him and what holds him back."

#

On his way to the kitchen, Frank saw several agents in blue jackets ransacking the house, ripping open furniture and kicking holes in the walls. Sitting at the kitchen table were Rex's mother and two FBI agents who clearly had not slow-played their position. What was wrong with these guys? What was going on with all of that hair gel?

"I'm sure you fine fellows would have gotten right to the bottom of this one, but I'll take it from here if you don't mind," Frank said. The agents shot him annoyed looks, but he ignored them and introduced himself to Mrs. Nash. When they'd left, Frank pulled up a chair.

"Now, Mrs. Nash, it's probably best to just forget whatever nonsense those two FBI buffoons just told you."

"Are you somehow any better?"

"Well, I do oversee operations in Latin America, so I'm at least familiar with the players," Frank said. "I may even be able to help Rex out of this jam, but I must tell you that he is in a tremendous amount of danger right now. If you want to help him, I need you to help me find him first. We believe he's still in Panama, but we aren't sure. Do you know if he has any contacts or childhood friends with a connection to Panama? He might try to reach out to them."

She shook her head. Frank nodded, and held out a card.

"If you hear from your son, I want you to tell him to call me. Tell Rex that I can help him, okay?"

She smiled and took the card.

REX NASH

March 15
Prince George's County, Maryland

Rex ground his cigarette out in the parking lot and walked into the auto shop. The first thing to catch his eye was a mounted baseball bat with a deep scratch and two rusty nails poking from its business end.

Dave Barese walked into the room, studying his clipboard. He didn't look up, but he grinned at Rex all the same.

"What's up, Dave?" Rex asked.

"Back from Panama already? Did you win?"

"Oh, it's still going on. It's been, uh, pretty intense."

"I guess so. You look like shit."

Rex pointed at the baseball-equipment-turned-weapon-of-war on the wall behind him. "I see you are still keeping things PG County."

"Ah, you know it," Dave said. "You think the bat is hard-core? Check this out."

He pulled a sawed-off shotgun from under the counter and handed it to Rex.

"Impressive." Rex handed it back.

"We get some unruly customers from time to time. My therapist said I needed to enhance my conflict-resolution tools. This one is my bad-attitude adjuster."

"I don't think that's what your therapist meant," Rex said.

"No way, man. He was right on. Zero conflicts for me now. People used to bitch and whine to me all the time. One look at that bat, though, and they're real polite. And if they're not, I have my contingency plan." He patted the gun. "Driving some nails through that evil baseball bat and mounting it on the wall, and starting to wave this beast around along with it really helped to open up some clear dialogue. Now everybody knows exactly what page I'm on. All about effective communication, my friend."

"Too funny," Rex said.

"Hey, man. Come see my new office."

Rex followed Dave into the garage, past the car lifts, and up a flight of stairs. Dave opened the door to a small room.

There was a big couch to his left beside a mini-fridge and a wine rack. Christmas lights were stapled on every corner of the ceiling, and a black light hung over a Salvador Dalí poster. Rex smiled as he took further inventory of the varied gadgets on the right: a TV, a PlayStation 4, a stereo system, a kegerator, and a coffee table with a bong resting atop it. To Dave's credit, there was at least an almost-clean desk, with a computer, by the window. Dave might have matured somewhat after years of being accountable to the responsibilities of owning a business, but his taste in decoration certainly hadn't.

"This is where I do all my, you know, office-type shit."

He pulled a couple of Coors Lights out of the fridge and tossed one over to Rex before cracking his own. "So... how's Panama? You're back pretty quick. Job finished up?"

"Yeah, about that," Rex said. A bit of fineness was in order. This wasn't something where you could just lay it all out there. That would scare the shit out of him. The less details the better. "Things may have gotten a little out of control down there. I'm... in a bit of trouble. Someone set me up, and my situation is pretty fucked. I need an off-the-radar place to lie low for a while."

"Whatever you need, man," Dave said. "I got you."

"Thanks," Rex said. "The reality is, you're the only one who can really help me. I can't even try to talk to anyone else."

"Seriously?" Dave asked. "Why not?"

"You're the only person I know that's enough of a caveman to have never used social media."

"You're right there." Dave shrugged. "I hate every form of that stuff. Seriously, it's lame."

"I can appreciate your stance," Rex said. "If I had asked anyone else I know for help, I would have been tracked down in about ten minutes."

"Social media is a nightmare," Dave said. "They just want all of your contacts, associations, politics, and whatnot. I don't want these people tracking me everywhere I go, every restaurant I enter, every purchase I make, every place I visit."

"I'd hate to see the file they'd have on you," Rex said, mockingly rubbing his chin as if he were pondering some great question of the universe. "Now, I can only guess, but I don't think it would be going too far out on a limb here to say that about ninety-nine percent of the information in your file would be porn and rub-and-tug-parlor related."

"Exactly. I'm the only who knows where all the best spots in town are, and I aim to keep it that way."

Rex laughed and cupped his hand over his beer to keep it from spilling.

"No, seriously, I'm not going to throw away all my privacy just to keep up to date with the latest selfies and pictures of stupid pets and ugly kids. All from a bunch of jerks I never gave two shits about in the first place."

"That's one way to look at it," Rex said.

"You know what you need to solve all of this?" Dave asked.

"What?" Rex asked.

"You probably just need to get laid. Bobby's got some wild girls over at his house tonight. Let's go crash that shit."

"Doubt that'll solve anything," Rex said. "I need to lie low until I can find a way out of this jam. Like, nobody sees me—not even random females."

"Stop acting gay," Dave said. "Nobody around here knows what continent Panama is on, let alone anything about what you were up to out there."

"I don't know; it's pretty serious," Rex said.

"Wait a second," Dave said. "How many hundreds of murders have there been in PG County alone this year? And how many of those do you think were solved outside of the ones where the guy was literally caught in the act, or it's some dumb fuck sitting there at the scene of the crime with the murder weapon in his hand? About fucking zero, that's about how many."

"Okay, okay. I see you there, but this is a whole international situation," Rex said.

"Yeah, exactly," Dave said. "How would anyone around here have the slightest fucking clue? Let me tell you something. I have nothing but cable news blaring through my shop twelve hours a day, so if anyone knows what's up, it's me. But I'll let you in on a little secret, just between me and you. For all that bullshit I have pumping into my ears six days a week, I still don't have even the slightest idea what the fuck is going on anywhere in all of America, let alone someplace outside of it."

"I get your point," Rex said.

"So, you ready to go?" Dave asked.

"Fine," Rex said.

#

Rex watched from the passenger seat of Dave's Escalade as they drove through their old neighborhood. From behind the wheel, buzzed, Dave fumbled with the radio and his phone. Rex took in the passing landscape as if he were seeing it for the first time. Growing up, he couldn't wait to get out of this shithole, but tonight he was glad to be back. Every landmark, store, stoplight, and street sign seemed to hold a new mystery. In Panama, he'd wondered if he'd ever get the chance to see them again.

"Rex! What are you, high?" Dave asked. "You haven't heard a word I just said."

"What? Oh, sorry."

"Like I was saying, Bobby found a bunch of super sluts from Baltimore, so your timing is perfect. He said they're all coked up and whacked out on E. They're running around the house naked and shit."

He handed Rex his phone. It was Bobby on a video call. Bobby turned his phone to reveal two scantily clad women giggling in the background.

"You see that shit?" Bobby said. "These girls are insane. Hurry up and get here."

Rex ended the call. "Bobby may be a lunatic, but I guess that's just the way things are these days," he said.

"Yep. It's *Girls Gone Wild* over there," Dave said.

"Hey, pull into this 7-Eleven for a second. I think I know that car."

They both got out of the Escalade and walked into the store. Rex headed to the clerk behind the counter and reached for his wallet. Dave veered off to the drinks on the back wall.

The blonde in line in front of Rex was buying a Pepsi. Her hair was long and natural, and she wore a halter-style pink sundress that highlighted her deep tan.

After she'd paid, she turned away from the counter and screamed.

"Jessica?" Rex said, stunned.

"Stay away from me, you jerk!"

"Wait, what? Not sure how I deserve that."

"Yes, you do," Jessica said.

Perplexed, Rex froze in place. He gazed at her, searching for some clue in her body language that might reveal what she was getting at.

He couldn't help but notice that she was in perfect shape. Her belly looked the same size as it had the last time he'd seen her.

"I thought you were pregnant."

"Pregnant? What are you talking about?" Jessica asked. "You really are a jerk! After what you did to me? The things you said? Just leave me alone."

She ran from the store, tears flowing. Rex rushed after her, but she hopped in her car and drove off.

Dave walked up behind him in the parking lot.

"Wow, man. What did you do to that girl?" Dave asked. "She was about to kill you."

"There's no reason for *her* to be pissed at *me*," Rex said as they got back into the car. "She dropped the I'm-pregnant-by-someone-else bomb via text message, then refused to answer the phone. She fucking devastated me."

"Well, why is she so pissed, then?" Dave asked.

"I don't know," Rex said. "She sure doesn't look pregnant any-more."

"So, she's just like a crazy bitch, or what?" Dave said.

"No, not at all," Rex said.

"Is this *that* Jessica girl?" Dave asked. "Haven't you known her your whole life?"

"Yeah," Rex responded.

"Then how can you be so confused over this?" Dave asked. "Don't project some false image onto her based off the type of trashy broads that hang out with Bobby and shit. Focus on what you know about *her*."

"It's conflicted," Rex said.

"Look, don't get caught up with a bunch of stress. That won't do anything but cloud your mind. Use some fucking logic," Dave said.

"Agree, but everything I thought I knew about her went down the drain when I read that text."

"Have a little faith," Dave replied. "Sometimes you just have to trust in what your gut is telling you."

"Yeah, but the world is telling me something much different," Rex said. He wanted to believe what Dave was saying, but how could he?

"Rex, you gotta push that noise out," Dave said. "That's how you get to the truth about things."

Push the noise out. Nothing felt true about this situation, and he needed answers. "I think you're right," Rex said. "Turn left at the next light."

#

Jessica's parents' home was large and secluded, with trees on either side.

"Hang back here for a minute," Rex said as Dave pulled into the tree-lined gravel driveway. "Call me, though, if anyone shows up."

"You sure?" Dave said.

"Yeah, just give me a second to talk to her."

All the windows were dark in the white colonial as Rex approached the front porch except for a single light emanating from the living room. Rex snuck up to the window and peered in. Jessica was alone in the middle of the living room, still wiping away tears as she talked to someone on the phone.

He walked around the side of the house, cracked open the door to the living room, and slid it closed as he stepped inside. She put the phone down on the coffee table, her back still to him.

"Jessica," he said.

She screamed. "What are you doing here?"

Rex held up his palms, hoping the gesture would calm her down. It didn't.

"Get out of my house!" Jessica yelled.

Rex's phone began to ring, and he tried to silence it. *I just need a second,* he told himself. The caller dialed again.

"Look," he pleaded with Jessica, shutting off his cell, "I just need to know why you told me you were pregnant. In a freaking text, for fuck sake."

"I never said anything like that," Jessica fired back. "Why would I say I was *pregnant*, Rex? What are you talking about? Did you ever think about those texts *you* sent *me*? You dumped me out of nowhere and then called me a worthless whore. You told me to *kill* myself. I hate you! Get out of my house!"

Footsteps came from behind Jessica. A figure emerged from the dim hallway and stepped into the living room.

Jessica turned. "Marco. About time! Rex stalked me. He followed me home."

"Who the fuck are you?" Rex asked.

The man pulled a 9mm handgun from his waistband.

Rex threw his hands in the air. *Chill*, he told himself. Was this Marco guy the boyfriend she'd mentioned in her texts? Hadn't she said his name was Ben? Whoever he was, it would be wise not to piss him off any further.

Marco raised the gun.

Rex froze still. Stay *calm*. No sudden moves.

"Don't shoot him!" Jessica said from where she stood between them.

Rex slowly nodded at Jessica. This was way out of control, but maybe she could diffuse the situation. He looked her in the eyes with confidence and encouragement, hoping she would come through.

"Get away from him!" Marco shouted. "He's dangerous." He lifted a hand gently, as if to embrace her. "Remember what he said to you in those texts. We talked about this."

Jessica hesitated and turned to Rex with a confused expression.

"He's only come here to hurt you," Marco said, behind her.

He reached out to her with one hand, and she slowly walked toward him. When she was within arm's reach, he swung the pistol hard into her face. Jessica crumpled to the floor.

Rex reflexively dodged left, out of the firing line. *Don't think, act*. He leaped forward and tackled Marco.

The moment before impact, Marco dropped the gun and grabbed hold of him, using Rex's own momentum to slam him down hard on the floor. As Rex struggled to regain his breath, Marco slipped his hand under Rex's arm and into a half nelson. Rex struggled to squirm free, but Marco grabbed his other arm and lifted him up off the floor before dropping Rex's head down onto the tile.

Blurred movements, shapes, flickering lights, and then... dim focus at last. Helplessly, Rex watched as Marco retrieved the gun from the floor and headed his way.

"You're a sucker, Rex." Marco stood over him, pointing the gun. "You can't win. You are a chump."

Rex knew he needed to move, but he couldn't. He tried to speak, tasting blood in his mouth. "Jessica?"

"Oh, your pretty little girlfriend here?" Marco smiled. "I did enjoy the sex. She was just so distraught after all those terrible texts you sent. Well, *I* sent them, actually, but no one's ever going to know that. She never even questioned why or how it was that I managed to appear in her life at that exact moment when she was the most vulnerable and needed someone to comfort her. Nothing personal, though, Rex. I was just doing my job."

"Job... for who?" Rex asked.

"The people who make the world run," Marco retorted. "You, on the other hand, are, as I said, just a chump. The only memory of you will be that of a lone-wolf lunatic loser who killed his girlfriend after going on a rampage in Panama. Your friends, your family... everyone will believe that you couldn't handle the pressure. There will be no dots to connect. They will quietly bury you in six feet of disgust and move on."

Rex tried to move, but Marco stomped on his chest and leaned in.

This is it. Rex closed his eyes.

He heard the roar of a gunshot and felt a warm spray of blood.

He opened his eyes to see what was left of Marco's head slumped to his chest as he fell. Dave, a sawed-off shotgun in his hands, stood in the doorway.

"Thank God," Rex told his friend. He rolled over, wiped the blood from his mouth, and crawled to Jessica, who was still motionless on the floor. He knelt beside her and kissed her forehead. Slowly, her eyelids fluttered open.

CHARLES LEE

March 16
Darién Province, Panama

Charles Lee pulled a handkerchief from his pocket and wrapped it around his finger as the black Ford Explorer made its way up a long driveway and parked in front of a mansion deep in the jungle. As the driver brought the car to a stop, Charles touched the tip of the handkerchief to his tongue and wiped a smear of mud from his boots. Stupid spic pilot. A helicopter could land anywhere. Did it have to be in mud?

Diego Dopazo strode from the mansion, flanked by two body-guards. Charles started to open the front passenger door, but another guard approached and signaled for him to stay inside.

Diego nodded at Charles's car before ducking into his own. When that car had left, the guard gave another signal, and Charles got out alone. The guard barked something in Spanish on a CB and waved him toward the entrance.

He straightened his tie, folded his handkerchief, and stuffed it back where it belonged. Two other guards escorted him inside.

He crossed a lofty porch where two armed guards stood, surveying a seemingly endless jungle.

"Charles," Edgardo said, standing as Charles entered a lavishly decorated living room. "Welcome."

"Edgardo Blades, in the flesh," Charles said. "Been a long time. I was beginning to wonder whether you were still alive or if I was dealing with a myth."

"Very much alive, my friend," Edgardo said.

"You're looking well, Edgardo," Charles responded.

"Come take a seat. Meet my associates, Temmy Vallarino and Armando Delgado."

Temmy, slightly built, was dressed in a fitted suit. At a distance, his conservative short gray haircut gave him a distinguished look. Charles walked over and shook his hand. "Nice to meet you."

Temmy smiled and patted his shoulder as they greeted.

"We have heard much about you," he said, in a deep raspy voice.

Charles nodded at the welcome, but up close he could see the man's wild eyes. "I'll bet," he replied.

He looked over at Armando Delgado, a short, portly man with round cheeks clearly reddened by alcohol consumption. "Armando, right?"

"Ah, yes." Armando extended his hand. "I have met with your partners many times before, but only in *los Estados Unidos*. Thanks for making the trip our way. I know it's not easy for you to get down here."

"Charles, anything to drink?" Edgardo asked.

"Oh, I'm fine," Charles said. "Thanks." He picked a chair and sat.

"So, how did the meeting with Diego Dopazo go?"

"He is on board," Edgardo said. "He knows what he has to do."

"Diego did express concern about a few things, however," Temmy said.

"Such as?" Charles asked.

"What if the plan fails?" Temmy said.

"But it won't, right, Charles?" Edgardo said. "We assured him that our American friends have it covered. You have run the polling backward and forward and assured us that, with President Martinez and Vasquez at each other's throats, Diego's victory is guaranteed."

"It is critical that Diego wins," Armando said. "Martinez was merely bad for business, but this guy Vasquez, he is a holy crusader. He could bring the whole thing down."

"The polls show we're right on track," Edgardo said. "We know it's working."

"Like Edgardo says, the plan is already working," Charles said. "Diego is positioned to win."

"There are other concerns," Edgardo said. "The situation with the American, this Rex Nash person, now that's a problem, my friend."

"That's not on me," Charles said. "Nash was not supposed to survive the blast."

Temmy shrugged. "Explosives aren't precise, Charles."

"Fair point. Now tell me, how did he get the drop on your guys at his apartment, and again at the hotel?"

"We were only working from your plan, Mr. CIA," Armando said.

"Look, Charles, I have to agree with Armando on this one," Edgardo said. "I can't believe this disaster was the best your team could come up with. I mean, there are fucking loose ends everywhere."

"Even the most perfect plan runs into problems if it's not carried out correctly," Charles said.

"*Mira*," Edgardo said, "you CIA dickheads are the same ones who missed 9/11, weapons of mass destruction in Iraq, you name it. Everything you guys touch turns to shit. We should have known better. You are the world's biggest fuckups."

"You really wanna go there?" Charles asked.

"Let me tell you something," Edgardo said. "You are not going to fuck me. I do the fucking in this relationship."

"Calm down," Charles said. "Nash is the most wanted man in Panama. He has no money, no friends, and no support. Where is he going to go?"

"What if he talks to Vasquez?" Temmy asked.

"Then Vasquez kills him before we do. Even better," Charles replied. "He's probably biding his time, looking for an opportunity to reach out to the State Department. But the minute he enters the embassy, he's ours."

"All right, Charles, I hope you're right," Edgardo said. "I'm trusting you. And I don't give my trust lightly. I don't forgive, and I don't forget."

A ding sounded on Charles's phone, and he turned away to check. A texted photo. He opened the attachment: Marco, bloody and dead.

Charles felt the blood rush out of his head. "Gentlemen..." He leaned over and put his hands on his knees. He took a deep breath. "We have a problem."

FRANK BAKER

March 17
PG County, MD

The harsh bite of the early morning cold was what Frank always re-membered most about hunting trips with his father. If deer season had been in the summer, he might have looked back more fondly on the experience. Mostly, he remembered those weekend hunting trips as a game of hurry up and wait. His father always seemed to have a better time than he did. The deer were always a few steps ahead of them, but Frank's dad, busy hunting the Wild Turkey in his pocket flask, didn't seem to mind.

They did tag a few. The killing never bothered Frank—it was just point and shoot. He had no illusions about where his food came from, and he admired the whole eat-what-you-kill ethic in-herent to the hunt. It was what happened afterward he found un-pleasant. Field dressing the deer always turned his stomach. The distinct musty smell exuding from the open carcass, the mealy gore spilling out—that stuff was pretty ugly.

The same smell of death engulfed Frank as he stood in the cen-ter of the crime scene in the Roark family's living room. He wanted to be anywhere other than there at that moment. But what other way could he get a handle on the situation?

He tried breathing through his mouth, but he could taste the smell of the corpse. A fly buzzed over him and he swatted at it. It sped away and landed on a dark red splotch on the couch, then flew to a chunk of scalp on the armrest.

Frank had seen enough. He turned away from the remaining half of Marco's face, but the sight of the body, crumpled on the tile floor and leaking blood, was burned into his mind.

Frank recognized the two FBI agents from Rex's mother's house. They grinned at him now from the other side of the room. Obviously, his nauseated reaction amused them. He hardened his stare.

"Big Frank," the blond agent said, "we were wondering if you could share your enlightened read on this one."

"You can probably guess why the ID was flagged in the system," Frank said. "One of ours, Marco. Judging from the clothes and watch, anyway. Tough to tell from the face, but it fits—at least what's left of it."

"That's why we called you," the dark-haired agent said. "But more important, what is his body doing here?"

"We put Marco on the girl a few months back," Frank said. "Nash was designated as a top-secret, potential national security threat long before he set off that bomb in Panama. We've been tracking him for a while now."

"So, how exactly do you want us to phrase that to the woman's parents?" the blond asked.

"Guys, the reality is... this doesn't look good for anybody," Frank said.

"We're not cleaning your shit up for you," the dark-haired agent said. "You're the ones who fucked up."

"It's not the parents I'm worried about," Frank said. "It's that we had a man on the case, and we still failed to put a stop to Nash before he struck in Panama. Then there's the letting him slip back into the U.S., and to top it all off, he takes out one of our own. There's no way we can let any of that information leave this room."

"Oh, so we're supposed to just play make-believe and pretend away the dead man on the floor?" the blond taunted.

"We're going to get Nash, you can bet on that," Frank said. "We just need to readjust our focus here. The Panama stuff is still classified in the reports, right?"

"Yeah, but a lot of people have seen it," the blond said.

"Well, that stops now. I'm raising the classification," Frank said. "Fully restricted, even from you guys."

"Are you out of your mind?" the dark-haired agent said. "We're not going to leave this up to you."

"You guys will still be the lead on this," Frank said. "It's just a matter of changing the narrative. What we have now is simply a jealous boyfriend who killed his ex's foreign lover."

"Without a connection to the events in Panama, we wouldn't have the authority to remain in control," the blond said. "It would become a gig for the local police."

"No," Frank said. "Nash kidnapped the girl, so that takes the case out of the police's hands and places it right back in your lap."

"We're going to have to pass," the dark-haired agent said. "That sounds like a hassle, and more important, we don't really like you."

"Look, you dipshits, when I'm at dinner tonight with the deputy director of your entire fucking agency, I'll be sure to mention how you couldn't be bothered," Frank said. "I'm sure he'll be impressed by your unique approach to matters of national security."

The blond's eyebrows raised with concern. "Okay, okay, calm down," he said and waved his hand in surrender.

Frank slowly nodded. "I thought so."

"What about the media though? the blond asked.

"You're worried about the media in Panama?"

"Nash made quite the splash in the papers down there."

"Did it make a splash in the U.S. media?"

"No, but what if—"

"I can assure you, the media isn't a problem for us," Frank said. "The only concern I have is that the two of you fully understand what needs to happen going forward. If you get an open shot on this guy, just remember that nobody needs to go wading through the murky details of a long public trial."

RAUL VASQUEZ

March 21
Panama City, Panama
(45 days left)

This was it.

Vasquez was about to step out onstage, and he knew the stakes. He'd given countless speeches before tonight, and he'd learned through years of practice how to bury the jitters better than anyone. It wasn't a talent he'd been born with—no, even through high school, the idea of speaking in public had been terrifying to him. He remembered having to give a presentation in front of his class at age fifteen and being unable to read the notecard because his hands shook so much. Because in tenth grade everyone had been required to take a communications class, he'd dreaded even going to school that year. No matter how hard he'd studied, when he stood in front of the class, his palms started sweating, his head spun, and he forgot what to say entirely.

He'd failed that class, and it had stung like hell, but his parents' reaction had been even more painful than receiving his grade. From their sad, steady looks, and the soft tone in which they'd told him it would be all right and that he could focus on math and science instead, it was clear that they thought he was socially impaired.

At seventeen, Vasquez noticed that his younger brother had started accompanying his father to work more often. Vasquez used to be the one his father had brought with him, but since his lack of interpersonal skills had been exposed, he'd been asked to tag along less and less. If he wanted to lead the family's company one day, he knew he'd need to overcome his fear of public speaking, and fast.

When Vasquez arrived at college that fall, he signed up for every communications class he could. He crashed and burned, earning a string of Ds, but he wasn't discouraged. Since he hadn't failed, he counted it as improvement—and enrolled in the very same courses the next semester. He even signed up for the debate team. In time, he grew to become a master of the art. He eventually found a way to transform all that fear, doubt, and anxiety into a confidence and dynamism that could capture a whole stadium's attention.

Vasquez looked around the holding room, uneasy. It wasn't the rows of desks and big chalkboards that triggered his unease. No, it was more the musty smell of old drapes and chalk dust that brought his mind right back to the embarrassments of his youth. He took a breath and tried to shake his panic. He walked up to a large window and pulled back the curtain to see the lights of TV crews surrounding the building's entrance.

There was Diego Dopazo, shaking hands and smiling like the slick bastard he was as he made his way inside. Watching him, Vasquez felt his trepidation vanish. He was ready for battle. He closed the curtain and walked over to his deputies and advisors and Charles Lee.

"Charles, I understand the argument, but it is something I cannot do."

"We've talked about this," Charles replied. "How many times did we go over it last night? Now is not the time to start going off the reservation."

"You don't understand Panama," Freddy broke in, addressing Charles. "The people, they *like* this kinda stuff. They want to see him get right in there and fight like a man."

"It is true. I have to take the gloves off," Vasquez said. "I can't just stand there and let Dopazo run his mouth with all that *mierda loca*. I will tell the people who he really is, and I will do it right there in front of everyone."

"That's not going to help anything!" Charles fired back. "I showed you the polling last night. You cannot afford to get into a conflict with Dopazo tonight. All that's going to do is push voters from you and back to Martinez. Your numbers aren't strong enough yet to take on either of them."

Vasquez could see the American's panic, but his mind was set. "That doesn't matter."

Charles put his hand on Vasquez's shoulder and looked him sternly in the eye. "Your only hope is to play the nice guy, above the fray," he said. "Let Diego and Martinez fight it out first. If they damage one another badly enough, you might just have a chance to sneak in at the end."

"Bullshit," Freddy said. "We are dealing with the biggest *corruptos* in Panama, and you say nothing? The people are going to think you're some kinda asshole."

Vasquez nodded. "And what if your polling numbers are wrong, Charles?"

"They're not. You can't argue with the math here," Charles said. "It's an unfortunate reality, but if Martinez and Diego don't somehow manage to sink each other tonight, we need to start thinking about which one of them you want to endorse. If you hit Diego too hard right now, it could leave you in a really bad negotiating position. Unless, of course, you want to just hand the election to Martinez?"

"I can't endorse Diego."

"You have to play it safe," Charles said. "Otherwise, you will also lose any chance to become vice president under a coalition ticket."

"No way. I won't do it," Vasquez said.

"You may not have a choice," Charles said.

"You want me to put on the big lie. Where's the logic in turning my back on everything I campaigned for?"

"Politics have no relation to morals," Charles said. "As they say, the promise given was a necessity of the past. The word broken is a necessity of the present."

"Maybe you need a little faith," Vasquez said. "I am listening to my gut for once. I know what needs to be done. I'm not giving in to weakness and fear, not this time. Tonight, I am coming with what the people of my country need to hear."

CHARLES LEE

March 21
Panama City, Panama
(45 days left)

After having to witness Vasquez rip Diego apart live in front of the nation for two hours, Charles was relieved when the night finally came to an end. He watched the TV crews swarm Vasquez as he stepped off the debate stage. The candidate squinted under the burning camera lights, searching for the exit. He looked miserable as he inched his way toward his motorcade.

As Vasquez retreated further from the building, the glow of the camera lights dwindled. Soon the reporters circling him seemed like a swarm of fireflies. The night crept in, swallowing the building. The front of the hall was pitch black, save for the cherry of Charles's cigarette.

It was just one day, Charles told himself. There was still a long way to go between now and the election. He ground his cigarette against the door and left.

A black Suburban pulled up as he approached the parking lot. Hearing footsteps behind him, he turned to see a solidly built man wearing a red baseball cap with the brim pulled low.

Something was off. Charles started walking in the opposite direction and did his best to look as if he wasn't avoiding anyone.

"Charles Lee?" the man called out.

He turned. "Who are you?"

The man stepped closer. "Virginia requires a moment of your time."

"What kind of shit is this?" Charles spat.

"Get in the car."

"I don't like the way this is playing out. Catch you another time."

"It wasn't a suggestion. Get in the car."

The rear window rolled down. Charles saw a familiar set of eyes looking back at him.

He sighed. "Ah, right," he said, putting on his best fake smile. "Good to see you, Frank."

Charles had expected Frank to show up sooner or later, but this was unusual. He took one last look around, hoping beyond hope to see something—an incoming meteor, the rapture, *anything*—to save him from having to get inside the car.

He assessed his chances of leaving the car alive. Probably seventy-five percent. But even lower if he didn't play along. Charles decided to play the odds.

#

Frank looked Charles over as he settled down next to him in the back of the Suburban. Nothing seemed different about the guy. Well, almost nothing. The same black ostrich cowboy boots and *Magnum, P.I.* mustache, but still he sensed something unfamiliar.

Frank had been in this business for decades. He'd watched his father live and breathe it for decades before that, and knew every tell in the book. He'd discovered countless deceptions offered up by world-champion liars and con men, so right now he saw right through Charles's bullshit façade to the fear and desperation underneath.

"How're you holding up down here, Charles?"

"I'd be a lot better if Vasquez had even the slightest ability to stick with a decision," Charles said. "The man has the memory and concentration of a fruit fly. He keeps changing his mind every time the wind blows. Last night, he was swearing up and down that he was all in with the debate strategy. A minute before he went on-stage tonight, he suddenly changed course and threw everything we talked about out the window. The guy is insane. There wasn't a single thing I could do at that point to bring him back in line."

"Well, maybe in those final moments you should have ensured the wind was blowing in our direction," Frank said. "Vasquez going rogue is the last thing we need on top of everything else."

"I'm not sure it'll matter too much in the end," Charles said. "Martinez and Vasquez are still securely poised against each other and fighting over the same pool of voters. The PRD votes in a block, so the only votes up for grabs are Martinez's and Vasquez's. Even if Vasquez makes some miraculous last-minute run, Martinez will still eat enough of his potential vote pool to hand this thing to Diego."

"Well, let's hope so," Frank said. "The situation with Rex Nash grows worse every minute. We have teams of people going through all the phone and text conversations of every person he knows, every social media connection follower, anyone. So far we haven't found a single mention that he's on the run, let alone anything concerning his whereabouts. At some point, whether it's him or the girl, one of them will stumble. Undoubtedly, they'll signal their location by using a credit card or sending an email. Then we've got them."

"When you do find him, it's probably best that we keep our folks at a distance," Charles said. "Use someone with no connection to us."

"Marco had a guy that he utilized to get close to the campaign, right?" Frank asked.

"Yes. Vargas, I think,"

"That's the one," Frank said. "I remember Marco calling him an ice-cold son of a bitch. I like that."

"Yeah, and he's also a psychopath," Charles said. "Hacked up some kid from the campaign to pieces with a machete. Kid's name was Alfanzo or some such. Guess he had seen more than he was supposed to. Vargas made it look like some kind of gang war deal. Marco was usually rock solid, but he said that one made him puke right on the street. Apparently when he looked up from his vomit, Vargas was staring right at him with the blood-soaked machete in his hand and a blank expression on his face, like a robot. Evil. Then he just turned to the kid and kept hacking. And on the way back, he pulled into a drive-thru and bought a fucking ice-cream sundae. Marco said the two of them just sat in the parking lot for twenty minutes with the guy eating that stupid sundae."

"He's hired," Frank said.

"And if something goes wrong and he gets ID'd, it doesn't go to us. Points right back to Vasquez."

"It's an uncomfortable and sordid situation all around," Frank said. "We need to be careful. Anyone connected to Rex Nash should stay off the radar until we get this under control. That includes you. I told Edgardo you would be arriving at his compound out in the Darién tomorrow morning."

"Isn't there any better place to disappear to?"

"I'm sending you there for two reasons," Frank said. "I want you out of sight, out of mind, and out of reach, but I also want you on deck to help clean things up if the need arises. Second, I need you to keep an eye on Edgardo. He may be becoming... ineffective. He's been afflicted with a growing sense of self-importance recently, a bit delusional. I'm hearing reports of him getting carried away. I mean, he's always been a pretty sick guy. But sometimes people like that sink too deep. They get drunk off the violence after a while. They think they're bulletproof because they've killed so often without consequence. In truth, the only reason they're still alive is that no one has found them even worth the time it takes to pull a trigger."

Frank pulled a briefcase from the floor and grabbed a pack of cigarettes from it. "Here, you'll need to take this with you."

"I have my own."

Frank waved him off. "Pull out the two in the left corner."

Charles did so and rolled one gently between his fingers. Something was lodged where the tobacco met the filter, a capsule of some sort.

"Appears you left a present inside."

"Yes," Frank replied. "Under the tobacco is hydroxide polisti-cate, liquid form. Now, the scenario I'm about to discuss is unlikely to occur, but it's best to be prepared in case it becomes necessary to remove Edgardo."

"What is this stuff?"

"It's a slow-acting poison," Frank said. "Sets off a chemical reaction in the body. It has an interesting effect. Eats away brain tissue."

"Rough," Charles said, wincing. "How long does it take to work?"

"Two to three days if you inhale it," Frank said. "If Edgardo smoked a cigar laced with it, for example, that would do the job pretty quick. If he simply ingests it through a drink, though, it could take up to a week. Inhalation is your best bet. It's quicker, and almost certain to be mistaken for a stroke. But if the time comes, take whatever opportunity presents itself."

"What's so problematic about an extended delay?" Charles asked. "Might be better to distance the reaction as far from the encounter as possible."

"Yes, but that would allow more time for him to notice the side effects," Frank said.

"Such as?"

"Well, as it happens, the testicles start to dissolve before the brain."

Charles gazed at Frank in horror. "You're kidding, right?"

"Nope. Just one of Mother Nature's quirks," Frank said. "If he inhales it, by the time his nuts start to corrode, he'll only have a day or so left to live."

"So if he ingests it, there's a week where he'll be walking around with an empty sack, wondering what happened," Charles said slowly.

"But then again, what's he going to do if he suspects you?" Frank asked. "Is he really going to tell someone to kill you because his balls disappeared?"

Charles shrugged. "Yeah, he might keep that info to himself."

"Whatever happens, be careful not to spill that stuff on your skin," Frank said. "If you lost your brain, you could probably get by, but you certainly can't make it in this business without your balls."

JESSICA ROARK

March 23
Eastern Shore, Maryland
(43 days left)

Jessica adjusted the passenger seat back slightly. Something was scraping her ankle just between the straps of her sandal. She wiggled her foot to shake off an itching sensation. The itching continued, so she reached down under the glove compartment and probed along the floor. Her hand brushed something. A receipt? A wrapper?

She extracted the papery object from her sandal and held it up to the orange, late-afternoon light beaming through the dirty car window. It gave the black packet a nasty gleam.

"Oh my God, gross," she said.

"What's gross?" Rex asked.

Jessica waved it at him.

"Is that—?"

"Yep, an open condom. What's left of it."

Rex pressed the button to unroll Jessica's window. "Get it out of here!"

Jessica flicked it out the window. It drifted like a butterfly, leaping over cars, twirling and flipping, before it finally fell out of sight. "Somehow I knew using a loaner car from that buddy of yours would end badly."

Rex shrugged. "Hey, we have to take what we can get, considering the circumstances. And we have a lot to thank Dave for."

"You know, that wrapper didn't *come* empty," Jessica said. "There could be a surprise lurking in here."

"Let's hope not," Rex said. "We're getting to the bridge. Nowhere to pull over, just guardrails for five miles."

"What if it's under your seat?" She laughed.

Rex lifted his leg and looked down.

"I don't care if I have to park this thing in Chesapeake Bay," Rex said. "I'm not dealing with that."

Jessica laughed and leaned over Rex's lap, then eyeballed the uncovered portion of the car seat in front his crotch. "Uh-oh. Best not to look, then."

"I'm not looking," Rex replied. "I don't want to know."

"Are you a hundred percent sure the beach is the right place to go?" Jessica asked. "Why not just run as far away as possible? We could go to California or some isolated mountain resort out in Colorado."

"Your parents' beach house should be fine for now," Rex said. "We just need somewhere quiet and safe to think things through."

"Yeah, it's empty and available, but it's still only a couple of hours outside of D.C.," Jessica said.

"The main concern is to get off the grid," Rex said. "If we rent a hotel room or swipe a credit card, it's the same as if we called the bad guys and gave them our location. We're up against a pretty vicious predator here. The World Wide Web is exactly what it sounds like—at the center of it, there's a spider waiting. And anywhere you touch the spider's web—you use a phone, a credit card, whatever—it vibrates, and tips the spider off. Once that happens, it's too late to evade it. The more you struggle, the more tightly caught you become, and the more the spider learns about you. The more it knows, the lower your chances of escape."

"Scary." Jessica shuddered. "I hate spiders."

"There's a flip side to it, though," Rex said. "See, while the spider lies lording over the unfortunate prey caught in his web, he's at his most vulnerable to those on the outside. He lets down his guard and misses the obvious. Death is sneaking up on him, and he doesn't even notice."

"Well, at least we made it over the bridge," Jessica said. "Better fill up the tank now. Nothing but farmland between here and the ocean."

Rex pulled over at the first gas station. "I need to use the restroom. Bad."

"Gas on me," Jessica said.

"As long as it's cash."

"Yeah, I know," Jessica muttered as Rex walked into the store.

He was surely telling the truth about the spider, but it all sounded so unreal. Marco, that monster. The horror he had put her through, that was real, as real as it got. Still, it didn't validate all of those conspiracy theories Rex was spinning. There had to be a more reasonable explanation for everything that was happening. He believed in what he said, but he'd spent too much time in that banana republic. It wasn't how things worked in this country. It couldn't happen here.

"Only use cash or else the spiders will get us," she muttered.

She hesitated, then pulled out a credit card. Ridiculous.

REX NASH

March 23
Eastern Shore, Maryland
(43 days left)

It was late afternoon when Rex and Jessica slipped past the last speed trap outside the old colonial town of Georgetown, Delaware, and onto the final stretch of U.S. 113 toward the shore. Rex immediately rolled down the car windows. He knew Jessica didn't like his nicotine habit, but if there was ever a time to smoke, this was it. The familiar smell triggered memories of what it was like to really relax, if only for the span of a cigarette.

He looked over at Jessica, who wrinkled her nose at him. He tried to blow the smoke out the window as best he could, but he didn't put it out. He would smoke it right down to the filter. It was either smoke or have his head explode from the pressure.

Jessica didn't say anything, just smiled and turned her head toward the open window. For the duration of the drive, there had been only the smell of exhaust and land—of small towns when they were near people, of trees and dirt and manure when they weren't. As Rex puffed away, he noticed a change in the air rushing through the car windows. It was redolent with the smell of saltwater. Rex smiled and kept smoking. He didn't chain them, not exactly, but left a space of maybe five minutes between cigarettes. A quiet, strange mood settled over them as they approached the ocean. It wasn't fear, and it wasn't dread. Nothing negative, really—more like a satisfying calm brought on by a momentary vision of beautiful normalcy amidst the eye of a great storm.

Jessica spun a lock of hair around her finger as she gazed at the wide open farmland and the changing colors of light on the horizon. The orange-tinted glow of the setting sun reflected off her skin, and the shapeliness of her body drew Rex's eyes. His glance lingered on her perky, well-formed breasts as the car began to drift rightward. Quickly, he yanked the steering wheel back in line and steadied the car. *Eyes on the road.* He exhaled deeply and tried to shake off the growing consciousness of his body's desire for Jessica. He rallied his mind to unleash a flurry of warnings, but when he looked at her again, the ever-present fears whirling through his mind concerning his current predicament faded away. While his future might seem irretrievably lost, at least in this moment he had everything.

There had been so much hurry in the last few days, so much anxiety, that Rex had forgotten just how lucky and in love he was. Watching Jessica as she stared out the window sparked memories of the summers of their youth spent at the beach all those years back.

He sensed that she was thinking about it, too, but neither of them said anything. Rex was keenly aware that they could die at any minute, and the fear had to be weighing on Jessica as well. But there was no one he'd rather die beside.

By the time they reached the beach house, Rex had made up his mind. He walked in the door with Jessica, still without a word, and turned the lock behind them. Then he kissed her deeply, and she melted into him. Without bothering to unpack the bags or even bring them in, Rex picked her up in his arms, and carried her into the bedroom. There, they escaped into each other's embrace and lingered in the passion without regard to time, safety, or paranoia.

Afterward, Rex kissed her forehead and stood to get dressed. "Be back in a second," he promised.

"I'll help you with the bags." She started to get up.

He stopped her. "No, I got it."

Rex went outside and smoked a cigarette before grabbing the first set of bags from the back seat. The air was cool yet comfortable, as the bitter cold of March had given way to the onset of spring. Taking one last drag from his cigarette, he paused to admire the vastness of the clear night sky and the endless number of stars that sparkled over the ocean.

Life was good. For now.

He grabbed the handful of bags next to him and left the rest of their stuff in the trunk for later.

Jessica had already plucked a couple of dusty bottles from the liquor cabinet and fixed some drinks. Nothing fancy, just bourbon on the rocks for Rex and a vodka cranberry for herself.

They sat in lawn chairs on the porch and listened to the ocean waves collapsing onto the shore.

"Give me one of those cigs." She grinned.

"You don't smoke," he pointed out.

"I know."

He fished around in his pack. "Last one."

"Oh, you should have it."

"Let's split it."

She took the cigarette from his hand, grabbed the lighter, and set fire to the end. Her cheeks expanded as she pulled in a shallow breath. She blew the smoke right back out.

Rex dismissively waved his hand. "It's better if you inhale."

Jessica giggled and took another drag. She let the smoke linger and waft between her lips before inhaling it in with a second breath. She quickly raised her hand over her mouth attempting to hold in the smoke as it spewed back out in a fit of deep coughs.

Rex wagged his finger. "Can you believe that there are people out there that try to claim this stuff isn't good for you? Not that health is a concern at the moment."

Jessica smiled. "I think we're gonna be okay."

"I'll make sure of it," Rex said. "I won't let anything happen to us."

"I know," she said, sounding confident.

He nodded as if he believed her. After a few more drinks, they went inside and sat on the couch.

"Did you want to watch something?" He nodded toward the old TV across the room.

"I have another idea," she said.

Rex reached for his drink. He noticed a dolphin sculpture as he plucked his beverage off the mahogany coffee table. It was resting next to a glass jar filled with conches and seashells.

"What is that?" He waved toward it. The sculpture was huge, heavy, and hideous.

"Oh," she said. "Jeez, I don't know. My parents bought it on one of their trips to the flea market. Silly."

"I figured," he said. "They're into that... artsy whatever."

"Functional art," she said. "It's a paperweight."

"If you say so. Ugh."

They spent the night in a guest bedroom on the second floor as it seemed like the safest room, the only one without a deck or a glass sliding door. It had just one window, which overlooked the driveway.

Rex slept off being drunk more quickly than Jessica, and found himself tossing and turning just after midnight. He tried to adjust positions carefully so he wouldn't wake her, but there wasn't any danger of that. She was snoring gently, and even her breathing was slurred.

Between the snores, Rex heard a slight rustling outside. *Probably raindrops against the trash cans.* But the noise wasn't coming from under the window—it sounded like it was coming from the living room. The distinct creak of floorboards sounded from near the kitchen.

He sat up as quickly and quietly as he could, but the bed still squeaked just a little. Now there was silence beyond the door. He searched in the darkness for the bag with the gun Dave had given him before they left.

It was still in the trunk of the car, he remembered. He peeked out the window but didn't see any signs of movement. He grabbed his car keys, then felt around for an object he could use as a weapon just in case, but his fingers connected only with clothes and coat hangers.

Fuck.

He tiptoed over to the door and cracked it, but he saw nothing in the darkness of the hallway. Slowly, he inched himself into the hall. All was silent, with only the glow of the night-light over the kitchen counter.

Rex pressed his back along the wall as he took furtive steps to the end of the hallway and peeked around the corner. Both the living room and kitchen were empty. Relief washed over him.

He pulled a big knife from the block by the stove and stood in front of the pantry, listening. He pulled the door open and leaped inside, jabbing in the darkness with the knife. Something hard and metallic banged against his bare foot.

Shit. He jumped away, bumping the shelves. Boxes and metal pots thudded and clattered to the floor.

He froze, expecting to hear a gunshot or feel the searing pain of a blade in his side, but again, there was only silence. He backed out of the pantry, knife ready.

Maybe he had imagined everything. As he started to regain his calm, he noticed an open notebook on the island counter. He stepped closer and inspected it under the night-light. The writing inside looked a lot like his own. Not exactly, but very close:

I'm sorry for what I had to do. Please don't be angry. I had to stop her from turning me in. I never meant for any of this to happen. I thought the explosion in Panama would take care of everything. I only realize now that it was all for nothing. There is no hope for me. That is why I have done this.

Please forgive me,

Rex

Where had this bullshit come from?

Had Marco tried to set him up with this before he'd attacked him and Jessica?

Jessica! He needed to check on—

A strong chemical odor—awful, like rubbing alcohol and bleach mixed together—was everywhere all at once. A shadow crept across the page, and he swiftly turned. A wet towel smothered his face, and blackness engulfed him.

#

His head throbbed. Rex opened his eyes and realized he was on the floor, his mouth taped shut. He tried to move his hands, but they were duct-taped behind his back.

Vargas slammed a pointed boot into his gut, and vomit raced up Rex's esophagus. Puke dribbled from the edges of the tape and trickled through his nostrils, but he had to swallow most of it. He tongued at one edge of the tape in a spot where the puke had burned the adhesive away, unpeeling enough of it to give him a hole to breathe through.

"You," Rex murmured.

Vargas smiled at him and walked over by the refrigerator at the other end of the kitchen island. He knelt down over something on the floor.

Jessica.

"Get off of her!" Rex tried to scream, but the words came out as an ugly gurgle.

Vargas got up and returned to Rex. He waved what looked like an oversized bandage over Rex's head and peeled the adhesive side off with his fingers.

"Know what this is?"

"Fuck you."

"I could've just shot you both, but you seemed really in love. I figured it might be a stretch for people to believe that you'd want to blow this pretty face of hers to pieces. Easier sell that you tried to make it painless, no? I'm not much of a writer, but I thought it would make your suicide note a little more—how you say in English?—touching. The handwriting is easy enough to fake with technology, but in order to really erase all doubt amongst the dumb fucks out there, we needed something... extra. It's an art. Not that anyone will ask questions. They almost never do. It's so rude to ask. People must respect your poor mother's privacy, after all."

"What's that supposed to mean?" Rex mumbled through the hole in the tape.

"Well, as you know, I worked as a cop for over twenty-five years," said Vargas. "I've seen a lot of ugly, ugly shit, Rex, and plenty of questionable suicides. But I've never seen anyone rewarded for chasing a case once it's closed. We call it a suicide and it's done. We wash our hands of it, and turn to something else. You would think the families would demand more, but no. They're the ones most willing to buy the story—the more absurd, the better. A bit counterintuitive, but there's a trick to it: don't make the dead guy look like a nice person. The uglier you make somebody's death, the more likely people are to believe it. Gives closure, in a way. Your own dear mom will lap it all up. Sure, she'll whine and moan and bitch and sob. It'll ruin her life. Hell, it'll probably kill her too. But deep down, she'll be thankful she remembers you as an evil monster. So much easier to grieve someone when you think they deserved to die."

Vargas lifted Jessica's shirt and pointed at a patch stuck to her exposed stomach. He winked at Rex, grinning. "Fentanyl. She's high as a kite right now." He slapped another patch on her belly. Jessica wriggled and tried to mumble something beneath the duct tape.

"Vargas, you piece of shit!" Rex flopped around, feeling like a fish on the deck of a boat.

"Hold your horses," Vargas said. "You'll get your turn soon enough."

Vargas shoved Jessica onto her back and sat on her chest, pinning her arms with his knees. He grabbed a huge, ugly hunting knife from his pocket and ripped it open. Rex squirmed, banging his shoulder against the floor as he inched toward Vargas.

"*Tranquilo*, Rex," said Vargas. "I'm not going to stab her. I said it would be painless."

He pulled a straw from his shirt pocket and used the knife to slice it in two. Gently, he inched the little straw up Jessica's nose. Then he grabbed another packet of fentanyl, cut it open, and carefully guided the powder through the little straw and into her nose.

Rex kicked around harder, moving just past the edge of the island counter. Vargas was preoccupied at the other end.

Rex pulled and pulled against the tape on his wrists. His arms were sweaty, and the tape was thinner than it should have been, though he couldn't break through it. He stopped, curled into a ball, and managed to bring his hands beneath his feet and around to his chest. A small tear appeared at the tape around his ankles. Rex pulled, and tugged at it quickly and quietly. Once the tear widened enough, he yanked on it as hard as he could. The tape split apart with a loud rip.

The sound of the tear caught Vargas's attention, and he lunged at Rex, but Rex kicked away from him and leaped to his feet. His eyes scanned the room and fell on the heavy dolphin statue. He ran toward it, Vargas scrambling close behind him, and grabbed it from the coffee table.

He turned around swinging, and the statue met Vargas's temple. There was a brutal crack as Vargas fell.

He could see the man's chest still moving. Raising the statue once again, he swung it down with everything he had and sank the base of the statue into the side of Vargas's skull.

REX NASH

March 24
PG County, MD
(40 days left)

Rex paced around Dave's office as his friend tended to Jessica's wounds. He stared at the business card in his hand as he listened to the person on the other end of a burner phone. The card had been buried in his wallet since the night he'd visited the Istmoto Pub back in Panama. The name on the front was Juan Gonzalas.

"Juan," Rex said, "the meeting needs to be with President Martinez directly, and only him. He will be very interested in what I have to offer."

"Nash, we would like to do this, but it will be difficult under the circumstances," Juan replied. "While you and I know with certainty that neither of us had anything to do with the bombing, no one else is quite as sure."

"That's why, for your sake, we need to get this done," Rex said.

"Not possible," Juan said. "Neither President Martinez nor I can chance even the slightest rumor of a meeting, let alone the risk of being spotted anywhere near you. You are radioactive."

"It needs to be outside Panama, for sure," Rex replied.

"More like the middle of the ocean."

"Maybe a chance encounter? Say, our boats just happen to pass by each other at a certain time?"

There was a pause. "You know, that just might work."

"I wasn't being one hundred percent serious with that suggestion."

"Yeah, I know, but the president does love being out on his boat," Juan said. "Let me handle the logistics, and I will get you out there."

"Deal," Rex said.

PRESIDENT MARTINEZ AND REX NASH

April 3
The Bahamas
(33 days left)

In the stern of a large boat floating off the coast of Crooked Island, President Martinez wiped sweat from his brow. The sun was merciless on his shirtless chest, with the gold chain hanging from his neck starting to sting his skin with heat.

He puffed on a cigar and chopped up bait with a butcher knife, throwing bits of bloody chum into the blue water as, behind him, crewmen worked fishing gear. There was a splash, and he wiped the water from his arm as a big fish gobbled up the bait. He huffed and stared at the empty blue sky through his sunglasses, looking for an approaching chopper, but there was no sign of it yet. He placed his cigar down next to the cutting board, picked up a bottle of vodka, and walked toward the edge of the stern, still looking to the sky.

As he crossed the deck, he lowered his gaze to a six-foot bull shark lying next to his foot. The shark's dark, dead eyes seemed to stare right at him. A feeling of uneasiness crept into the president's mind. He wondered what was behind those eyes, and whether the lifeless predatory creature somehow knew a secret about his fate. He swiftly raised the vodka in his hand and took a long swig. At last, he heard the helicopter.

#

A voice crackled in Rex's headset, and his stomach turned with anxiety as he pondered all that could go wrong with the upcoming encounter.

"Rex, look over to your right and you should be able see them now," the helicopter pilot said.

Up until this point of the flight, Rex had been rock solid. The high level of adrenaline pushing through his blood had made him feel nearly invincible. He looked down through the glass at two luxury fishing yachts in the clear blue water.

"Start getting ready," the pilot told him. "This will be a little tricky. Nothing too much, but we are not landing on the deck, so be as quick as you can getting down. Whatever you do, don't jump. Those rotor blades aren't made of foam."

Minutes later, two security guards helped Rex onto the deck of the second boat. Three crew members worked to fasten a boom swim lane, a netted enclosure attached to a line of buoys, between the vessels to hold the sharks and jellies at bay. Two faceless riflemen—Rex could only see their silhouettes and guns—were stationed on Martinez's boat.

He looked across and waved. Martinez stepped up to the boom swim lane and leaped into the water. The guards escorted Rex to the side of the boat and motioned for him to jump in as well.

"*Vamos!*" one guard said. Rex swam toward Martinez with sure, swift strokes, knowing that both shooters would keep their weapons trained on him. The roiling feeling in his stomach returned as he reached the middle of the enclosure.

"What a surprise to see you here in the middle of the ocean like this," Martinez said.

"Think of the chances," Rex replied.

"Well, what do you have to say for yourself?"

"You know you are going to lose the election, right?"

"You know when this conversation is over, I'm going feed you to the fucking sharks, right?"

"That may be, but you are deep in third place, and Diego is way out in front with three weeks left. You can't win."

"Juan said you had something to offer."

"The presidency," Rex said. "But five years from now."

"And how is that?" Martinez said.

"Diego drops out; Vasquez wins and supports your return in five years."

"You want me to sit things out for five fucking years?" Martinez said. "Never."

"You've been in office too long," Rex said. "Two terms back-to-back can turn people into real assholes."

"You are too late," Martinez said. "I made that transformation long ago."

"Vasquez wins, and you return to the presidency in five, but I need your help to make it happen," Rex said.

"Last I remember, Vasquez still thinks you tried to kill him," Martinez said.

"We both know Diego was behind the bombing," Rex said. "Only you have nothing to tie him to it right now."

"And what do *you* have?" Martinez said.

"His hired assassin's dead body in my girlfriend's living room," Rex said. "Plus the guy's cell phone, with Diego Dopazo's and Charles Lee's numbers in it."

"Strong," Martinez said.

"It's still not enough," Rex said. "I need your help to identify any ties between Charles Lee and U.S. agencies, assuming your security apparatus can obtain a link."

"What's the angle?" Martinez asked.

"I can get support through my contacts in Congress, but I need proof of where this leads back to," Rex said.

"I can get the info on Charles Lee without much trouble," Martinez said. "The rest is on you."

"I can bring Vasquez on board," Rex said. "The congressional heat over Charles will force Diego's backers into cover-up mode. They'll have to push him out of the race."

Martinez wiped a strand of snot from his nose and pulled it into the water. He stared Rex in the eye and quietly treaded water. For an entire minute, the only sound Rex heard was the clicking of the fishing rigs. Martinez started to breathe more heavily, straining harder to stay above water with each stroke of his arms. Finally, he nodded. "Talk to Juan. He will get you back to the U.S."

REX NASH

April 11
Washington, D.C.
(27 days left)

As Jessica parked just in front of the Russell Building on the Senate side of the Capitol, Rex could see the strain and worry she tried to hide behind a smile.

"All right, this is it." He unbuckled his seat belt and searched under his feet until he found a manila envelope.

She reached over to hug him as he lifted his head, her eyes welling. "I love you," she said.

Rex kissed her. "I love you too. Don't worry. Everything is going to be okay."

He got out of the car, took a deep breath, and looked up at the long series of steps to the entrance. Inside were two cops: one working the metal detector and the other the X-ray machine. *Shit.*

"You! Halt right there!" a voice called as he walked toward the metal detector.

Rex stopped but didn't turn around.

"Don't move!" the cop yelled, one hand resting on his holster. "Turn and face the wall!"

He raised his hands in the air and did as he was told.

"Now, slowly put your hands behind your back."

He complied.

"Rex Nash, you are under arrest for crimes against humanity," the policeman said. "And for being an all-around bi-aatch."

Rex dropped his hands and lifted his middle finger. "Ronnie, you asshole!"

His friend was dressed in full uniform, pointing and waving like a third grader on a sugar high. Ronnie clasped his other hand over his mouth, holding back howls of laughter. Chuckles sounded from the other cops behind the checkpoint.

Rex sighed and shook his head.

"Man, Rex, I had you scared," Ronnie said, walking up. "Sweating like a—"

"You have no idea."

"It's been a while," Ronnie said. "What's going on? Last time I saw you, you were wrecking cars in the middle of downtown. You getting a beach house again this year?"

"Maybe. I have a meeting with Senator Sheehan right now, though."

"The new head of the Intelligence Committee, huh?" Ronnie said. "Hope you didn't cause some international incident with all them hookers down in Panama. A buddy of mine from the Secret Service got in real big trouble for doing just that down in Colombia. Bet you made him look like an amateur."

"Not exactly," Rex replied. "How do I get to the senator's new office from here?"

"Second floor, Room 237. Down the hall on your right."

"Thanks."

His heels made loud, echoing claps on the marble as he moved down the corridor. Inside Room 237, the receptionist directed him to the senator's personal office. The seal of the U.S. Senate was displayed in the center of the blue carpet. Miniature flags stood on Senator Sheehan's hardwood desk. She smiled, stood, and extended her hand as Rex walked over to her.

"So, what's all of this about my favorite campaign manager working in Panama?"

"Forget about me. Congratulations on your new appointment," Rex said.

"Well, thanks," Senator Sheehan said. "Moving up in the world."

"About Panama. I brought a few things you need to see." Rex handed her the manila envelope.

#

Frank Baker didn't notice that the phone receiver was digging into his ear until he felt a throbbing pain. "Yes, I understand, Senator," he said. "We have been monitoring the situation. In fact, we were in the process of preparing a report for you, but as you know, this is all highly classified material."

"Well, that's very convenient, Frank," Senator Sheehan said. "A little more urgency would be nice. I really don't appreciate having been kept in the dark about this, especially considering the players involved."

"We will do better in the future."

"I'm sure of it," the senator said, letting out an annoyed sigh. "Well, where is this Charles Lee person right now?"

"The thing is, it seems he has pulled off a disappearing act for the moment, but we *will* bring him in and make sure he faces justice," Frank said. "We're sending in our guys to shut down Diego Dopazo as we speak. The more quietly we handle this, the better—but we will handle it, ma'am."

#

Senator Sheehan hung up the phone and looked at Rex. "Your suspicions about Charles Lee were correct, Nash," she said. "The CIA says they've had him under watch as a potential rogue agent for some time."

"They're saying it was just Charles acting all by himself?" Rex questioned. "That doesn't sound right. What about Marco?"

"Please don't turn into a conspiracy theorist on me here," Senator Sheehan said. "They said Marco was just doing what he thought was his job."

"Pretty fucked-up job," Rex said.

"Yes, but Charles had authority over him," she said. "Everything at the CIA is so compartmentalized that it's not easy to keep track of anything that's going on over there, let alone something like this. They said Charles had a deeply underwater mortgage. It's not too hard to imagine how it could happen, given the territory he was responsible for. I mean, think of all the corruption that goes on in those places over in Latin America. His desperate finances really should have been a red flag to the CIA, since people like that can be easy targets for temptation. It certainly is embarrassing to the Agency. But in the end, he really was just a lone rogue actor."

"Got it," Rex said.

"Hope you understand the need for us to keep this quiet, right?" Senator Sheehan asked. "We don't want people getting a distorted perception."

FRANK BAKER

April 11
Langley, Virginia
(27 days left)

Frank Baker reached under his desk to power off his computer. He dug the fingers of his other hand into his left pocket until he heard his keys jingle. After distinguishing the one with a small round head, he looked up at the framed picture of his father and unlocked the bottom drawer of a filing cabinet. Inside, resting on a ream of copy paper, was a bottle of Macallan single malt. A crystal tumbler sat next to it.

Frank had never been much of a scotch drinker. It was an old man's drink, and it tasted like gasoline. He kept the bottle in the drawer only in honor of his father.

He didn't remember his old man drinking much when he was little. Maybe a couple of gin and tonics at the yacht club on Gibson Island, and only in the summer, when they held sailboat races. The scotch came much later. His dad started pouring a glass every evening after coming home from work, and just as invariably, to his mom's dismay, fired up a cigar. When he got even older, he liked to turn his hearing aid off so he could keep sipping scotch and puffing away, oblivious to his wife's complaints.

Now Frank poured himself a double and placed the bottle on his desk. He took a deep swig and tried to relax. A loud knock shook the door. He raised his head and quickly pulled the bottle off the desk.

A tall gray-haired man about twelve years his senior opened the door and stepped into the office. "I got your message about the call with Senator Sheehan," he greeted Frank in a deep, raspy voice.

"We have a real mess on our hands," Frank said. "We're out of time, and the Dopazo situation is untenable. A Vasquez win puts us in a very risky situation."

The man sat down in the plush chair before Frank's desk. He pointed at the tumbler. "What's that you have there, Frank?" he asked. "Scotch? Oh, your daddy used to love that stuff. Don't be rude. Go ahead and pour me a glass already."

When his dad had put a few more back than usual, he'd muse aloud about what his life might have been like had he fought in the war. What if he'd faced down machine-gun fire on the shores of Normandy or at the Battle of the Bulge? He'd never made it to the front lines, spending most of the war in D.C., working to enhance public support. OSS had sent him out on a few low-key missions in Central and South America, but while fascism and communism had indeed taken root there, Frank's father had known the real battle was elsewhere. The Panama Canal had remained safe, and the war had been an ocean away.

On nights like those, his father had called him spoiled and had reminded Frank that he'd been taken ice skating or for rounds of golf at the country club. And he always brought up the exorbitant cost of boarding school. At the end of his tirades, he'd pour another glass. Then he'd take a deep swig, sit back in his chair, and smile warmly. When the glass was finished, he would show Frank a rare moment of affection, with a half-hug or pat on the head on his way to bed.

Frank retrieved another glass from the drawer now and poured the man a drink.

His guest took a sip and turned the glass in his hand thoughtfully. "Frank, politicians come and go," he said. "The bureaucracy and the apparatus that surrounds them lasts far longer. I think maybe Charles has allowed Edgardo's fixation on having his own man on the throne and his paranoia over Vasquez to sidetrack our focus here. Edgardo is getting old and erratic. Maybe it's time for a change."

"Maybe, or maybe not, but I'm very worried about the situation with Charles," Frank said. "We have to put him somewhere way off the radar. Change his appearance or something."

The man took another sip and placed the glass on the edge of Frank's desk. "Power is mostly an illusion, but it addicts you like a drug. Once obtained, you have to fight increasingly hard just to maintain the high. Charles is a loyal friend, but we have committed ourselves to a path. We gave away the power of choice in favor of the illusion. The greater the illusion grows, the less we can wield it, and the more we become slaves to it. Believe me, Charles understands this more than anyone."

CHARLES LEE

April 21
Darién Province, Panama
(15 days left)

Charles dangled a lit cigarette over the rail of the balcony as he watched the sun set over the jungle behind Edgardo's Darién estate.

Suddenly, Edgardo cursed from inside the living room at a volume just loud enough to hear from the balcony. "So, you are *absolutamente comprometidos* to this, Frank?" Edgardo shouted next.

Charles glared in at him through the balcony's sliding glass doors. Edgardo pulled the phone away from his ear and turned it off. He crossed to the center of the living room to a table that held an unopened box of Nicaraguan cigars. While he opened the seal on the box, he waved one of the guards over and whispered something to him. After extracting a cigar, he walked toward the sliding glass doors.

Charles turned away as Edgardo joined him on the balcony. With a nervous glance over the jungle-covered foothills, he ashed his cigarette over the rail and watched it fall like snow, fluttering with the breeze down into the gully below.

"I have not had a good cigar in a long time," Edgardo said.

"I didn't know you smoked," Charles replied.

"Cigarettes are disgusting," Edgardo said. "That stuff is addictive. I do enjoy the occasional cigar, though. I just opened a new box. Go ahead and take one if you want."

"Sure, thanks."

Charles stepped inside the living room and approached the table, surreptitiously pulling another cigarette from the pack in his pocket. He looked back nervously at Edgardo to make sure he was out view.

Selecting a cigar from the box, Charles carefully broke the vial of poison hidden inside the cigarette. A clear odorless liquid dripped out over the top layers of cigars. He hastily stuffed the remnants of the cigarette and vial safely back inside the packet and into his pocket.

He felt a tap on his shoulder.

"Do you have a light?"

"Yes, but I need a cigar cutter."

Edgardo reached inside his pocket and pulled out his lucky bone-handled stiletto.

Charles's eyebrow raised. "A little overkill there?"

Edgardo grabbed the cigar and gestured out toward the balcony. "What can I say? I'm a caveman. I like to intimidate."

"You always were old school," Charles said.

Edgardo sliced the sharp blade across the tip of the cigar and handed it back as they walked outside.

"Charles, how long have we known each other?" he asked. "A long time, yes?"

"Many years," Charles said.

"I spoke with Frank," Edgardo said. "He's concerned about some things."

"About what?" Charles said. "Was that him just now?"

"Yes. He told me you may have gone rogue."

"Rogue?"

"Those were his words, by the way."

"What the fuck are you talking about?"

"Frank seems to think you got involved with some bad people."

"I'm not sure I get the joke."

Edgardo shrugged. "This is the tale Frank chose to create. There is nothing I can do."

"Listen, Edgardo. Whatever you think—"

Something wrapped around his neck. He put his hands up to it. A rope. He could feel Edgardo's security guard pull it tighter and tighter from behind him. He struggled, helpless and gasping for breath. The noose tightened.

A piercing pain shot through his chest. His eyes glanced downward and saw a bone knife handle protruding from his rib cage. Edgardo pulled the knife out and stabbed him again. Charles squirmed and shook, but the guard just squeezed and grappled harder, pushing him halfway over the railing.

"I'm CIA," Charles said, gurgling. "You... can't do this."

He sensed Edgardo's blade run through his gut two more times. Then he felt the pull of the guard's arms swinging him over the railing and the squeeze of the rope that held him up.

"Such a distorted perception of reality can be deadly, I think." Edgardo nodded to the guard. "Let him go," he said, and walked away.

Charles was consumed by two overwhelming feelings. The first was a heavy sense of regret, and the other was a sinking feeling in his stomach, as if he'd just jumped off a high dive. Those feelings were soon replaced by the quick and intense pain of his internal organs being crushed on impact.

REX NASH

May 5
Panama City, Panama
(Election Day)

Rex stood alone in the center of a backstage holding room behind the ballroom at the JW Marriot in Punta Pacifica, Panama City, watching election returns on a small TV. The rumble of the crowd in the ballroom and the honking of horns and chanting outside from the overflow crowd that was beginning to surround the hotel were growing increasingly louder.

The press secretary walked in. "It's time," she said.

Rex nodded. He adjusted the front of his coat and straightened his tie. "What did Bill Casey think about the messaging in the draft poll?"

"He asked why you wanted to spend so much money polling in New Hampshire, South Carolina, and Florida two years out," the press secretary said.

"Well, Bill doesn't know it yet, but—"

"They're signaling for you right now," she interrupted. "You need to get onstage."

Rex walked down the dark hallway that led to the stage. Jessica stepped toward him from the edge of the stage and gripped his hand. She smiled, and he kissed her.

"Showtime," he said, as they took the stage together.

The spotlights were blinding. All he could see was the podium and the silhouette of a figure behind it. The figure pointed at him, and the crowd roared.

"There are so many who helped us win the presidency tonight, but I want to give a special thanks to my campaign manager and good friend, Rex Nash!" Vasquez said.

DIEGO DOPAZO

Weeks Later
Darién Province, Panama

Even set to full blast, the air conditioner was no match for the dense humidity of the Darién jungle. For over an hour, cycles of wisps and whines had belched from beneath the dash, yet only a mild, damp breeze trickled through the vents.

Then there it was, at the exact point where Diego Dopazo's hair met the top of his forehead: a drop of sweat. He stared into the mirror on the passenger seat visor and watched it roll down his face.

"Por qué ahora?" he muttered.

He quickly wiped his brow as the car rolled to a stop. A figure approached his window, and a wide, bald head partly obscured by large aviator sunglasses peered in at him. The man wore a white fishing shirt and had an AK-47 slung over his shoulder.

"Buenas tardes, Señor Dopazo," the guard said.

"Buenas," Diego replied as he stepped out of the vehicle. The man accompanied him to the front of the estate. As he approached the steps, another guard announced his arrival via walkie-talkie. He raised his hand and signaled for them to wait.

As they stood there, Diego noticed that the guard with the AK-47 was wearing a peculiar pair of black ostrich cowboy boots with rusted brown leather calves. They seemed familiar, but he couldn't say why. Diego stared at the boots. A crusted, dark purple streak was splattered along the side of the heel.

"Oye, *mi amigo,* your boots have blood on them," Diego said.

The guard looked down. *"Mierda. Gracias."*

He laid his weapon down on the step and pulled a handkerchief from his pocket, which he wrapped around his finger and spat on. He lifted his foot onto the step above his gun and wiped the blood away.

"Vámonos," the guard with the CB shouted, waving Diego toward the door.

He was directed into a lavishly decorated living room, where he was greeted by Temmy Vallarino and Armando Delgado. An empty bottle of dark rum rested on the coffee table, with another newly opened bottle on the sideboard. Armando's chubby cheeks glowed red, and Temmy's smile stretched to the edges of his long, narrow face. It looked like they'd been there a while.

Diego picked up a tumbler and filled it to the brim with ice. The ice crackled and popped as the warm, amber-colored rum flowed over pockets of air trapped inside.

"So, where is Edgardo?" he asked.

"He left to take a call," Temmy replied.

"Frank?" Diego asked.

Temmy shook his head. "I don't think so."

"Take a seat," Armando said. "Edgardo will be back soon enough."

Diego joined them in a jovial conversation about their favorite baseball teams and telenovelas. The more the conversation veered into the trivial, the more unsettled he became. He watched Armando carefully as the man ranted on about the officiating of the Yankees-Marlins game the night before. Diego hadn't seen a single game that year, but he smiled and nodded with each point.

Where was Edgardo, that erratic and unpredictable fuck?

The constant unknowing with the guy was bad enough, but who knew what the sick, crazy piece of shit had in mind next? Whatever it was, Diego had a feeling it was going to be bad.

The snap of a stiletto shot across the room. Edgardo placed the knife in his pocket as he strolled in from the balcony, puffing away on his cigar. "About time you showed up, Diego." Edgardo walked to the center of the room and took a long pull, blowing the smoke across the room in Diego's direction.

Diego turned his head and swatted at the smoke. "Getting to this place unnoticed is easier said than done these days."

Edgardo strode over to an end table beside Diego's chair and smothered the tip of his cigar in the ashtray resting next to an open box of cigars.

"Yes, I know. But if I held Temmy and Armando here any longer, they would have drunk the rest of my good rum. Then what kind of situation would I be in?"

"Let's not think of such crazy nightmares." Temmy chuckled and wagged a long, narrow index finger.

Armando winced and gulped back the contents of his glass. He patted the top of his wide, round belly and put his glass down on the coffee table.

"So, what is to be done with Vasquez?" Diego asked.

"Edgardo, have you talked to Frank yet?" Temmy asked. "What's his thinking?"

"That's a good question. I'm waiting to hear from him, but he's taking his sweet time," Edgardo said. "Too much time."

"I think we should finish what we started," Diego said.

"That's unwise," Temmy replied.

"You can't afford to let him loose with that kind of power," Diego said.

"Certainly not," Armando said.

"So we have to take him out," Diego said. "The sooner, the better."

"And rattle the people from their slumber?" Edgardo asked. "They were told to believe it was all the doing of this person Rex. Once that's fallen apart, suddenly there's another explosion? Do you not think such an occurrence would be overly illuminating?"

Temmy endorsed Edgardo's words with a quiet nod and leaned forward. He turned his beady eyes toward Diego. "Our business is that of darkness and confusion. Without these things, we are not long for this world."

"Isolate Vazquez in darkness, drive confusion, and keep him chasing shadows," Edgardo said.

"Yes, things will remain as they are. Nothing changes," Armando chimed in.

Diego folded his arms. "How is that going to work any better? I still say we kill him."

Edgardo looked over at Armando with a mischievous smile. "War is peace, freedom is slavery, ignorance is strength."

"Oceania had never been in alliance with Eurasia?" Armando said.

Edgardo winked. "Precisely."

Temmy raised his tumbler. "To Edgardo, the media's mythical drug lord who has never once sold any drugs."

"They make me out to be some kind of pirate," Edgardo said, "smuggling this over here and that over there. It's all very strange."

"Sordid business. A bunch of low-life street rats and ignorant rabble endlessly killing each other over table scraps," Armando said.

"Some of those street rats happen to be my clients," Edgardo warned. "If they knew about who you are, they might not hold you in the highest of esteem, either. I wonder what they would think if they knew the truth about that dam you had blown to pieces. How many hundreds of people had to die in that explosion to keep the price of iron ore where it is? There were a million other ways it could have been done, but you said this was how your clients wanted it."

"So I was overly colorful in my language." Armando shrugged. "No offense intended. The drug industry does have its uses, after all—dark currency and that kind of thing."

Edgardo turned to Diego. "Tell us, how could you fail to understand the nature of our methods after being acquainted so personally with them?"

"It was only a suggestion that we kill him. How could I know the inner workings of your minds?" Diego said.

"How would you know?" Edgardo replied. "I remember a young, upcoming politician who one day took a fateful trip abroad. To Miami, in fact."

Diego clenched his fist. "Edgardo, no. Don't do this," he begged.

"Maybe you should have beaten Vasquez on your own. Maybe then such secrets would be of greater value," Edgardo said.

Diego felt his stomach roil. He wiped some of the new sweat from his forehead.

"Let's hear this," Temmy said.

Diego scowled at him and mouthed, *What the fuck?*

Edgardo patted on the knife tucked inside his pocket. "Maybe I carve you up and feed you to Armando and Temmy here?"

"Yes, yes, you should," Temmy said.

"That way, you might be worth something to somebody," Edgardo said.

Armando stood and walked over to the table next to Diego. He reached his hand into the cigar box. "This is going to be good. I think I should enjoy one of Edgardo's cigars while listening to this story. Much appreciated, Edgardo." He glared down at Diego as he plucked one out.

"Yes, and pass the rum this way," Temmy said.

"Smoke away, my friends, that's what they are for," Edgardo said. "Not the most expensive brand in the world, but good enough."

Diego peered over at the box, in search of an idea about what he might say that could divert the conversation from the secrets of his past. "I smoke that brand all the time. They're excellent. Nicaraguan, grown in that rich volcanic soil. It gives the tobacco a nice earthy flavor. I don't know why people even bother with overpriced Cuban trash."

Armando put his hand over his belly, and his stomach let loose a long, audible growl. "I think I ate too much at lunch," he said. "Maybe I'll have one a little later." Armando stuck the cigar in front of Diego's face and smiled. "Here."

Diego snarled back at him and grabbed it. "Just get on with it, then, Edgardo."

"So, this young politician, we will call him Diego, loved to revel in all the hard-earned female attention he gained after winning that seat," Edgardo said. "Particularly females who were not his wife."

"At least it wasn't a guy. Good for you, Diego," Temmy said.

Diego glared at him.

"Once upon a time, one of these mistresses revealed to Diego that she was pregnant."

"Aww, that's cute," Armando said. "One of your girls, Edgardo? Why do you never send these women out on the prowl to hunt down dirt on me? It's not fair."

"Unfortunately, no," Diego said. "She was an intern, the daughter of a friend and supporter of my campaign."

"Yes, and like a true gentleman, the politician promptly forced the man's daughter to get on a plane to Miami. He then made her go to one of those American clinics where they take care of that kind of thing."

"Okay, yes, problem solved," Temmy said.

"Well, the voters of Panama have considerably different views from the voters of Miami about such matters. For this politician's district, in particular, it would undoubtedly be a career ender, should the truth ever reveal itself. That whole dynamic is why my investments in these clinics in and around Miami and the D.C. area provide such a wonderfully continuous flow of names and information."

"Ruthless," Armando said.

"Any time a name from our database of politically sensitive persons or their associates is entered into either our payment systems or medical records, an automatic notification is generated," Edgardo said. "Just like that, this politician was firmly within my grip. But he did not know that yet, did he, Diego?"

"Obviously, no," Diego replied.

"Would you like to tell them the rest of the story, what the politician did next?" Edgardo asked. "Having it told in your voice would bring so much more to the story."

"No, that's okay."

"Are you sure?"

"I'm very sure."

Edgardo abruptly winced and adjusted his sitting position as if he had pulled a muscle in his leg. "From what I understand, this girl was not altogether pleased following the procedure. Is that right?"

"No, she wasn't."

"She threatened to tell her father, is that what it was?"

"You don't understand," Diego began.

"What's that old saying again?" Temmy said. "If a tree falls in the woods..."

"If a politician kills a young woman in Miami and no one sees it, did it really happen?" Armando said.

Diego reached for a cigar from the box and nervously rolled it back and forth between his fingertips, unlit.

"Maybe, maybe not, but someone did see it," Edgardo said. "The minute he left—" Edgardo paused and placed his hand over his groin area. He took in a deep breath and resumed. "The minute he left the clinic with the girl, we had someone tailing him and taking pictures all along the way." Edgardo stopped again. Something was clearly paining him. He rested his hands on his knees and hunched over the edge of the chair.

Diego stared curiously at Edgardo, wondering if he was about to vomit on the carpet.

"It was quite a surprise, what turned up in those pictures." Edgardo lifted his head. "And now, Diego, you're all mine." He stood and pulled his knife out of his pocket.

"Hey, Edgardo, calm down," Temmy cautioned.

Edgardo ground his teeth and slowly walked toward Diego.

"Edgardo?" Armando said. "You seem ill. Is there something wrong with you?"

Edgardo glared back at him and pointed the knife in his direction.

"I've wandered this earth a good deal longer than you," Edgardo muttered through a clenched jaw. "With time, all forms of random maladies and ailments build. You should mind your words if you wish to live long enough to experience them."

He smiled and continued slowly lurching his way toward Diego. "You have to know taking out Vasquez at this point is a fool's errand, yet you lust for his death all the same. Still chasing after the illusion." He pointed the knife toward Diego's chest. "You have no power. You never did, you never will. You are my slave."

"Come on, Edgardo, that's enough," Armando said.

Edgardo clenched his jaw again.

"One of many slaves," he added through his teeth.

"Hey, it's not my call." Diego held up his hands. "I am up for whatever you want to do."

"Here, give me that cigar," Edgardo said.

He pulled the unlit cigar from Diego's hand and cut an opening with his knife.

"There, that's how you cut a cigar the right way," Edgardo said.

He handed the cigar back to Diego and patted him on the shoulder. "We are hardly the most ruthless operators out there. And you, my friend, are a long way from the foulest of creatures under our control. Yes, we can contain Vasquez. It is not required that we remove him from the presidency. Rather, we remove the presidency from Vasquez."

Temmy stood and picked up his empty tumbler. "*Exactamente.*"

"*Perfecto,*" Armando said.

Temmy walked toward Edgardo and Diego. "Now this is something we can all drink to. Let's open another bottle." He pulled a gold Zippo lighter out of his pocket and handed it to Diego as he continued past.

Edgardo slowly hobbled back toward his seat. He placed a hand on the armrest and leaned on the chair. "*Qué mierda,*" he grunted. "I must have pulled a groin muscle somehow."

"Oww," Temmy said. "I know what that's like."

Diego flipped the gold lighter open and lit the end of his cigar as he watched Edgardo struggle to get seated. *Good, I hope it grows worse. Then again, wounded animals are twice as vicious. Better that he remains in good health, at least until I leave.*

"Gentlemen, I have become extremely uncomfortable," Edgardo said. "I might have to leave you to yourselves for a while."

Diego raised an eyebrow. A red ember lit the end of his cigar as he pulled in several rapid puffs.

"I apologize, but it's almost a feeling of being repeatedly kicked in the balls."

"Terrible. You should take a painkiller," Temmy said.

"At a minimum, pure morphine is needed for such a thing," Armando said.

Diego felt a bitter taste in his mouth. "Edgardo, are you sure these are real Nicaraguans?"

"Of course."

"It doesn't taste right at all."

Edgardo's eyes turned wild, burning with fury. "Frank, you son of a bitch."

REX NASH

Fenwick Island, Delaware
Three Months Later

The eighteenth pin was one hundred fifty yards away, and beyond that, the ocean. It was late in the day, and remnants of the storm that had passed through earlier clung to the roots of the tall grass. Droplets of moisture spread over the tips of Rex's shoes as he waded deeper into the rough and angled out the perfect shot. He took a breath of the salty air. The aroma reminded him of Jessica and the beach.

He pulled back the seven iron and swung. The head of the club connected just under the ball, sending it upward high and soft. He followed the trajectory as it hovered over the clubhouse and dropped down just over the top of the green.

"Fantastic shot, Rex!" Rev. Abasolo called out.

When Rex arrived at the green, he spotted a ball on the fringe and headed toward it, putter in hand.

"Oh no, this is me." Rev. Abasolo pointed toward the pin. "That's you over there."

Rex's ball was a foot out. "Wow, I'll take it."

"How long will you be in the Bahamas?" the reverend asked as he attempted to read the multiple breaks between his ball and the stick.

"Two weeks. Do I need to mark this?"

"Go ahead and putt it. I need a little more time with this, anyway."

"No gimmies with you, huh?" Rex grinned.

"Human beings need to step away at times and remember who they are," Rev. Abasolo said. "Wounds of life are continually inflicted upon us, and the traumas we inflict on others only fester until confronted."

"I hope you've put as much philosophical thought into how you're going to sink your putt from that distance. You might need a special prayer to make that one."

Rev. Abasolo smiled indulgently and stood over his ball. "Now this will be a work-free trip, correct?"

"Correct."

"Even if el presidente calls?"

"Especially then."

Rev. Abasolo glanced up. "The trauma, it's all still with you. I can almost see it on your face."

Rex shrugged.

"You can either choose to offer forgiveness and seek repentance or be pulled into a spiral of vengeance and denial."

Rex tapped the ball in the hole. "I'd almost rather just walk away from the fight altogether."

"It's the lies we accept just as much as the lies we tell that pull us down into darkness."

Rex leaned over and plucked his ball from the cup. "Hey, at least I can say I survived the Lighthouse Sound course."

"Survived is right. Rex, this course you chose, it's been brutal to say the least. Which hole was that, Impossible Par Three?"

Rex started walking back to Rev. Abasolo. "The fifth hole? Right on the edge of the water?"

"Yes, where the ocean winds whip over that small, twenty-yard green," Rev. Abasolo said.

"Eighteen yards, I think," Rex said. "Looking at it from the tee, it was basically a bump with a flagstick."

"I lost three balls in the water on that one," Rev. Abasolo said. "Even with the extra pack you gave me, I'm down to my last. It's a beautiful course all the same, though."

"Try as one may, Father, this politics game is a bit like blowing into the wind, or trying to hold back the tide," Rex said. "Throw in the evolution of hi-tech mass media and the ever-deepening levels of propaganda that it brings, and there will come a point where people won't have the ability to distinguish up from down anymore."

"There is always a struggle. It's the way things have always been," Rev. Abasolo said. "Get your own act together first, then inspire others. Give them the truth and they will follow."

"What if the truth is out of reach?" Rex asked. "Is the game lost?"

"No, the battle continues." Rev. Abasolo tapped the ball with his putter, sending it wide to the right of the hole. It slowly curved along with the incline, then fell dead center and sank into the cup.

"Okay. After that putt, I do believe in miracles," Rex said.

"The Lord is on my side for this hole, at least," Rev. Abasolo replied. "Now, one through seventeen, that was clearly the devil's work."

"But how does the battle, as you call it, continue if truth is inaccessible?" Rex replaced the flag and started back toward his cart.

Rev. Abasolo put a hand on his arm. "As St. Paul the Apostle explained, ever since the creation of the world, the invisible existence of God and His everlasting power have been clearly seen by the mind's understanding of created things."

"Okay," Rex said.

"And Paul goes on to talk about how those living in remote places, unexposed to the gospel or the law, can still demonstrate the effect of the law engraved on their hearts, to which their own conscience bears witness. In other words, the fight is never over because the darkness can never extinguish the truths within us all from the start."

Rex drove the cart up to the clubhouse, where Jessica was talking with the club manager about their upcoming wedding reception.

"Father Abasolo," she said, as he and Rex climbed out. "Welcome to Fenwick! Thank you so much for making the trip all the way up here." They exchanged a hug before Jessica slipped under Rex's arm.

"Are you ready?" Rex asked.

Jessica nodded. "You bet." She kissed him, her diamond ring glittering in the late afternoon sun.

THE END

ABOUT THE AUTHOR

JONATHAN R. SNOWLING is a novelist, screenwriter and political consultant. He is the author of the 2022 novel Distorted Perception and the 2018 screenplay True Artist. Filming for the movie True Artist began in April of 2018.

As an author Snowling draws insights from his unique experiences as a top tier Political Consultant. He was named "International Consultant of the Year" by the American Association of Political Consultants (AAPC) in 2015.

Snowling has served on state, federal, and international races in Texas, Virginia, North Carolina, Louisiana, South Dakota, Washington State and Central America. He is undefeated (5-0) as a Campaign Manager in open seat races.

He steered an upset victory for Juan Carlos Varela in the race for the Presidency of the Republic of Panama. He spent two years on the ground in Panama as a General Consultant and Campaign

Director guiding Varela's campaign to impressive victories in both the 2013 presidential primary and the 2014 general election.

He received both the AAPC's Campaign Excellence Award and Campaigns & Elections Magazine's Reed Award for "Best International Campaign" due to his work in Panama.

Born and raised in Maryland, he received a Bachelor's degree in Political Science from The University of Maryland, College Park. Snowling later earned an MBA from George Mason University's School of Management in 2011.

Follow Jonathan on Twitter @JonSnowling

CPSIA information can be obtained
at www.ICGtesting.com
Printed in the USA
LVHW112110020622
720141LV00013B/107/J

9 798985 581362